Murder After Hours

A Meadowbank Mystery

Margaret Alty

Published 2013 by arima publishing

www.arimapublishing.com

ISBN 978 1 84549 579 4

© Margaret Alty 2013

Printed and bound in the United Kingdom

Typeset in Garamond 12

Swirl is an imprint of arima publishing.

arima publishing

ASK House, Northgate Avenue

Bury St Edmunds, Suffolk IP32 6BB

t: (+44) 01284 700321

www.arimapublishing.com

Chapter One

Brian and Melissa were married on Friday, the eighteenth of May, which coincided with the re-opening of the restaurant in the Market Square. The Salmon's Rest restaurant had been closed for almost a year following the hasty departure of the previous owners and had, for one reason or another, been difficult to sell. Now, at last, the residents of Meadowbank had a choice and didn't need to drive up to The Royal Oak hotel if they wanted to go somewhere else for a meal. The new proprietors, Harry and Barbara Wood, came from London: a couple in their early forties and, although with a number of years' experience in the restaurant business, had never lived outside London before. For those people in the town with an inbuilt pessimistic view on life, this fact didn't bode all that well in their considered and much-discussed opinion for either the Woods or, indeed, for Meadowbank; their presence reminding them, somewhat unfairly, of what had happened during the relatively short time Peter and Danielle Taylor owned the business.

The marriage had taken place in Winchester's registry office and Brian and Melissa had chosen to celebrate in a slightly different way. Not for them the formal meal, although Brian had suggested they could hold their reception in the restaurant at The Royal Oak, but Melissa had told him she much preferred for them all to come back to The Market Inn instead. Although, as wedding receptions went, it was even more unusual in that both the bride and groom, together with their barman, Derek Frost, spent a good part of the time behind the bar serving drinks to their guests, it was obvious by the radiant smiles on Melissa's face she had never been happier. Brian also, with memories of his first disastrous marriage fast diminishing, looking at her now felt exactly the same. He was being given a second chance and the love he felt for his new bride that afternoon, surrounded by their friends and relatives, was complete. He had never seen her look so lovely; her short blonde hair curling softly against her cheeks, flushed with excitement now that the brief civil ceremony was over and they were back in the familiarity of Meadowbank, also the creamy lace dress she had chosen for this special day was perfect, emphasising her slim figure. Brian Morrison, he thought to himself, you are indeed a very lucky man.

Across the road, in The Salmon's Rest, the atmosphere was much more subdued, but for their first luncheon, Harry and Barbara were not disappointed. All twenty tables had been taken and the bookings for that evening already looked promising. Apart from the *a la carte* menu, they had selected an introductory set luncheon of a cold consommé soup and a seafood platter, followed by a sundae of first-of-the-season strawberries with the thick clotted cream brought up from Devon earlier that morning by Barbara's parents who were spending the weekend with them, more as morale support than anything else. Harry and Barbara were already aware that not everyone in Meadowbank actually greeted them unconditionally; also, they knew about the history of the restaurant; who had owned it before them and the circumstances of how it came to be on the market. Due to the fact that Peter Taylor was now serving time in one of Her Majesty's prisons they didn't meet him at the completion of the purchase, but the London estate agents had introduced them to his wife, Danielle, who, while not being exactly complimentary about the town and its people, making it abundantly clear to them both that she didn't like Meadowbank one little bit, did assure them of the profitability of the business. But, even without this recommendation and before they had studied the accounts for the period while the Taylors had been there, once they had viewed the restaurant they had immediately fallen in love with it. The fact that moving out of London was an entirely new venture for them hadn't deterred them in the slightest. Many of their friends, including Barbara's parents, had tentatively warned them they may find it difficult to adjust to the country life, but their minds had already been made up. They were both determined to make a go of the business. It was what they wanted: a complete change and away from the proverbial rat race.

They had decided to make very few changes to the restaurant, being entirely happy with the Italian decor of the vibrant Mediterranean colours: red, mustard, blue and green and all cleverly merging with the Parisian-style in the red and white checked tablecloths and matching cushions on the suede covered banquettes. Danielle Taylor had been generous in the final sale; she had taken very little with her and Barbara had remarked to Harry after they had exchanged contracts that this was probably because she didn't want any reminder of when she was living there. They had read about the Meadowbank murders as they had been graphically described by the media, but at that time, neither of them had even heard of the town and like most people in London and the provinces, the news was superficial to their daily lives; the interest lasting only as long as the next sensational headlines hit the press. When they were told by their agents of the Salmon's Rest being on the market, although the name of the market town in the heart of Hampshire did sound familiar, they didn't believe there could be any sort of stigma attached to the restaurant itself. As Harry had commented in his characteristic dry way, it wasn't as though any of the murders had actually taken place on the premises. Also, when they had been talking to Danielle Taylor they didn't take the time to reflect what it must have been like for her to find out that her husband was a murderer. Harry and Barbara, a down-to-earth and prosaic couple, didn't believe in ghosts, even although there had been a few of the local residents quick to tell them what the atmosphere had been like in the town around the time the murders came to light. All of this retrograde stuff had nothing to do with them; they were newcomers to Meadowbank and were confident that in time they would be accepted and no longer treated as outsiders. At least, that was what they hoped.

At the same time as the wedding guests were preparing to toast the newlyweds and their friend and neighbour, Simon Grant, was taking a photograph as Melissa with a guiding hand from Brian cut into the two-tier wedding cake, the new tenants drew up outside the end terraced house across the square.

Surprisingly, no-one in the town knew who had bought number twenty-eight, but somehow, given their insatiable appetite for wanting to know what was going on around them, plus their ability to find out all they could, they had reached the conclusion, although still to be proved, that the property was being rented by the new owner. As the whole transaction had been carried out by London estate agents, and not by Town & Country in Meadowbank, they had no valid reason for such an assumption, but on this occasion they happened to be right.

As with the new proprietors of The Salmon's Rest, Johnnie Baker and his girlfriend, Felicity, were newcomers to Meadowbank, although Johnnie did mention to her on the drive down from Manchester, he had been there once. It had been a few years before they had met; in the days when he had been in the rock group and they'd been touring in the south of England and had found the town by accident after taking a wrong turning off the M27. It had been the middle of the summer he'd said, and after spending the evening drinking in the first pub they found, had decided to camp out that night in a picnic area they found half-way along the road leading out of Meadowbank.

Clambering out of his pride and joy; a white open-top Peugeot, albeit over eight years old now and with too many miles on the clock, Johnnie dragged out their various pieces of luggage, including his much coveted guitar and fumbled in his jacket pocket for the keys to the house.

'Well, Felicity,' he said, 'here we are. What do you think?'

'Give me a chance,' she said, joining him on the narrow cobbled pavement, 'we've only this minute got here! A bit of a sleepy hollow though, isn't it? Let's see what the house is like, shall we?'

'Oh,' he grinned at her, 'that will be fine; Mr East wouldn't buy any old rubbish; you should have realised that by now, Felicity.'

'Come on then,' she laughed, giving him a slight push and picking up a couple of the bags at their feet, 'let's find out. Funny though,' she added frowning, 'about that message from Mark last night. Why do you think he changed his mind about joining us, Johnnie? He was all for it a couple of days ago. Mr East isn't going to be happy when he hears.'

'I've no idea,' Johnnie said, finding the key to the front door, 'but no doubt Mark would have had his reasons.'

'Odd though,' she persisted, 'we've got on well with him these last few months. He could at least have spoken to us and told us why.'

'True,' he said, opening the door and pushing back a pile of junk mail which lay in a discarded heap on the hall floor, 'but, Felicity, don't forget, although he also lives in Manchester, we don't really know him all that well.'

'I still don't understand why he should have backed out the way he did – one text message on his mobile and that's all; we'll probably never see him again.'

'Listen,' he said, turning round to look at her, 'drop it, Felicity; it's none of our business, but you are right, though,' he added, leading the way along the narrow hall and into the kitchen, 'I don't think Mr East will be pleased. Anyway, let's face it, Mark isn't our problem.'

'I know,' she said, following him, 'we've got enough to think about at the moment.'

*

Chief Inspector Brenda Masters put down the report she had been reading and looked out of the window. The front of the Meadowbank Police Station faced the whole length of Market Square as far as the church. May was one of her favourite months; the winter, which this year had been particularly severe, well and truly behind them and with the long summer months to look forward to. The cherry blossom had been out for some weeks now and the pavements on either side of the stone steps leading up to the main door of Saint Stephen's had a soft sprinkling of tiny pink petals.

Three o'clock was chiming as she allowed herself for a brief moment to take in the tranquil scene; the town, at this time of the afternoon, almost deserted. In fact she was thinking, the last few months had been relatively quiet, with no more than the odd domestic fracas to contend with and one isolated case of an attempted break-in, but nothing serious and certainly not on the escalating scale which had affected Meadowbank almost without any let-up since the previous summer. And now, she thought, dragging her eyes away reluctantly from the window, it would seem judging by the report which had that morning arrived from New Scotland Yard they may be in for another wave of crime; the potential gravity of what it implied could prove far more difficult to control or prevent, requiring considerable effort and skill throughout the whole of the south of England. Up until now Meadowbank had managed to avoid the universal drug problem; at least there had been no cases reported which inevitably meant Brenda had little first-hand experience of knowing the best way to proceed. The report had disturbed her; it was so rare to hear directly from New Scotland Yard; those eighty-odd miles along the motorway to London may just as well have been several hundred miles away, but according to them pockets of drug rings were being set up along the south coast and further inland. There had been a spate of robberies reported from pharmacies and drug stores; not only in Southampton, Portsmouth, Winchester and Petersfield, where over the past six months a total of thirty-six reports had been received, but more recently word had come in from the smaller towns in the southern counties, including Lyndhurst in the New Forest and further east and almost running parallel with the motorway, Botley, Wickham, Denmead and Havant and spreading as far west as Bournemouth, Poole and Plymouth.

Brenda was on the point of calling Ian Ash into her office when the main phone on her desk rang.

'Yes, Sergeant?' she said and waited to be put through to Chief Inspector Gerald Carpenter, her counter-part in Winchester.

'Good afternoon, Brenda,' he said, 'I hope you are having a good one.'

'Passable, Gerald.' she said. She had known him from when she had first joined the force and although they hardly ever met up, seldom having any reason to, they had worked together on more than one case when the support from his team in Winchester had been invaluable to them tucked away in Meadowbank. 'I've just finished reading the report from New Scotland Yard; I expect you've got one as well.'

'Yes,' he agreed, 'came this morning; makes grim reading, doesn't it? Mind you,' he went on in his usual brisk way, 'we've had a spiralling drug problem here for a while now, somewhat spasmodic I have to say and not too difficult to break up; mostly kids and not too bright in hiding what they're up to, but this is something totally different.'

'It appears to be well organised.'

'I'm sure it is; anyway, Brenda,' he continued, 'that isn't why I'm phoning you.'

'No?'

'I've just received a call from Manchester; they were called out earlier today to one of the service flats in London Road. I don't know how well you know Manchester?'

'Not all that well.'

'Well, one of the cleaning staff found the body of a young man; at first she thought he was just unconscious, assuming, as there was an empty bottle of whisky next to him, he'd had too much to drink the night before —'

' — but he wasn't?' Brenda interrupted, having a good idea by this time what was coming next.

'No,' Gerald said quickly, 'he was dead alright and had been for several hours; at least since around ten last night. He had either taken something, we're still waiting for them to get back to us on the substance, or it had been administered to him, but too early to say.'

'But you think it's murder?'

'I think it's more than likely, yes.'

'And you believe there is a connection with us here in Meadowbank?'

'It's a possibility, Brenda,' he said, 'and if there is, his death could have something to do with this drug ring business, although it's no more than supposition.'

'Why?'

'For a number of reasons,' he started to explain, speaking slower this time, as if he was still collating his thoughts and trying to put them in some sort of order for her, 'Mark Astley, that was his name, was already known to us. He came from Winchester originally, went to school here, although he was more often than not playing truant. A bit of a tearaway. He would have been twenty-eight now, but he'd been a young offender, petty crime, you know the kind of thing: supermarket thieving, the odd bottle of whisky and packet of cigarettes from off licences and breaking into parked cars and doing a bit of joy riding and this was before he was old enough to have a licence. In fact, he spent most of his early teens in Borstal; didn't do him any good of course and after that he left Winchester, went up north, but still couldn't keep out of trouble. He was involved in a large post office robbery in Leeds about six years ago, did time, only nine months though and since he came out of prison he more or less went to ground. All we did know, and that was only because he had signed on with the social security, was that he was living in Manchester.'

'And was he into drugs?'

'Not to any degree; nothing heavy, marijuana, stuff like that. I suppose you could say he was a dabbler; he seemed to get his kicks from breaking into properties and damned good at it he was too.'

'And why do you think he could have been involved in this latest drug ring alert? According to the report they're scattered around the south of England.'

'I know, but apart from the way a number of these robberies have been conducted, to my mind they appear to bear his particular stamp, also it looks as though he had been planning to join up with a couple of his friends in Meadowbank.'

'I see.'

'You're thinking it might be a coincidence?'

'I doubt it, Gerald.' Brenda said, unable to keep the smile from her voice. Like all of them in the force the very word coincidence was strictly taboo. 'How did you learn about this anyway?'

'Apparently,' he said, 'the officer who called at Mark Astley's flat this morning found his mobile; it had slipped down between the cushions on one of his chairs, and he hadn't deleted the last text message he made.'

'Which was?'

'To quote verbatim: "Sorry, Johnnie, but I am unable to join you and Felicity in Meadowbank as planned tomorrow.".'

'Nothing else?'

'No; brief and to the point.'

'You have this Johnnie's mobile number?'

'Yes, but up to now, we've done nothing with it. I wanted to confer with you first, hear what your reactions would be.'

'Well,' Brenda said, 'it looks as though it's encroaching on my patch.'

'Partly, yes.'

'It would give us a stronger lead, Gerald, if you could find out about that number.'

'That's been done already;' he said, 'I've got the number here,' are you ready, Brenda?'

'Yes, Gerald, fire ahead.' she said, taking a clean sheet of paper from her pad.

'It's 07721 345 290 and the mobile was purchased in the HMV store in Manchester six months ago by a Mr John Baker of Flat 4a, forty-six Deansgate, Manchester, not far from the Granada television studios.' he added.

'You're going to tell me that Mr Baker is no longer at that address, aren't you?'

'Are you a mind reader, Brenda,' he gave a quick chuckle, 'but you're quite right. He vacated the premises, handing in the keys to the agents, yesterday at eighteen hundred hours.'

'And if he and his girlfriend; that is if it is his girlfriend, could be his wife, is with him, the pair of them may be in Meadowbank as we speak. And,' Brenda went on, 'if they are, we'll find them.'

'Good,' Gerald said, 'it looks very much as though, along with the Manchester end, we'll be working together on this one, Brenda. Have you got any immediate thoughts on how you're going to proceed?'

'Not exactly,' she said thoughtfully, 'but if you are right, and these two have something to do with any of the drug rings in the south, I don't think it would be too clever to alert them to any suspicions we may or may not have about them.'

'That had occurred to me as well,' he admitted, 'put it like this, Brenda, our main criteria is to be vigilant and actually prevent any break-ins; to alert them might prematurely flush out whoever is in control of these setups.'

'I agree, of course. But, Gerald,' she continued, 'I think we would, that is if Manchester wants us to get involved, and as an initial step, speak to them both and find out what they know about Mark Astley and why he was planning to come south. See what they come up with.'

'Which could be interesting.'

'Quite.'

*

It was well after five before the wedding reception broke up which didn't give them long to clear away the debris of plates and glasses before their normal opening time of six-thirty.

'There's really no point in closing now.' Brian said to her when the last of their guests had gone.

'I suppose not,' she agreed, filling the dishwasher with the first lot of glasses, 'but it was a great party, wasn't it?'

'The best!' he smiled, 'Even although we were on the go all the time. Mind you, love, if we'd held the reception up at the hotel, it would have been quite different.'

'Don't I know it! But, honestly, Brian, although it has been hard work, it's been worth it and everyone seemed to enjoy themselves.'

'It looks as if we have some early customers, Brian.' Derek said, bringing over a couple of empty glasses he had found on one of the window ledges.

'It doesn't matter,' Brian said, 'we're almost straight.'

The young couple hesitated for a moment in the open doorway, their eyes adjusting from the bright sunlight to the relative gloom inside the pub. Brian didn't remember seeing either of them before, although the man, in his mid to late twenties he guessed, did look vaguely familiar.

'You are open, aren't you?' he asked Brian, 'We've only arrived in Meadowbank this afternoon and weren't sure about your opening hours.'

'We are, yes,' Brian smiled a welcome, 'normally it isn't until six-thirty, but we've had a special function today, so our usual routine is somewhat out of kilter. Anyway,' he went on, giving the bar a final wipe and putting down some fresh beer mats, 'what can I get you?'

'I'll have a Heineken; what about you, Felicity,' he said, turning to the girl beside him, 'your usual?'

'Please, Johnnie.'

'And a glass of Chardonnay.' he said to Brian.

It was still not six-thirty, but their first two customers must have acted as magnets because no sooner had Brian served them, a crowd of their Friday night regulars converged on the bar. The couple, he noticed, remained where they were; rather than sitting down at one of the tables which he thought a little unusual. It wasn't as though they appeared to be a talkative pair, wanting to get into conversation with anyone else. Brian had been in the business long enough to suss out the different types of people who had, over the years, come into his pub: there were a number of categories, but in the main either those who merely wanted a quiet drink or the more garrulous who liked nothing better than to get into conversation with anyone who would listen to them.

An hour later and the two were still there, Derek having served them another round. By now, Brian was sure he had seen the man before, although he felt it must have been some time ago.

'You say you've just arrived?' Brian asked him during a brief lull from serving.

'That's right,' he answered, 'we've moved into one of the houses across the square.'

'Number twenty-eight.' the girl quickly put in.

'Alison Moore's house;' Brian commented, 'we heard it had been sold recently.'

'We're only renting.' the girl supplied.

'Well,' Brian said, 'I hope you'll be happy here. Is this the first time you've been to Meadowbank?'

'Yes,' he said unhesitatingly, 'we don't know this part of the country, but when the estate agents told us there was a house available for rent here, we thought it would make a change; didn't we, Felicity?'

'That's right, we did,' she answered slowly, 'a new place and new people.'

'Well,' Brian repeated, 'you'll find us an easy lot to get on with. It shouldn't take you long to settle in.'

'I'm sure it won't,' she said, 'you do seem to be very busy. Is there any chance you may be looking for extra staff; I've been working in a pub in Manchester for the past year?' she added.

'Sorry to disappoint you,' Brian smiled apologetically, surprised at the direct approach. Surely the pair of them hadn't come to Meadowbank on spec? Jobs were not all that plentiful, with still a number of young people unable to get work, although there could be a chance during the summer months for some temporary work, 'but as far as The Market Inn is concerned, we're okay. You could ask at The Bridge Inn; they do a good trade and Mrs Gallier, she's the landlady, might want some extra help.'

'Thanks, I'll go along there tomorrow.'

'Failing that,' he suggested, wanting to help, although at the same time not quite making up his mind about them. There was something which was not gelling and as he stood facing them both, he couldn't quite work out what it was. She seemed genuine enough: a pretty dark-haired girl with elfin features and not as tarty as some of the young people who came into Meadowbank at the beginning of the season looking for work, but it was her boyfriend he couldn't quite take to. He was groping around in his mind to find a word to fit him and the only one he could come up with, while probably unjustified, was shifty. It was the way he seemed to have the off-putting habit of not looking at you straight in the face, as though he was doing his best to keep his distance. It was only an impression, and the more Brian thought about him, the more certain he was becoming that not only had he seen him before, but there was a connotation, an unpleasant one at that, but he couldn't, at least not yet, put his finger on it, 'you could try The Royal Oak hotel,' he went on, giving his attention to the girl, 'it's on the Stockbridge Road only five miles or so from the town. It's just possible they may have a vacancy. Probably worth a try.'

'Thank you,' she said, 'you've been really helpful. By the way,' she added, formally making to shake his hand, 'I'm Felicity Carter and this is my partner, Johnnie Baker.' pulling him towards her to complete the introduction.

He does not want this Brian thought immediately, not missing the flash of irritation which crossed the man's face. Why? Let it go, Brian, he said to himself; he's probably just an unsociable type; nothing all that unusual in that, was there?

They didn't stay much longer after that; Brian was at the other end of the bar when they left and the girl waved to him, but not him. Johnnie Baker didn't look back and kept walking until he was outside and on to the pavement.

'You're looking very thoughtful.' Melissa said to him when they'd gone.

'Was I, love?'

'You know perfectly well you were, Brian Morrison,' she smiled, nudging him in the ribs, 'I can always tell when there is something on your mind.'

'Is that so?'

'Yes, it is. It's to do with the couple who've moved into Alison's old house, isn't it?'

'So, you've heard then?'

'Of course. Our band of regulars has been doing their best to enlighten me. Don't ask me how they found out,'

'No doubt they saw them arriving and put the proverbial two and two together.'

'And,' she suggested, 'this time, made four.'

'Something like that, yes.'

'So, Brian,' she persisted, 'what's bothering you?'

'It's not exactly bothering me, Melissa,' he said slowly, 'it's just that I'm positive I've seen him before, that's all, and yet when I asked him whether this was their first visit to Meadowbank, he said it was.'

'Perhaps he has a double.'

'Could have, I suppose, but it's not often I forget a face. That chap has been in here before; I'm ninety-nine per cent sure of it, although I can't remember when it was, but it must have been at least four or even five years ago.'

'But, if so, why would he deny it?'

'A good question and there was another thing.'

'Yes?'

'He was very quick to say he'd never been in Meadowbank and when he did, I couldn't help noticing the look his girlfriend gave him. It was no more than a glance, but she was surprised, Melissa. She really didn't expect him to say that; oh, she tried to cover it up, in fact, confirmed straight away that neither of them knew this area.'

Chapter Two

Jacqueline Wellings, senior sales consultant with Town & Country Estate Agents, had a nine o'clock appointment the following morning, arrangements having been made to meet the clients outside the property. Number Two The Mews, one of the two-storey town houses on the Stockbridge Road on the outskirts of Meadowbank, had been empty since the beginning of the year, but due to the complicated legalities following the sudden death of the owner, had only recently come on the market. As Jacqueline's new manager, Martin Frame, had confidently predicted when Town & Country had been given the sole selling rights, interest would be keen; Mr and Mrs Cyril Howarth, who were now waiting outside the front gate of Number Two, were the fourth prospective buyers in less than a week. Jacqueline, pulling up behind their brand new Volvo Estate couldn't help wondering how genuine their intentions were. Having lived in Meadowbank considerably longer than her manager, she held a more pragmatic point of view, feeling the current influx of enquiries were more likely to be out of curiosity, possibly verging on the macabre, given that the murder of the late owner actually took place inside Number Two, than with any real intention of wanting to purchase the property.

She had already met Cyril Howarth earlier in the week when he had called into the agency and he now introduced his wife to her: a thin, sharp-featured woman in her mid-to-late forties who, once she had shaken hands with Jacqueline, could hardly curb her impatience to view the house. Here was a woman, Jacqueline decided, who knew immediately what she wanted and whether she was aware of the relatively recent history surrounding the property it was impossible to tell. Normally, at least in Jacqueline's experience, prospective, at least genuine prospective buyers, played down their initial enthusiasm; it was all part of the purchasing game. To appear too eager conveyed they were entirely happy with everything they saw, but more importantly, with the price being asked. She could tell by Cyril Howarth's expression, one of barely constrained annoyance, as he tried, without any success, to convey to his wife to be less exuberant.

Jacqueline unlocked the front door and gestured for them to go in. There was a faint mustiness in the hall and without saying anything she led the way through to the lounge, opening both the front windows and the French windows leading on to the paved terrace at the back of the building. Already, after such a short time, the whole place had that air of neglect. Houses really needed to be lived in she thought and not for the first time. It was always the same; no matter how attractive the interior of any property might be, it needed people to breathe life into the atmosphere. Jacqueline made it a point never to make apologies; there was no point in her opinion of stressing the house had been empty for months and it needed to be aired or any other platitudes when it was blatantly obvious to anyone they were truisms and didn't require emphasising.

'I like it; I really do. What do you think, darling?' Mrs Howarth said, doing a mini-pirouette in the centre of the dining room and tugging impatiently at her husband's sleeve.

'Hold on, Angela,' he said, pulling her hand away, 'we haven't seen the rest of the house yet.'

'We'll go upstairs, shall we?' Jacqueline suggested diplomatically, feeling slightly embarrassed by the woman's over-the-top behaviour. 'We haven't looked at the kitchen and the utility room yet, but we can do that when we come down.'

'Good idea, Miss Wellings.' he said. 'In case you're wondering,' he added, as they went back into the hall, 'we do know what happened here.'

'And you don't feel this off-putting?' Jacqueline asked him; deciding it was best to come to the point at the beginning of any negotiation, far better than trying to hide something which would soon emerge, if not before they began negotiations but certainly not long after they moved in.

'Not in the least.' he said without any hesitation.

'And your wife?' she asked; by now Mrs Howarth had reached the top of the first flight of stairs, her eagerness to see the rest of the house apparently paramount to her.

'When my wife, Miss Wellings,' he gave her an old fashioned lopsided smile, 'sets her heart on anything, nothing, and I repeat absolutely nothing, will stand in her way. Believe me.'

They didn't spend long upstairs, Angela Howarth sweeping through the master bedroom and the other rooms giving them no more than a cursory glance, not even pausing long enough to look out of the windows, which, in itself, Jacqueline thought unusual. *Everyone,* without exception, looked out of the windows of a property they were thinking of buying. It was usually the first thing they did when they entered a room; it was instinctive and she had never known anyone before not to be interested in what the various views would be like and those, especially from the rear of the house, were splendid.

In the distance; the symmetric green and brown squares of farmland and off to the extreme right, the ancient roofs and chimneys of the Old Manor and immediately in front, the River Test. The river flowed swiftly at this point, having gathered momentum from the salmon leap further upstream at the Mill, Simon Grant's property, until it reached the natural curve at the back of Saint Stephen's church, gradually losing pace to flow more sedately under the bridge in the centre of Meadowbank, to eventually join The Solent. A peaceful scene; she'd always thought so, from when the town houses had been built and she had shown the first buyers round; Town & Country, having again, secured the sole selling rights.

'What do you think of the view, Mrs Howarth?' Jacqueline asked her when, for the first time, she had managed to steer her towards the window in one of the bedrooms on the second floor.

'Lovely.' she answered quickly, dismissively, immediately turning away.

'This room would make an excellent study, Miss Wellings, although I don't think I would get very much work done. I'd be continually staring out of the window.' Cyril Howarth said and then frowning as his mobile rang. Pulling it out from his pocket, he apologised and walked away from them both to answer it.

'Shall we go downstairs now?' Jacqueline suggested to his wife, sensing he wanted to be on his own when he took the call.

It was several minutes before he rejoined them. Jacqueline had shown Angela Howarth the kitchen, explaining the various pieces of built-in equipment and the utility room with a door leading to the integral garage and were back in the dining-room, when she saw him standing in the open doorway. She didn't know how long he had been there; she hadn't heard his footsteps either coming down the stairs or on the parquet floor in the hall. But, it was the set expression on his face which alerted her; something was wrong. His former easy-going manner had gone and she could see he was making a supreme effort to control his emotions. Angela Howarth didn't appear to notice any difference in him, hardly looking up when he spoke to her; his voice not quite steady, to ask if she had seen everything she wanted to.

'Yes, darling,' she said, 'and as you know, my mind is quite made up. In fact, Miss Wellings,' she added, turning to Jacqueline, 'I absolutely knew this was the house for us; even before I came inside this morning. I actually sent a text message to my son on Thursday to tell him so.'

'Miss Wellings, thank you for your time and as my wife has told you, she likes the house very much.'

'Much more than that, Cyril,' she put in, 'I *love* it!'

'Quite.' he said and Jacqueline noticed how pale he had become. She wanted to do, or say something to help him; put him at his ease, but never having been in such an awkward situation before, was at a complete loss for words. He'd had a shock; that was obvious.

'Mr Howarth,' she began tentatively, 'perhaps you would like time to think about this before reaching a final decision.'

'That's considerate of you, Miss Wellings.' And she could tell he was aware she had seen his distress, also, she could read appreciation of her understanding on his face.

'Oh, really, Cyril! Let's not waste any time. Someone else will come along and we'll lose this wonderful house!'

'Alright, Angela,' he managed to smile at her, but it was a poor attempt and, embarrassed, Jacqueline looked away. 'you'll get your house; I promise. I'll phone you after lunch, Miss Wellings,' he said to her, taking his wife's arm, 'there are a number of things I need to attend to first.'

*

Felicity was not having a productive morning. As the landlord of The Market Inn had suggested, she did go along to The Bridge Inn but, although Mrs Gallier had been friendly enough and didn't appear to mind being asked if she needed extra help behind the bar, she had told her the business didn't warrant additional bar staff, even on a part-time basis.

After leaving there, she drove up to The Royal Oak, parking at the rear of the hotel and walking round to the main door. She didn't really know what to expect; perhaps an old-fashioned rundown country house hotel, but as soon as she walked up the shallow flight of steps and through the glass swing doors, she realised how wrong she'd been. The Royal Oak was the epitome of sophisticated grandeur; from the rich dark panelling, the high ornate ceilings and the crystal chandeliers, to the black and white floor tiles leading up to the reception desk. Even that was different to most hotels she had been in: a smoked-glass top, crescent-shaped, in polished oak with a polished brass rail running around the whole length of it. All a bit stuffy for her taste she decided walking up to the desk.

These were her first impressions and she was wondering what it would be like to work in such a subdued atmosphere, where the few people she had seen appeared to whisper rather than talk and even the music coming from the lounge bar, had been turned down to its lowest level. Not a local radio station either; nothing so pedestrian as that, trying to work out what the tune was. Mantovani or something equally as ancient she decided and waited to meet Sandra Watson.

Even before Sandra Watson spoke to her Felicity realised she'd made a mistake coming up to the hotel. Not only was it not her scene, but she immediately recognised the type of woman who was now striding towards her. It wasn't only the arrogant, head held high, shoulders back kind of walk or the impeccably tailored grey and white pin-striped two-piece and the statement-making low-heeled black patent leather shoes; it was the disdainful haughty expression on a face devoid of any warmth whatsoever which got to her. It was blatantly obvious to Felicity that she hadn't so much as passed the first hurdle.

'My receptionist tells me you were asking if we had any vacancies?' she asked, without any introduction and certainly no formal shaking of hands.

'That's right,' Felicity answered, 'I've had bar experience, also I've done some waitressing.'

'I see,' she said, the dark eyes taking in every single item Felicity was wearing. She probably knows what colour my knickers are! Felicity thought. 'you say *experience*,' she emphasised, not taking her eyes away from her, 'but I would need to see your curriculum vitae even before I could begin to consider you for any vacancy we may have.'

'I'm sorry,' Felicity said and not in the least bit sorry; all she wanted to do was leave. Even if this woman, the receptionist had called her the manageress, did offer her a job, there was no way she could work here. It would drive her mad! Felicity had had a number of jobs since leaving school, some of them better than others, also many of her employers had left a lot to be desired, at least in her opinion, but the manageress of this – of this *mausoleum*, well, she would be impossible to work for. 'but,' she explained, 'I don't have a c.v.'

'Really? How extraordinary. I think you should consider getting one made out, my dear, otherwise you're going to find it extremely difficult, if not impossible, especially if you wish to work for such an exclusive hotel as The Royal Oak.'

'Thank you, I'll do that.' Felicity said, making to walk away, assuming the so-called interview was at an end.

'When you do, Miss -?'

'- Miss Carter; Felicity Carter.'

'Miss Carter,' she continued, 'I would suggest you arrange an appointment through my receptionist. Incidentally,' she added, 'I trust you have a permanent residential address in Meadowbank?'

'Of course,' Felicity answered sharply, finding her high-handed assumption that she was some kind of vagrant insulting, 'we're renting a house in the Market Square.'

'We?'

'My *partner* and I,' she emphasised; two can play at this game she thought, not that it was any of her business in any case, 'number twenty-eight as a matter of fact.'

'Number twenty-eight,' she repeated, 'that sounds familiar; yes, of course,' she went on, her scarlet-painted lips tightening, 'that was where Alison Moore lived, wasn't it?'

'I'm sorry,' Felicity said, longing to get away, 'I have no idea.'

'Well, it was and that young lady, she happened to be our receptionist, let us down badly, leaving right at the beginning of our busy period. You say you didn't know her?'

'No, I've never heard of her.'

'Hmmph, all I can say, Miss Carter, that can only be in your favour.'

What a cow! Felicity thought minutes later when, finally having made her escape before the manageress could get into her stride. Obviously Alison Moore wasn't exactly at the top of her popularity list, but then, Felicity thought, pulling out of the car park, who would be, working for her.

Drawing up at the traffic lights at the edge of the town, she wondered how she would be able to put up with living in such a tight-knit community; it wasn't going to be easy. Nor for Johnnie either, but then he didn't have much choice; Mr East called the shots, also he paid Johnnie's wages and the money was good. There could be no argument about that. A few more months, that was all it would take, providing everything continued to do as well as it had so far and then they would be able to move somewhere else, somewhere warm perhaps. But, meanwhile, she needed to find some sort of work to occupy herself; from what she had seen up to now there didn't appear to be much on offer. She had tried the two pubs, nothing doing there and as far as the hotel is concerned she had already dismissed that possibility.

Back in the Market Square and passing the one and only decent looking restaurant they had both seen since they arrived yesterday, the thought occurred to her that it may just be worth her while making a few enquiries. Nothing ventured and all that. The morning couldn't get any worse she decided, parking a few hundred yards from The Salmon's Rest restaurant.

Many of the tables were already occupied and it wasn't yet midday. A really pretty place was her immediate reaction, reminding her of the holiday Johnnie and she had had last year in Italy: the colours especially; the blues and greens of the Mediterranean, also the stone archway at the back of the restaurant which led on to a small tiled courtyard with huge pots of geraniums and other flowers she didn't know the names of.

'Good afternoon,' a short red-haired woman greeted her as soon as she stepped inside, 'table for one?'

'No, I'm sorry,' Felicity said, 'perhaps I should come back later when you're less busy.'

'You're not selling anything, are you?'

'Not directly, no,' Felicity smiled, 'except I was wondering if you had any vacancies for a waitress.'

'We could have,' the immediate response surprising her, 'but as you say, now isn't the best of times. I tell you what, why not come back later; after two should be a lot quieter and we can have a chat.'

'I will, yes and thank you. My name, by the way, is Felicity Carter.'

'And I'm Barbara Wood and that's my husband over there, behind the bar; Harry. We've only been open for one day and as you can see we are a bit rushed off our feet, so if you'll excuse me –'

What a difference five minutes make Felicity thought going back to the car and driving the short distance back to twenty-eight. It would be really convenient too; literally on their doorstep. It didn't matter all that much what the wages were, so long as she was occupied, that was the main thing.

*

'How did it go this morning, Jacqueline? Did they sign on the dotted line?' Martin Frame asked her, leaning languidly against her open office door.

'I believe it went reasonably well.' she said, selecting her words with care, although she realised she was probably wasting her breath. There had been many times when Martin's predecessor, Rodney Blake, had exasperated her by his persistence; wanting to know the ins and outs of what sale she may be handling, especially if they were for one of the more expensive properties on their books, but she had always been able to mentally shrug this off somehow, but these days she was finding her reaction towards Martin extremely difficult to handle. After Rodney's death in January, Martin had been transferred from their office in Guildford and even from his first day as manager of Town & Country she had taken exception to his manner. She hadn't discussed this with anyone, mainly because there was no one she could discuss it with. It wouldn't have been fair to inflict these personal prejudices on Gregory because, if she was being honest, that is what they were. She was finding as the weeks went by, Martin's comments, including his supercilious attitude to any of their less well-off prospective buyers who came into the agency, brash and unprofessional. Also, she rather suspected she wasn't the only one to think this way; she had caught the embarrassed expression on Gregory's face more than once when, as soon as these clients' backs were turned, Martin would make some disparaging and undeserved remark. Even their new receptionist, who had only been with them a couple of months and had never known Rodney, had looked up once or twice, no doubt not quite understanding where Martin was coming from. Jacqueline had been working with Gregory for more than three years now; he was good at his job, although up to now he had been handling rentals only, but she was hoping to persuade Martin to transfer him to the selling side of the business; their agency was thriving and she was sure their budget could support an extra member of staff to take on these lettings, but so far, waiting for the right opportunity, she hadn't broached the subject with him. 'Did the Howarths find anything wrong with the property, then?' he was asking.

'No, they didn't; on the contrary, Martin, they appeared to like it very much and Mrs Howarth, in particular, was delighted with everything.'

'So, what's the problem?'

'As far as I know there is no problem,' she answered, doing her utmost not to rise to his bait, 'Mr Howarth is going to phone me after lunch to give me his final decision.'

'Jacqueline,' he said, pulling himself upright and coming over to her desk, 'do you happen to know what time it is?'

'Yes, of course I do. It's ten minutes to three.'

'Unless he's in the habit of having a very long lunch, I don't think you're going to hear from him.'

'I wouldn't go as far as to say that.'

'Wouldn't you? Well, I would. I won't suggest, even remotely, Jacqueline, that you may have lost the sale by not putting just a little bit of pressure on Mr Howarth. You know the spiel; I'm sure I don't need to remind you.'

'Martin,' she said slowly and taking a deep breath, 'if, as you seem to be saying, the sale does fall through, so be it.'

'So be it!'

'Yes, that's what I said and that's what I meant. It is not my practice to put pressure on a client, force him or her to make a decision they may not be ready to make. I've been in the property business for some years, as I am sure you are aware, and I have a good track record and one, I might add, I am proud of.'

'We will see, Jacqueline. In my considered opinion, this agency requires some pepping up; it's tired, lacking the necessary umph! We are here, all of us in fact, for the sole purpose of making money for the agency and ultimately for ourselves and we can only do that by selling property!'

'I'm fully aware of that, Martin,' she said quietly, 'and theoretically you are quite correct; now, if you don't mind, I have a number of phone calls to make.'

'I hope you have taken on board what I've been saying, Jacqueline.'

'I've taken on board everything you've said, Martin,' she said, keeping her voice level, but realising what she was about to say to him had to be said and the sooner the better, 'if you're dissatisfied with the way I work, I would like you to tell me.'

'What does that mean?'

'Quite simply,' she answered, 'it means if you are not, then I'll have no alternative, but to hand in my notice.'

'Come on, Jacqueline,' blustering now and walking back towards the door, 'no need to over react. A bit of constructive criticism never did anyone any harm.'

Perhaps fortuitously at that moment the telephone on her desk rang and picking up the receiver she swivelled round in her chair to a position where she couldn't see him. Ironically and perhaps timely it was Cyril Howarth on the other end of the line.

'Good afternoon, Mr Howarth.'

'Good afternoon, Miss Wellings,' he said, 'I apologise for taking so long to get back to you, but we've had some rather sad news.'

'I'm sorry; I thought you may have done.'

'You are a perceptive woman,' he said, 'you see, I had to break it to my wife after we left you this morning. That wasn't easy -' he hesitated for a fraction of a second, but Jacqueline didn't interrupt, allowing him the time he needed, 'the phone call I had was to tell me her son, Mark; my stepson, had died.'

'I don't know what I can say.' she said slowly, all too aware that Martin was still in her office and no doubt trying to understand what was happening.

'There really isn't anything anyone can say,' he said, 'Mark was only twenty-eight, no age at all, and up to the time we heard the news, they still didn't know what happened; whether it was suicide or -' again, he paused, 'or,' he continued, 'it was foul play.'

'But this is absolutely dreadful! Dreadful! How distressed you and your wife must be. I can't even begin to imagine what she must be going through.'

'It was a tremendous shock, of course, but he's always been a bit of a handful, ever since he was a young lad, although it was still a shock.' he repeated.

'I appreciate you phoning me, Mr Howarth; I would have fully understood if you hadn't. You must have so much to do.'

'It's true, we do. The funeral and everything, but my wife is still adamant, Miss Wellings, she wants us to buy the house; in fact, in many respects she seems more determined than ever. It could be that by staying here in Winchester where Mark was brought up would always be a constant reminder of everything. I don't know. Do you understand?'

'I think so.'

'I am going to be pretty well tied up with the various formalities over the next few days,' he went on, 'but can I make a formal offer and naturally pay the deposit on the property as soon as possible?'

'Of course, that's no problem.' Jacqueline said quietly, 'I'll get the papers drawn up this afternoon; they need to be signed of course. Would you like me to bring them to Winchester and you and your wife could sign them together, would that help?'

Cyril Howarth listened without interrupting and when she had finished, she could tell by the long intake of breath, in some way she had taken a load off his mind. Poor man she thought; I'm sure the last thing he wants to be doing right now is negotiating the first stages of buying a property. Before ringing off, he gave her directions on how to find where they lived on the outskirts of Winchester and arranging a time shortly after six that evening.

Replacing the receiver, Jacqueline looked up, wishing she had the office to herself, but Martin was still there, in exactly the same position as earlier, but this time with a wide grin on his face.

'Sounds as though you've clinched it, Jacqueline.'

'As you say, Martin,' she said doing all she could to keep the distaste from her voice and, taking her handbag from the desk drawer, stood up, 'I've clinched it and now, if you'll excuse me, I'm going out.'

*

'So, Ian, what do you think?' Brenda asked him later in the afternoon,

'You've read the report from New Scotland Yard; also, I've told you what Winchester have come up with.'

'As far as this drug business is concerned, ma'am,' he said, 'it's a pity the report is so sketchy. All it tells us is where the robberies have taken place and how they're spreading through the south and that's about all.'

'I know,' she agreed, 'but perhaps that is all they do know, except, as they described it, pockets of the drug rings have been set up which would indicate they could be acting as some sort of centres.'

'For receiving the drugs you mean?'

'Yes, but also for the distribution of them. Where do they go from there? Presumably they will be contained within the country.'

'I suppose it depends on where they'll get the highest street value for them.'

'Major towns and cities I should say,' she said, 'which rules out all the smaller towns.'

'Like Meadowbank?'

'And many others, yes. But, Ian, the worrying aspect of it all,' she went on, 'is that it's spreading and so far, the way the robberies have been carried out, on a professional scale I mean, they still remain unsolved.'

'You're right,' Ian agreed, 'they sound as though they are highly trained, working as small teams maybe, but presumably they must report to someone in control.'

'Eventually,' Brenda said, 'someone will slip up; get too smart or too greedy, perhaps talk out of turn, that sort of thing, but we can't afford to wait for that to happen. They have to be stopped before it reaches epidemic proportions. I believe it's far more than merely being vigilant; we're up against a large network of crime here; I'm certain of that. Also, I don't think we should entirely discount these smaller towns as having only one use.'

'You mean when these pharmacies are relatively easy to break into?'

'Yes, perhaps bases are being set up initially in them before the drugs are distributed further afield.'

'When you think about it,' Ian put in quickly, feeling the first stirrings of interest. Although he had complained about being over-stretched during the series of events in Meadowbank since last summer, he had begun to feel bored in recent months with practically nothing happening;

at least nothing he could really get his teeth into, 'As a base, Meadowbank would be well placed geographically; only a matter of miles away from either the M3 or the M27.'

'True,' she said, 'which brings me to what Chief Inspector Carpenter was telling me. He was quite convinced you know that a number of these break-ins bore the stamp of Mark Astley. Apparently, he'd had a long track record and had the ability of entering a building, taking what he wanted and then going without leaving any trace of having broken into the place. I suppose that in itself is quite rare which often meant several hours or in some cases days would go by before these drugs had been missed. He started at an early age remember.'

'And,' Ian said, 'he had intended to come here.'

'Quite, and then changed his mind, almost at the last minute. Odd that.'

'This Johnnie Baker, ma'am,' he said, 'you've decided not to call him?'

'Not yet, Ian,' Brenda said, 'we need first to know where the pair of them are. If we did and he is up to no good, it could very well alert him and then we'll never find him, at least not in Meadowbank.'

The phone ringing at that moment interrupted them. Why was it, Ian thought, this invariably happened, just at the point when they were trying to work their way through to formulating some line of strategy: talk about breaking the thought process!

'Alright, Sergeant,' Brenda was saying, 'put him through. Hello, Gerald .... no, it's perfectly alright. Ian and I have been going through the various aspects of this latest drug business ....'

Brenda wasn't on the phone for long; most of the time saying little, until finally bringing the call to a close: 'Well, Ian,' she said, looking across the desk at him, a small smile on her lips, 'that was interesting.'

'Yes?'

'Apparently, Mark Astley had a text message from his mother on Thursday morning to tell him she and her husband were planning to move to Meadowbank to live and were going to view a house here this morning, also that she had already set her heart on them buying it.'

'As you say, interesting,' Ian said, 'perhaps that was the reason he pulled out from coming to Meadowbank?'

'Could have been. If he had been planning to stay in Meadowbank, having his parents in the same town could have been too close for comfort for him. They're called Howarth by the way,' she added, 'Cyril and Angela Howarth. He's her second husband, although they've been married for years and Cyril Howarth is fully aware of Mark Astley's criminal background.'

'In that case,' Ian suggested, 'all the more reason for Mark Astley to stay away; his stepfather would bound to have been suspicious, at least wondering why he should have chosen to live here.'

'Yes, they hardly ever saw him. Their home is in Winchester, that's where Mark Astley came from originally, but after his spell in Borstal, he went north; his latest address being in Manchester.'

'I've been thinking.'

'Yes?'

'If Johnnie Baker is here, I guess it would be normal for the pair of them to go to one of the pubs at some time and you know what people are like in Meadowbank; any newcomer is immediately of interest to them. They like nothing better than to find out as much as they can about them.'

'That's a good idea,' Brenda said, 'so, what about this evening, then? Do you want to do the rounds, or shall I?'

Chapter Three

There were three pharmacies in Meadowbank: a new Superdrug in Bridge Street; White's The Chemist at the lower end of Market Square and The Meadowbank Pharmacy, next door to The Salmon's Rest restaurant. Victor York, the pharmacist, had lived in the town for a number of years. A quiet man; he didn't mix socially, which meant no-one had been able to find out a great deal about him. He wasn't married, although from time to time, a woman around his age, early fifties, would appear; this, naturally, leading to wild speculation among those who had nothing better to talk about. No-one had come up with what could be the most logical answer, considering the close resemblance between them, that she was his sister, but that would have been far too mundane an explanation and wouldn't have appealed to their over-active and lurid imaginations. They hadn't even been able to find out the lady's name, with the result she was referred to among themselves as Victor's woman.

The Meadowbank Pharmacy stayed open late two nights in the week, Saturday being one of them. The hour between six and seven was always quiet, when most of the shops in the town, including the mini-market in Bridge Street, were preparing to close up for the weekend, and Christine Saunders, Victor's assistant, grateful for the brief respite until the evening surgeries were over and they would have an influx of prescriptions to deal with, made them both a coffee before making a start to reconciling that day's takings in the software which had recently been installed on their main computer.

'That's funny.' she muttered under her breath, looking closer at the screen, 'Something's wrong here, Victor.' she said to him.

'What is, Christine?' he asked, leaning over her shoulder to see better, 'Don't look so worried; it's probably only a blip in the system.'

'It could be I suppose.' she admitted, but continuing to stare at the screen, not entirely convinced. 'But, I don't understand; look, Victor,' she said, pointing at the screen, 'there's the entry for the last assignment of pharmaceuticals we had delivered on Tuesday.'

'Yes.' and she recognised the impatience in his voice. While not exactly computer illiterate, she knew Victor's dislike of computers, usually leaving that side of the business to her. As he had often said to her in that supercilious way he had at times; he was a pharmacist, a dispenser of medicine, not a computer operator.

'Well,' she started to explain, wishing he wouldn't breathe down the back of her neck in that way, finding the strong smell of the peppermints he was addicted to, unpleasant, 'the figures of the last two items are not right. We received four cartons of amphetamine tablets and two of morphine phials but there are only two cartons of the amphetamines and one of the morphine listed.'

'Have you checked them against the invoice?'

'Yes, here you are,' she said, handing him the invoice, 'I've pencilled round both items.'

'You don't think you may have made a mistake when you keyed them in?'

'I didn't, no.'

'You sound very sure, Christine.' he said and to her relief standing back.

'I am,' she insisted, 'for the simple reason I took a print-out immediately I keyed them in; just as I always do. It's my way of checking that my figures match those on the invoices we get. I always do that, Victor. And,' she added, giving him the sheet of A4, 'here you are, and if you look at the top, you'll see the time and the date of the entry; eighteen hundred hours, the fifteenth of May.'

'I see,' he said, giving the print-out a cursory glance, 'as I said, a blip. You know yourself, Christine; the installation of new software can play silly games sometimes.'

'Should I give the technician a ring on Monday?'

'Oh, I wouldn't. Too premature; let's see if it happens again. No point calling him out unnecessarily.'

'It is worrying though, wouldn't you say?'

'It could be, but this time it can be easily rectified. All you have to do is change the figures to the correct ones, Christine.'

Christine was on the point of disagreeing with him. To rectify the problem was not as simple as that and she was surprised, even given his disinterested approach to correct accounting procedure, by his suggestion. She would, she decided, going back into pharmacy to serve the evening's first customer, take the time to reverse the whole entry and key it in again; that way, the whole transaction would be clear to the auditor when he came later in the year, also, if it did happen again, she would call the technician in herself.

*

Simon Grant and his wife called into The Market Inn for a drink before going across to the restaurant for a meal, Eliza mentioning as they pulled up outside the pub, how odd it would seem going into The Salmon's Rest again as the last time had been when the Taylors had it and how it would be bound to remind them of how much had happened since then.

'Including our own marriage, my darling,' he said, leaning over and kissing her, 'no regrets?'

'No regrets, Simon.' she smiled at him.

The evening was warm and the door of The Market Inn had been left open. Already, although only seven o'clock, the pub was beginning to fill up with customers bringing their drinks outside with them. By this time, having lived in Meadowbank for almost a year, Eliza recognised many of them and as she had felt almost from the first moment of arriving in the town, unbelievably comfortable when she was among them. She had never once felt an outsider, and had often, over the months, wondered why this was, knowing how other newcomers were often treated by the hard core of locals who made it quite obvious they didn't like change of any kind and that included anyone new arriving in their midst, especially taking up what they jealously regarded as their local, whether it was here, in The Market Inn, or Isobel Gallier's pub in Bridge Street. In her more cynical moments, which were rare, she put it down to the fact she was married to Simon, whose parents had originated from the town, owning the old mill which now belonged to Simon; his parents, on their retirement, deciding to make a new life for themselves in France.

'Hello, Eliza! Hello, Simon!' Melissa called out to them over the top of the customers waiting at the bar to be served. Eliza spotted Inspector Ash among them, mainly because he was a good head taller than most of the others. There was something a little incongruous about him in here she thought; out of context she supposed, wondering what it must be like for him; when being a police officer meant he was hardly ever off-duty and in his leisure hours merging in socially. It can't be easy, she concluded.

'There's a free table, Eliza,' Simon said, 'if you would prefer to sit down.'

'No, it's alright,' she said, 'I want to have a word with Melissa anyway; thank her for yesterday.'

'Of course,' he answered over his shoulder to her and leading the way between a noisy crowd in the centre of the room towards the bar, 'I think everyone in Meadowbank must be in here this evening!'

'Saturday night, Simon. It's traditional!' she shouted above the babble of voices surrounding them, competing with Phil Collins trying also to make himself heard with "A Groovy Kind of Love".

'Is that what you call it?' Simon yelled back at her and grinning. 'What a racket!'

Eventually they reached the bar and he was able to order their drinks: a wine for Eliza and half a lager for himself. There was something special about an evening in early summer Eliza decided looking around her; people acted quite differently, perhaps it had something to do with being able to shed the heavy overcoats, scarves and fleece-lined boots, especially this year, when it seemed winter was going to last forever. There had been too many days when the sun had been unable to penetrate the low grey cloud and this had definitely affected the mood of even the most resilient of person. But now, with the lighter evenings and the promise of many more to come before the clocks had to be changed once again, everyone seemed to be emerging from their partial hibernation during those long dark winter evenings.

'It was a lovely wedding, Melissa.' Eliza said to her, 'And thank you so much for asking us.'

'Yes,' Simon added, 'Brian is a very lucky man and you, Melissa, were a lovely bride.'

'Oh, Simon,' she laughed, 'please, you're making me blush.'

And it was true; Melissa was blushing. What a lovely young woman she is Eliza thought; totally unaffected and Simon had been right. Melissa had looked lovely and so very happy.

'Hello, you two.' Brian said, coming over to them. 'How are you?'

'We're fine, Brian,' Simon said, 'some crowd, eh? How on earth do you cope?'

'With difficulty,' Brian chuckled, 'but then it's always the same at Bank

Holidays.'

'Do you know,' Eliza said, 'I had completely forgotten that Monday is a holiday. If I had still been in London that would never have happened.'

'It just shows how contented you must be, Eliza.' Brian smiled, 'Simon,' he went on, 'I'm glad you've come in tonight because there's something I want to ask you; it's been puzzling me.'

'What's that?'

'Well,' Brian went on, 'do you see those two by the window; I mean the younger one.' he added.

'Yes.'

'Do you recognise him?'

'Er – I don't think so – but, wait a minute,' he said, 'I believe I do. It was a few years ago though.'

'I knew it!' Brian said, 'I said so to you, love, didn't I?' he asked, turning to Melissa.

'That's right, you did.'

'Why,' Simon asked, 'is it important?'

'I don't know about important,' Brian said slowly, 'but he and his girlfriend came in here yesterday, after you had all gone, apparently they had only arrived; they're renting Alison's old house and when I asked him whether he had ever been in Meadowbank he denied it. I thought it funny you see, because I was convinced I had seen him in here before, but that was about all I could remember. He didn't have the same girlfriend though; I'm sure about that.'

'He was part of a group.' Simon said.

'What?'

'They were four of them and there was a girl. Don't you remember, Brian? They kept themselves to themselves, but someone in the bar mentioned later after they had left that they were touring and had taken a wrong turning off the motorway and found themselves driving through Meadowbank and decided to have a drink before finding a place for the night.'

'What a good memory you have, Simon.'

'Oh, not really,' Simon smiled dismissively, 'some people are more memorable than others I suppose, but there is something else I do remember, though.'

'What was that?'

'I shouldn't really be saying this,' he began and Eliza could tell by his expression he was reluctant to say anything further, 'but the following morning; that was when we heard about the break-in at Major Tilsly's.'

'I do now, yes.'

'Mind you, it's only supposition, but the police never did find out who had been responsible. I'm sorry, Eliza,' he smiled at her, 'here we go again; like two gossiping washer women!'

'If you'll excuse me,' Melissa butted in, 'but I must give Derek some help; we've some more customers coming in.'

'You're busy,' Simon said, 'we do realise that, Brian; anyway, I hope I've solved your puzzle?'

'You have, yes, but you've only given me more to think about.'

'Why? It was some time ago; it must have been at least four or five years.'

'I know, but what I'm wondering is, why has he come here to live? Meadowbank doesn't seem to be his sort of place; too quiet, I would have thought. Oops, Eliza, tittle- tattling; I apologise.'

'Don't, Brian,' she assured him, 'it's understandable. His girlfriend isn't with him this evening though, is she?'

'Felicity? That's what she said her name was; Felicity Carter and he's called Johnnie Baker. She asked if we needed any extra bar help actually, so she may have found something already. I suggested she tried either The Bridge or up at the hotel.'

'I pity anyone who works for Sandra Watson.'

'Well, Simon,' Brian said wryly, 'it depends how desperate she is to find some work.'

'Who's the man he's talking to; I don't think I've seen him before?' Eliza asked, 'Oh, dear,' she added, trying to stop smiling, 'I'm at it now, it must be catching, this thirst for local knowledge.'

'Cheeky!' Simon grinned, 'But talking about thirst, shall we have one more before going across the road; we've time, I booked a table for eight-fifteen.'

'He's the new owner of Bill and Valerie Green's old house,' Brian told them as he poured their drinks, 'I don't know his surname, but I heard someone call him Charlie the other evening and that he comes from

London.'

'Another newcomer to Meadowbank.' Eliza smiled.

'As you say, Eliza,' Brian chuckled, passing their drinks across the bar to them, 'another newcomer to Meadowbank.'

*

'Are you still at work, Victor?'

'I've another two hours to go yet, Charlie. Where are you phoning from?'

'I'm at home now,' Charlie East said, 'but I've spoken to Johnnie this evening, given him his final instructions.'

'Does he know about Mark Astley yet?'

'I don't think so; at least he never said anything. He's still a bit miffed about the text message he got from him on Thursday.'

'And you didn't enlighten him?' Victor asked, thankful there were no customers to interrupt him; what he had to tell Charlie was important and needed some considerable thought before any steps could be taken, but it looked very much as if the situation, from what Christine had uncovered this evening, needed addressing one way or another and pretty damned quickly at that.

'No, I didn't. He'll hear soon enough. Astley's death hardly merited any mention on the nine o'clock news. So, you could say, I'm not to know. It isn't as if I was next of kin!'

'Someone would have been though.' Victor was quick to point out. There were times when Charlie was just too bloody smart and not for the first time since he had known him, he hoped he wouldn't get too smart.

'Yes, that's right. He had parents in Winchester.'

'He didn't come from Manchester then?'

'No, he moved up there some years ago; he was still in his teens with already a police record. He told me once he wanted to make a fresh start.'

'Well, he did that alright, didn't he?' unable to keep the cynicism from his voice.

'You can say that again,' a dry humourless chuckle on the other end of the line which sent a shiver down Victor's back, 'anyway, no doubt his demise will be in the Sundays tomorrow.'

'No doubt. So, who has Johnnie got working with him tonight?'

'No-one. He's on his own; I couldn't get a replacement in time, Victor.'

'And you consider he'll manage without any backup?'

'Johnnie Baker is good, Victor; don't underestimate him. In fact, in many respects he's even more skilled and, of course, as it has transpired, more circumspect, than Astley. No, you've nothing to concern yourself about there; he'll deliver alright.'

'And what about Felicity Carter?'

'What about her?'

'Can she be trusted?'

'You know, Victor, you really are becoming an old worry-guts. Those two have been together for the past three years. She's not stupid; far from it. She's got too much to lose by, shall we say, talking out of turn or to the wrong people.'

'If you say so.'

'I do, Victor, I do.'

'That aside, Charlie,' Victor began and wondering what sort of reaction he was going to get, 'it looks as though we may have a problem on our hands here.'

'Explain.'

'Christine has found one of the discrepancies in the assignments.'

'Hell!'

'So far, it's only in the one we had delivered this week; she hasn't spotted any of the others yet.'

'This is not good, Victor.'

'I know that perfectly well,' he said, 'that's why I'm telling you.'

'Okay, let us recap,' Charlie put in, 'so, she has discovered one shortfall. And what sort of explanation did you give her?'

'I suggested it could have been a fault in our new software.'

'And did she swallow that?'

'I think so, but she's worried, Charlie.'

'*She's* worried!'

'She wanted me to call in the technician to check through the system, but I told her to wait; see whether it happened again.'

'Spare me from these over-zealous computer operators.'

'Christine is actually more than that,' Victor protested, wondering now whether he could have handled this better on his own, but he really didn't have much of a choice, 'she's worked for me for the last five years. She is super-efficient, inclined to be somewhat pedantic at times, but she is an asset to the business and never complains about the long hours she has to put in; not like some.' he added, remembering past assistants he'd had working for him and how they used to grumble when asked to work late, even although it always meant more money for them.

'No-one is infallible, Victor.'

'I know.'

'We can't simply dismiss this development and merely hope she won't take it into her head to check back through the records, because if she did, well -' he paused and Victor knew it wasn't for effect. Charlie East was worried and that made two of them he thought, more aware than ever of the inevitability of it all, '- well,' Charlie continued slowly, 'that's anyone's guess, I suppose, but we can't afford to let that happen. You do realise that?'

'I could crash the system,' he suggested, the idea suddenly occurring to him.

'You could, yes,' Charlie said, 'but surely you would have to bring in your technician to re-install for you?'

'Ye-es.'

'These guys are trained computer technicians, Victor; they have the ability not only to locate the problem but they would soon detect if it had been done deliberately, so that wouldn't be such a good idea, unless Christine is sufficiently skilled to re-install the system. Do you think she would be?'

'As to that, I have no idea,' Victor sighed, 'and there's one thing I do know and that is I wouldn't be able to.'

'There you are then. We are stuck with the situation and that means we have no alternative but to deal with it in our way.'

'I don't like this, Charlie.'

'There are a number of things we don't like in this world of ours, Victor, and in my opinion in this particular instance, you will, quite frankly, just have to lump it.'

'You as well, surely?'

'Wrong.'

'What the hell do you mean?'

'I think you understand me quite well; that side of the business is your responsibility. It always has been, right from the start. Look at it like this, Victor, it has been a lucrative sideline, there is no disputing that for one minute, but the main source of income has needed considerably more skill and expertise and I shouldn't have to spell that out to you. No,' he continued, 'and to speak bluntly, technically speaking you have been cooking the books.'

'And passing on the goods to you.'

'Yes, that's true, but you try and prove it, Victor. Just try and prove it.'

'You bastard!'

'You are not the first person to call me a bastard, Victor, and I don't suppose you will be the last. I'm going to ring off now; I've had a long day. We'll talk next week and you can tell me then how you've resolved your problem.'

*

'I'm so glad they haven't changed anything too much,' Eliza remarked, once they were seated and had been handed their menus, 'apart from the pictures and, of course, Danielle's wonderful collection of Italian plates, it looks more or less the same.'

'It's quite rare, isn't it,' Simon said, looking around the restaurant, which at that time in the evening looked particularly attractive with the sun shining through from the walled terrace at the back of the building, 'usually, the first thing people do is practically strip the place and then, whatever atmosphere it had is entirely lost.'

'I know,' she said, opening the menu and glancing down the list of choices, 'but the food is bound to be different, though. What are you going to have, Simon; a steak?'

'How did you guess, darling?' he smiled at her over the top of his menu and thinking how lovely she looked: she had unclasped her glorious auburn hair, much longer than it had been when he had first met her, falling now well below her shoulders and tonight, he noticed, she was wearing the same dress as on that first day he had brought her to The Salmon's Rest: a soft pale lilac with panels of lace in a deeper shade; the colour enhancing her creamy complexion and he knew it was one of her favourites. 'But you're right of course,' he went on, 'and I bet you are

39

going to have the lamb cutlets.'

'You won't believe this,' she laughed softly, 'but I was going to have chicken chasseur and then only seconds before you spoke, I changed my mind, deciding instead to have the lamb!'

'Clever, eh?'

'Very!'

Barbara Wood came over to take their order and at the same time she introduced herself, asking if everything was to their liking.

'Perfect, thank you,' Simon replied, 'I'm Simon Grant and this is my wife, Eliza.'

'What a pretty name; it reminds me of Eliza Doolittle, but I expect you've been told that before?'

'A few times!' Eliza laughed.

'And how are you and your husband settling into life in Meadowbank?' Simon asked.

'Very well,' Barbara answered quickly, 'and as you probably know already, this is only our second day and, so far, we've been quite literally rushed off our feet, but fortunately our new waitress, Felicity, is helping us now.'

'The girl who brought our menus over?' Eliza asked her.

'That's right and she is new in the town as well, so you could say the three of us are on a learning curve!'

'Well,' Simon put in, 'we wish you the best of luck. As far as Eliza and I are concerned, and probably many others in Meadowbank, it is good to have the restaurant open again. We've missed it.'

'Thank you very much, Simon,' she said, 'if you're both ready, I'll take your order now, shall I?'

They both decided to start their meal with the 'chef's special' of chilled chicken terrine on a bed of iceberg lettuce, thinly sliced cucumber and cherry tomatoes with a dressing of Italian vinaigrette and a bottle of wine from the Bordeaux region of France.

'It would seem Brian was right,' Eliza said, raising her glass, 'the girl he was talking about did manage to find a job.'

'Yes,' he said, it didn't take her long. Anyway,' he grinned, 'she's bound to be happier working here than under the beady eye of Sandra Watson.'

'It could have been infinitely worse though,' she chuckled, 'she could have been working for Danielle!'

'Oh, yes, that's a point. She wouldn't have lasted five minutes! Do you know, in the short time Danielle and her husband were here I honestly lost count of the number of waitresses she'd hired and fired!'

'Poor girls.'

'Poor Danielle.'

'Yes, poor Danielle; I wonder where she is now.'

'No doubt back in Paris. I don't believe she was ever happy living in England and I did hear she had divorced Peter.'

'I'm not surprised!'

'Well, he'll be out of harm's way for some time to come; courtesy of Her Majesty's prison service!'

'Shall we change the subject, Simon. I really don't want to think about that dreadful time.'

'I'm sorry, darling,' he said, immediately contrite, 'not very tactful of me. But, it is ancient history now.'

'I know.' she nodded.

'Isn't that the man who was in The Market Inn earlier, Eliza? He's just this minute come in.'

'Yes, it is,' she said, following his gaze, 'what did Brian say his name was again?'

'Charlie something.'

'And that he had recently arrived in Meadowbank. If you ask me, Simon, there does seem to be rather a lot of them all of a sudden.'

'When you come to think about it, I suppose there are.'

'That's odd.'

'What is?'

'Well,' Eliza said, a frown appearing briefly across her forehead, 'he seemed to know the guy he was with in The Market Inn; they did appear to be deep in conversation, but obviously he doesn't know his girlfriend because she's at his table now and he has barely looked at her.'

'Perhaps he doesn't know her,' Simon suggested lightly, but Eliza was right he thought; it did seem a bit odd, 'we could be reading too much into the importance of whatever they were talking about. They may have only met recently, or something.'

'It's possible.' she said slowly, but he could tell she didn't think so. The trouble was he thought, too much had happened in the town in a relatively short time and they had become accustomed to sudden and tragic events, also discovering people were not as they first appeared.

'Come on, Miss Marples,' he laughed, 'have some more of this delicious wine.'

'I don't think Miss Marples drank wine, Simon.'

'Cheeky!'

'That's twice you've called me that this evening, Simon Grant!'

The meal lived up to their expectations: his filet of beef was cooked exactly as he liked and Eliza said she was glad she had chosen the cutlets. It was after ten when they finally left the restaurant, having by then been introduced to Harry Wood. As with the Taylors before them, it would seem that Barbara was responsible for the catering side of the business, while her husband was front of house, dispensing drinks and generally making sure their customers were being looked after. They were a likeable couple Simon decided as they walked back across the square to the car, and they should do well in Meadowbank. He had meant what he had said to Barbara Wood; many of them had missed having a good restaurant in the centre of the town. As much as he and Eliza enjoyed eating in The Royal Oak's restaurant, they did find the manageress' manner a trifle overbearing and not always conducive to a relaxing evening. Sandra Watson didn't exactly do herself any favours he decided, which was a pity. A little like Danielle who could be autocratic at times, but then there had possibly been a deep-seated reason for that, one being she hadn't been happy living in Meadowbank, even from when they had first arrived.

They had a final drink before going to bed; Eliza going upstairs first, leaving him to make sure all the windows were securely fastened. He was standing at the open kitchen window, leaning on the ledge, and enjoying his last cigarette of the day when he heard the sound of a car in the distance; the engine growing louder as it approached the mill. Probably one of the guests returning to the hotel Simon thought, looking across towards the road and waiting for it to pass by the gates. It was the only space, unless from an upstairs' window; any other part of the road was obscured by the high beech hedge bordering the entire length of the front of the property.

The car was travelling at high speed and the view Simon had was brief, but long enough for him to recognise the man who was driving; impossible to see the make, only that it was an open-top. Johnnie Baker was on his way either to the hotel which was only a hundred yards or so further along or he was going as far as Stockbridge. There was nowhere else on that stretch of road.

Chapter Four

Johnnie was up before Felicity the following morning and had already been across the square to the newsagents for the Sunday papers before she finally surfaced.

'You're up early, Johnnie,' she said, padding barefoot into the kitchen and leaning over to kiss him, 'couldn't you sleep?'

'Not all that well,' he said, looking up at her. She was wearing one of his old tee-shirts and with her hair a tangle and standing on end the way it did each morning when she had just woken up, she looked incredibly young. She took down a mug from the rack above the working top, filling it to the brim with the freshly made coffee, before sitting down beside him and pulling one of the newspapers over towards her.

'How did it go last night?' she asked, 'I didn't hear you come to bed, so it must have been late.'

'It went okay.'

'Just okay, Johnnie?' she said, a tiny quirky smile hovering at the side of her mouth.

'Let's say everything went according to plan.'

'Even without Mark?'

'Don't remind me,' he grimaced, 'and I must admit, if he had been, it wouldn't have taken as long as it did. It was almost light by the time I got back to Meadowbank and although we've only been here since Friday, I've already worked out if any of these old biddies had seen me what they would have been thinking.'

'It's a bit like living in a gold fish bowl.'

'Too true,' he agreed, 'anyway, Felicity, it won't be forever, but how was your evening?'

'Busy and hectic, but I enjoyed it. They're nice people; Barbara and Harry, very easy going, and when I compare them with that cow up at the hotel, I think I had a lucky escape. Mind you, even if I had produced my curriculum vitae, as she so eloquently put it, she may not have had a job for me anyway.'

'That's alright then.' he said abstractedly, glancing at The Sunday Telegraph's headlines.

'I tell you who did come into the restaurant last night, though.'

'Who?'

'Mr East.'

'Well, I suppose he has to eat somewhere, Felicity.'

'I know, but he acted as if he had never seen me before.'

'He would have had his reasons I expect,' Johnnie said, looking up from the paper, 'maybe he thinks it best to keep any contact between us to a minimum.'

'Yes, but you were with him earlier, weren't you? In the pub, I mean.'

'That's true, but the place was packed, Felicity. I doubt whether anyone even noticed us.'

'What did he have to say about Mark pulling out?'

'Very little, actually. He didn't appear to be concerned one way or another, only that he would have someone else lined up for next week, that was all.'

After a couple of sips of coffee, Felicity went upstairs to shower and, refilling his own mug, he settled down to read what had been happening in the world. The front page news was gloomy and predictable; the main headline being that they were planning to send more troops out to Iraq, followed by yet another furore in the House of Commons; some controversy about the number of illegal immigrants being given long-term sanctuary in Britain. He was half-way through the paper before he read about Mark; only a few lines at the bottom of a page, he could have quite easily missed it: "Mystery Surrounding 'Suicide' in Manchester", Johnnie read slowly, absorbing every single word, "Police were called to the home of Mark Astley, twenty-eight, early Friday morning following the discovery of his body by the cleaner. A neighbour has come forward to say he had been woken shortly before midnight by noises coming from Mr Astley's flat. The cause of death has been given as a drug overdose, although there is no evidence to support the deceased was an addict. Enquiries are continuing and at this stage of the investigation, whether the drug, the substance of which has yet to be confirmed, had been administered to Mr Astley, foul play has not been ruled out."

So, Johnnie sighed, leaning heavily back in his chair, they got him. They finally got him. Mark had been pushing his luck for a while now and it had only been a matter of time before the 'big boys' discovered what he had been up to. The siphoning off at the beginning had been mediocre, and presumably un-detectable, but Johnnie knew these had increased a hundred fold over the last six months or so, but he hadn't said anything to him, hadn't even made any attempt to warn him. Not that there would have been much point; Mark had made up his own rules and always had done since the very first day he had met him. Johnnie hadn't been entirely honest with Felicity when he had introduced Mark to her at the beginning of February. All she knew was that he would, from then on, be working with him and, although she was aware of what that work was, she didn't know a great deal more. Johnnie never told her where he would be going on those nights when he left late and returned in the early hours, but she recognised the risks he was taking each time and had learned to live with them. She was as keen as he was to have enough money to be able to change their lifestyle and the fact that it involved the stealing of drugs to achieve this goal, she had told him she accepted this, also that she was prepared to accept the consequences if he should ever be caught. That had been good enough for him.

Felicity didn't know Mark and he went back a long way; before he had met her and as far back to before the post office raid. Mark had been unlucky there and to give him his due Johnnie thought, taking a sip of the now luke-warm coffee, he hadn't shopped him. He could have done; quite easily, but then, that had been one of the good things about Mark; in spite of his shady background he had often shown a sense of honour; there was no other way he could think of to describe it. Mark had been basically a loner and had told him very little about his early years, except that he had been brought up by his mother; his father having left her before he was born, although from what he had said, his stepfather had more than made up for any lack of having a real father around the place during those formative years. Johnnie always reckoned Mark must have been born with a rebellious streak, refusing to conform, and then being brought up in respectable middle-class suburbia, it had all been too heavy for him. Too stifling, perhaps. Johnnie could only make guesses, but it had been obvious to him Mark had craved for the something unobtainable: it wasn't just the money and drugs weren't important to him; he just wanted to be different. Well, Johnnie thought philosophically, getting up from the table and pouring the last of his coffee down the sink, he had certainly been that alright.

'Okay, Johnnie,' Felicity said, coming in, 'I've still over an hour before I need to be at the restaurant; shall I make us some fresh coffee?'

'In a minute, Felicity,' he said, walking over to her, 'I've something to tell you first.'

'What's wrong?' her eyes wide with alarm as she looked at him.

'It's Mark,' he said quietly, wishing there was an easier way of breaking the news to her, but there wasn't, 'he's dead.'

'Oh! No! No!' she gasped putting her hands up to her mouth, the colour immediately draining from her face and he put out an arm to steady her until she was sitting down.

'It was in the paper,' he said, sitting down next to her and putting an arm around her shoulders, 'they found him on Friday morning in his flat; quite early I think it must have been.'

'But, Johnnie,' so softly he could scarcely hear her, but he could tell how much she was trying to keep calm, realising what a shock it must have been for her; for him as well, but to a lesser degree. It wasn't as though he was used to sudden death, but Johnnie had no illusions about the people he was working for and had learned to watch his back, but it was entirely different for Felicity. She was a good four years younger; she'd lived a pretty sheltered life before they had met and he was beginning to realise how difficult it would be for her when she eventually learned, as she undoubtedly would, why Mark had been killed. 'what happened to him? Did they say?'

'A drug overdose, apparently –'

'- Mark didn't take drugs.' she interrupted.

'I know that,' he agreed, 'they didn't say much else, except that, to quote them, they haven't ruled out foul play.'

'You –' stumbling over the words, 'you mean, he could have – could have been murdered?'

'Yes.'

'You believe he was, don't you, Johnnie?' she asked, looking up at him and waiting for him to say something. But what the hell could he say? He knew too much and he wanted to protect her, keep the knowledge to himself, at least for as long as he could. If the police found anything to link Mark with him, the last thing he wanted was for Felicity to have to be subjected to a barrage of questions. The authorities would know of

Mark's prison record and surely it would only be a matter of time for them to trace anyone he had been associating with, especially recently. The inevitability of what could happen was almost overwhelming.

'Felicity,' he said at last, taking her hands in his, noticing how cold they were, 'I honestly think that the least you know about Mark at the moment the better.'

'Why?'

'Because of his background, that's why,' he sighed, 'I don't want to alarm you, goodness knows that's the last thing I want to do, but there is a chance if the police are really going to go down the road that Mark's death wasn't suicide, they will be looking for any friends he may have had, or anyone he worked with for that matter.'

'I see,' she said softly, 'Johnnie, listen to me. I love you; you know that and I want more than anything for us to stay together. Also,' she went on, 'I am fully aware of the work you are doing for Mr East and I've already told you I accept all of this. In other words, I can live with it. And, as far as Mark is concerned, well –' hesitating for a second, 'I realise he had a criminal record and you don't need to worry about me. You can trust me, Johnnie; I'll never say anything I shouldn't if and when we have to answer any questions.'

Johnnie waited until Felicity had left for the restaurant before phoning Charlie East. Normally he would have waited for him to make the contact when he'd completed a job, but the situation that morning was far from normal. Mark Astley was dead. That was an indisputable fact and whether Charlie was directly responsible or not didn't make a great deal of difference. Either way, he must have known about it yesterday and, for obvious reasons, had said nothing. But now, it was his turn to play a game of strategy: if he didn't phone him and tell him what he'd read in that morning's paper, this could be construed to mean, he not only suspected who was responsible for Mark's death or, but far more importantly, had known what Mark had been up to, which could ultimately lead Charlie to suspect he had something to hide. The fact he was entirely innocent and had always played fair with all his dealings was neither here nor there. Charlie East was far from stupid.

Charlie answered as soon as he had finished dialling his number and didn't sound too surprised to hear from him, which could mean he was expecting the call.

'Good morning, Johnnie,' were his first words, 'how are you?'

'I'm okay, thanks, Mr East, but I've just read the newspaper report about Mark Astley.' Johnnie said, deciding to come to the point.

'Ah, yes. So have I, Johnnie. Sad business.'

'Very. It would seem they may be considering it wasn't a straightforward drug overdose, Mr East.'

'Yes, that's the implication.'

'A bit sudden though.'

'Murder usually is, Johnnie; that is, if it was.'

'It doesn't explain the text message though, does it?'

'How do you mean?'

'Well, according to the report, one of Mark's neighbours was disturbed by noises coming from his flat. This must have happened late on Thursday night, perhaps not long after he sent that text to me. It doesn't make sense.'

'When you've lived as long as I have, Johnnie, you will come to the realisation that not a lot makes much sense in this crazy world. However,' he went on, making it abundantly clear he had no intention of continuing the conversation, 'presumably all went well last night?'

'Yes, no problems.'

'Good, hold on to the goods for a couple of days then, Johnnie and I'll be in touch for them to be handed over as usual. Alright?'

'Alright, Mr East.'

'I see your young lady has found herself a job.'

'That's right; the restaurant along the road from us.'

'That's convenient. Well, Johnnie, I'll ring off now and I'll be in touch during the week.'

*

The church bells were ringing for the Sunday morning service when Ian called Brenda. He was phoning from the office, having decided to spend a couple of hours clearing his desk, something he felt sure he was going to find difficult to do during the following few days if, as he was beginning to think, events surrounding this drug business were about to unfold.

'I'm glad you phoned, Ian,' Brenda said, 'I was just going to give you a ring actually to find out how you got on last evening.'

'Much better than I had hoped, ma'am,' he said, 'those two are here alright. In fact, it would appear they're renting Alison Moore's old house in the square.'

'How on earth did you find that out?'

'Chance really,' Ian said, 'I overheard Simon Grant talking to Brian Morrison; the place was so busy, I really don't believe they even saw me standing practically next to them. It would seem that Brian recognised Johnnie Baker when he and his girlfriend went in there on Friday afternoon, shortly after they had arrived in Meadowbank incidentally, but couldn't remember when it was.'

'Yes?'

'But Simon did remember. Apparently it was about four years ago and Johnnie Baker had been part of a rock group; it sounds as if they had been spending the summer touring; anyway they called into The Market Inn, having taken the wrong road off the motorway.'

'So,' Brenda said, 'we know where they are living; that's the main thing, Ian.'

'Yes,' he agreed, 'but there's something else, ma'am; the time when he was last here just happened to be the night of the break-in at Major Tilsly's place.'

'Good grief!'

'Exactly.'

'I wasn't involved in the case,' she told him, 'but of course I remember the details and we all knew about Major Tilsly's art collection. We were never able to discover who broke in that night.' She went on and he could hear disappointment in her voice. Even after all this time and this was before she became Chief Inspector, but she still felt keenly about an unsolved case. 'But whoever it was, managed to get away with four paintings; they weren't in the gallery with the main collection, but in the hall, also several pieces of silver tableware.'

'And the major didn't hear a thing?'

'No, perhaps just as well if there had been more than one of them.'

'I wonder whether Mark Astley was with them?'

'Could have been I suppose; in fact, Ian, I think it would have been more than likely. Remember, he did come from this part of the country and he would have known about the Tilsly estate, bound to have done, in fact.' she added.

'Did you know that the Greens' house had been sold, ma'am?'

'No, I didn't, but then there were never any for sale notices outside. Why do you ask?'

'Because,' he started to explain, 'Johnnie Baker was with the new owner in the pub last night. They weren't at the bar, but sitting down at one of the tables. It was Brian Morrison who mentioned he'd bought the property.'

'Did you catch the man's name?'

'Not his surname, no, only that he's known as Charlie.'

'That shouldn't be too difficult to find out. For a man who insisted he had never been in Meadowbank before, Johnnie Baker seems to have settled down rather rapidly.'

'Exactly.'

'What about his girlfriend; was she with them last night?'

'No, she wasn't. By the way,' Ian went on, remembering what Brian had said, 'there was a girl with the rock group, but it wasn't Felicity Carter.'

'Perhaps that was why Johnnie was being evasive; didn't want to make his girlfriend jealous.'

'Could have been.'

'Anyway,' she said, 'we've got a bit more to go on. We can now go ahead and speak to Johnnie Baker, find out how friendly he was with Mark Astley and why he had been planning to join them here. Also, Ian,' Brenda continued, 'this rock group interests me. They could have been using it as a cover; quite a smart idea, if you think about it. Touring the country and at the end of a session carrying out a number of lucrative robberies on the way! I'll give Gerald Carpenter a ring in a minute and see if it's possible he can get hold of a photograph of Mark Astley. Perhaps someone may recognise him as being with them that night.'

'Four years isn't all that long ago.'

'No, it isn't,' she agreed, 'and I'll get the file out for you on the robbery, Ian. Mind you,' she went on, 'there's isn't a great deal on it, but at least it will give you some background to work on.'

'Every little helps, ma'am,' he said, 'I'll go along and have a word with Johnnie Baker, shall I? See what sort of answers he comes up with.'

There was a white Peugeot outside number twenty-eight; it had been there the day before Ian remembered, pressing the front door bell. Although an old model, it was still unaffordable by most of the people in and around Meadowbank. Having recently traded in his Renault for a two-year-old Volvo, he had been staggered at the increase in the insurance premiums and in spite of his no-claims bonus. If the Peugeot did belong to Johnnie Baker, whatever line of business he was in must provide a healthy income, he concluded.

The man who came to the door was about his own age, Ian guessed; in his late twenties, slim-build with a thick mop of dark brown hair and looked remarkably like Hugh Grant. He was wearing jeans and a plain white tee-shirt and if he was surprised to see a complete stranger standing on his doorstep on a Sunday morning, he gave no sign, merely waited patiently for Ian to introduce himself.

'Good morning, sir,' Ian began, 'I apologise for disturbing you at the weekend, but I'm Inspector Ian Ash from the Meadowbank constabulary and there are a number of routine questions I would like to ask you.'

'The police?'

'Yes, but first of all,' Ian put in, 'is your name Johnnie Baker?'

'Yes.'

'May I come in, Mr Baker,' he asked him, trying at the same time to fathom out the expression on the man's face, but it was impossible. Johnnie Baker was revealing nothing, at least not so far, 'better for both of us perhaps.'

'Of course,' Johnnie Baker answered, opening the door wider and gesturing for him to go in, 'I daresay everyone in this town knows who *you* are, Inspector.'

'Meadowbank is a relatively small town and some could think it was one of the disadvantages, but you get used to it.'

'I'm not sure I will.' he said, leading the way through the hall towards the kitchen. 'Sit down, Inspector,' he said, 'would you like a coffee; I was just about to have one.'

'No thank you, sir. As I said, this is purely a routine visit and I won't take up too much of your time.'

'That's alright,' he said, sitting down on the chair opposite to Ian and pushing aside a couple of mugs, 'it's Sunday and the one day in the week when I make it a point not to work.'

'Right,' Ian nodded, 'I am here concerning the recent death of a man called Mark Astley who was, we understand, a friend of yours.'

'I wouldn't exactly have called Mark a friend, Inspector; certainly not a close friend.'

'You've heard about his death?'

'Only this morning,' Johnnie Baker said, 'I read about it in the paper.' he added, pointing to a crumpled copy of the Sunday Telegraph at the end of the table.

'How well did you know him, sir?'

'Nobody knew Mark all that well.' adroitly side-stepping the question, 'I first met him; oh, it would have been almost ten years ago, I reckon. He had just moved up to Manchester and we got talking one evening in a pub; as one does.'

'We need to locate anyone he may have known, Mr Baker; this should help us put together a picture of his life, mainly because the manner of his death is inconclusive. You've read the article, so you'll know that already. It is possible he may have taken his own life, and if that was the case, as he didn't leave any suicide note, we have to find out why. What are your thoughts, sir? Was he the sort of man who would take such drastic steps?'

'I have no idea, Inspector. Reading about it this morning was a shock naturally, but as I've already said, I didn't really know Mark.'

'Although he had been planning to visit you here, in Meadowbank?'

'How did you know that?'

'He hadn't cleared the last message he made on his mobile, that's why.'

'Of course. The text he sent to us.'

'Do you know why he should have changed his mind, virtually at the last minute?'

'No, he gave no explanation.'

'Did this surprise you, sir?'

'Well, it did, yes.'

'This visit, Mr Baker,' Ian insisted, 'was this to be a short stay?'

'I think so, at least initially. He had been saying how fed up he was with living up north and wanted to have a change.'

'Itchy feet?'

'He could have had.' again giving nothing away. Johnnie Baker was, Ian decided, a man in total control of, not only what he said, but of his facial muscles. A difficult nut to crack.

'What sort of work did Mark Astley do?'

'I suppose you could have described him as an entrepreneur, Inspector. He'd have a go at anything.'

'Such as?'

'Selling, mainly. He could have sold sand to the Arabs!'

'And when did you last see him?'

'It would have been about a week ago; we had a drink together.'

'Was he working then?'

'No, Inspector, he was one of the many unemployed.'

'And your line of business, sir?'

'I'm in finance; freelance and, in case you're wondering, I work from home. One of the lucky ones,' he added, 'I don't need to commute.'

'Had you and Mark ever worked together?' Ian asked him, not entirely satisfied with such a loose description, but deciding to leave it and move in a slightly different direction.

'I don't know whether you would call it *work* exactly,' he emphasised, 'but we were part of a small rock group for a while.'

'When was this, sir?'

'About five years ago.'

'And,' Ian asked, 'the other members of the group; are you still in touch with them?'

'No; I haven't seen either of them since we wrapped up the group.'

'And, Mark Astley; did he?'

'No idea, Inspector. I would say it was unlikely, though. There would have been no point. The only thing any of us had in common with each other was music, and apart from when we were performing, we hardly ever met up socially.'

'Perhaps you could give me their names, Mr Baker.'

'Sure; no problem; they're Danny Howarth and Katie Brownlea, but I don't know where they're living now.'

Howarth; could this Danny Howarth be related to the Howarths Brenda had mentioned? Not such a common name, Ian thought, jotting the names down in his notebook.

'That's alright, sir,' he said, 'we should be able to find them. There are only a couple more questions.' he said, making to close his notebook.

'Yes?'

'You arrived here, I believe, on Friday with a young lady called Felicity Carter; is that correct?'

'Yes, that's right; we did;' a brief frown appearing. He hadn't expected that Ian thought, doing his utmost to read into the change of expression, but without any success; Johnnie Baker was well practiced in the art of concealment; that was obvious. 'why do you ask?'

'Because, sir,' Ian started to explain, 'I'm wondering, as you vacated your flat in Manchester early on Thursday evening, why you didn't decide to travel south on the same day; it's motorway for most of the way and the journey wouldn't have taken more than five and a half hours, six at the most.'

'Oh, I see,' he smiled, 'well, there is a very simple explanation for that, Inspector,' he said, the smile remaining in place, 'Felicity didn't finish work until late that night and as we had already done all our packing, we thought it would be a good idea to spend the night in an hotel and enjoy the luxury of having our breakfast cooked for us the next morning before we set off.'

'And the name of the hotel, sir?'

'The Grand; it's in the centre of the town.'

'Yes, I know the hotel. You say Miss Carter was working?'

'She was a barmaid at The Pig & Whistle in Market Street.'

'And how did you spend the evening, sir?'

'I had something to eat in McDonalds and a few beers in The Pig & Whistle while I waited for Felicity to finish.'

'And what time was that?'

'Sorry?' the return of the frown, but lasting a fraction longer this time.

'What time did Miss Carter finish work?'

'Oh. Shortly after the pub closed at eleven.'

'And then you both went to the hotel?'

'That's right; we both went to the hotel.'

'And you didn't go out again that night?'

'No, Inspector,' he said slowly and deliberately, looking at Ian straight in the face, 'and I didn't call round and see Mark either.'

'I would like to have a word with Miss Carter,' Ian said, choosing to ignore the jibe, 'I shall need to have her corroboration of what you've told me.'

'Felicity isn't here, Inspector; she's working at the restaurant along the road, The Salmon's Rest.'

'And what time do you expect her back?'

'Hard to say,' he said, 'she only started there yesterday and that was in the evening, but not before three.'

That was unfortunate Ian thought, standing up from the table and preparing to leave; he had no alternative but to wait until later to speak to her and, if Johnnie Baker was hiding anything, the pair of them would have had ample time to make sure both their stories tallied. A pity, but couldn't be helped, although he had managed to glean something: the names of the other two in the rock group, also the hotel where he said they had spent the night and the pub where his girlfriend worked. Ian did know The Grand, having once spent a night there himself and, if Johnnie had gone out any time during the night, it was more than possible the staff on the desk would have noticed. So, he concluded, walking back along the road to the Station, the visit hadn't been entirely non-productive.

Chapter Five

The Meadowbank Pharmacy didn't open until nine-thirty on Monday mornings, but Christine, having spent most of the previous day worrying over the discrepancies in what she had considered to be a faultless system, never having experienced any problems since it was implemented four weeks ago, wanted to get into work before Victor. She hadn't exactly worked out why she was behaving so furtively; it wasn't as though she was blaming him in any way, but she knew only too well he would tell her she was wasting her time. Probably wiser then, she rationalised, for him not to know.

Switching on the computer, she waited for the screen to come to life, pulling a blank sheet of paper towards her; if there were any other errors she would need to correct them and that would have to be done later when she had more time. It took her longer than she had thought it would to work through the various entries, mainly because of having to break off periodically to make sure she was aligning the figures on each of the invoices with their corresponding entries in the system. There they were again; changes in the amounts of deliveries of the same drugs each time. Surprised she hadn't noticed them previously, but as she continued to check and knowing now what to look for, perhaps it wasn't all that surprising she concluded. Working quicker now, Christine carried on, checking also a number of entries prior to the new software and sure enough they had continued; systematically and regularly, back, as far as she had time to look, to February. This was no fault in the software, neither was it a blip as so glibly suggested by Victor. He was the only person who could have done this; there was no-one else. What she had discovered appalled her and at the precise moment as she logged off, she had no idea of what she could do; part of her wishing she hadn't been so insistent in getting to the bottom of it all. She should have left it alone, but of course it was too late now. There was no point in talking to Victor, no point whatsoever; he would only deny it. She had to face the unpalatable fact she was working for a man who was manipulating the accounts for his own gain. There was no other logical reason.

Victor arrived in the pharmacy at exactly the same time as the first customers and saying a brief good morning, she went over to the counter to serve them. The following couple of hours went quickly and it was almost midday when she was able to have a break, by this time Victor was also serving. Going back into the dispensary which also doubled up as their office, Christine switched on the coffee pot. Clearing a space on the desk for the coffee mugs she remembered, the breath catching in her throat, that she hadn't put the invoice file back on the shelf, also she hadn't closed it, leaving it open at the last invoice she had been checking. The file was still there, exactly where she had left it, but it was closed. She was absolutely positive she hadn't done that. She had been in a hurry, running out of time, and after she had switched off the computer to open the front door of the pharmacy, had meant to come back and tidy the desk up, but those first customers had already been waiting outside. The sheet of A4 with her scribbled notes wasn't there. He had taken it; he must have. He would now know what she had been doing. With hands that shook, she put the file away, wondering at the same time whether he would say anything to her. In many respects she hoped he would; it would be out in the open then and she would know immediately what his reactions were. But, and here she had to stop; she didn't want to know what it would mean if he remained silent and made no comment. She hadn't even considered what was happening to those missing drugs. They weren't just numbers in a computer system; they represented several hundred amphetamine tablets and phials of morphine and that was only going back as far as the beginning of the year. How long had he been doing this? And, literally, right under her very nose! He had been taking such a risk, she thought, even although they had always used the same family firm of accountants and conducted their own stock-take at the end of each accounting year; it still remained an incredible risk and what if someone had discovered what had been going on? The thought made her gasp at the enormity of the implication; she could have been blamed and not Victor.

Christine didn't know how she managed to get through the remainder of the day. Fortunately, as often on a Monday, they were both kept fully occupied, having little time to say very much to each other and at six-thirty when she was leaving, Victor was on the phone, giving her a wave as she left the pharmacy.

Brian Morrison was opening the doors of The Market Inn and smiled at her as she walked across the road. Encouraged, especially after spending the day in such mental turmoil, she decided on the spur of the moment to go in for a drink. It was not as if she particularly wanted one, but she didn't want to go home either, at least not yet. She felt the need to be among other people, not necessarily to talk to anyone, but to feel part of a crowd. She had so much to think about and she was putting off that moment when she would have to decide what she should do. There was one thing she decided, following Brian into the pub, she couldn't go on like this; worrying and wondering when Victor was going to say something as surely and inevitably he must.

She took her wine over to one of the tables far enough away from the windows. She didn't want to sit where she would be looking more or less directly across the square to the pharmacy, nor did she want to see Victor when he left. He wouldn't be coming in here, that was one certainty. Victor York was not exactly a pub sort of man, but again, what sort of man was he, she thought and making a conscious effort to put him out of her mind, took a sip of her wine.

As she sat there, watching the evening customers arrive and doing her best to relax, she suddenly thought of someone who may be the best person to give her advice. Christine had been working for The Meadowbank Pharmacy since she left college, fifteen years ago, some time before Victor took the business over and had always enjoyed working for his predecessor.

Jack Wilson had taken early retirement; Christine had not known why and she would never have asked him, but it could have been to look after his wife, whom, she had heard had died a couple of years ago. He lived in Winchester Road, at the far end of the town and although she had seen him occasionally it had been some time since she had spoken to him. For some reason he didn't come into the pharmacy, but this was probably understandable; not everyone liked going back, too many memories, especially if they had been happy ones. She would give him a ring now; it was still early and she didn't think he would mind, but the more she thought about it, the more convinced she was that he could be the right person to confide in.

She took her mobile from her bag, also the small address book she always carried with her, turning the pages until she came to the number she wanted. He answered immediately and she could tell by the smile in his voice he was pleased to hear from her, although no doubt somewhat puzzled as to why.

'Christine,' he said, 'this is a surprise? How are you?'

'I'm fine, Jack,' she answered, wishing that was true; she felt far from fine, 'and how are you?'

'Apart from getting old, I can't grumble!' he chuckled. Jack Wilson wasn't even sixty yet, so he could afford to make light of his advancing years, she thought, smiling to herself.

'I'm sorry to bother you at this time of the evening,' she went on, 'and I do hope you won't mind, but I really need to talk to you.'

'Something's wrong, isn't it, Christine?' his voice changing instantly and she could easily imagine the genuine concern on his face.

'I believe there is, Jack and I think you are the only person I can talk to. I need some advice.' she added.

'I understand, my dear. You have your own transport, don't you?'

'Yes.'

'That's good; well, why not drive out, that is if you're free at the moment, and I'll give you directions on how to find the house.'

As easy as that. How kind he was and without asking any questions either. He had recognised her distress and, being a patient man, would wait until she arrived.

*

White's The Chemist in Stockbridge reported the theft of a substantial amount of prescribed drugs at ten that Monday morning; this was followed ten minutes later by a similar call from one of the other chemists in the town, but the news didn't reach Meadowbank until much later in the afternoon when an excited sales assistant in White's telephoned her boyfriend, Derek Frost.

Derek, having just come on duty, didn't have a chance to mention this to anyone until well after seven, but the people of Meadowbank, over a period now of several months, having become accustomed to hearing news of a more sensational nature, didn't consider either of these incidents as being particularly interesting and, apart from the usual handful of regulars, who immediately came to the conclusion that the robberies had been carried out by a London gang, quickly dropped the subject.

Simon and Eliza, returning from a day of meetings in London, called in for a drink on their way home and heard about the robberies from Melissa.

'So,' Melissa concluded, pouring out Eliza's wine, 'that's the latest. Apparently,' she went on, 'according to Derek's girlfriend, there was no sign of any break-in at either of the pharmacies.'

'Sounds like professionals.' Simon commented.

'Must have been, I suppose,' she nodded, 'but when drugs are being stolen it does make you wonder where they are going, doesn't it?'

'Is there a drug problem in the area?' Eliza asked her, raising her glass to Simon before taking a sip.

'Not as far as I've heard,' Melissa said, 'but I hope this doesn't mean we are in for a spate of robberies of this kind.'

'When did they happen?'

'Some time on Saturday night, Simon.' she said and then having to move away to serve some new customers.

'Saturday night.' Simon muttered under his breath.

'Sorry, Simon, what did you say?' Eliza asked.

'I didn't mention anything to you at the time,' he said, turning to face her, 'but when I was locking up on Saturday; it would have been almost eleven by then, I saw that chap, Johnnie Baker, drive past the mill.'

'He could have been going to the hotel.' she suggested.

'A bit late, wouldn't you have said?'

'Oh, dear.'

'I know.' giving her a rueful smile, 'It doesn't sound good, does it.'

'We *are* only surmising though,' she warned him, putting a hand on his arm, 'we could be quite wrong.'

'And if we're not?'

'I don't know.'

'Well,' he said, 'it won't be the first time you and I have been faced with this kind of problem; either to speak out or not.'

'Can you be sure it was Johnnie Baker you saw?'

'It was Johnnie Baker alright,' he said quickly, 'he had the top down, Eliza. Also,' he added, 'I recognised the car he was driving, a white

Peugeot and if you look out the window you'll see there is a white Peugeot parked outside Alison's old house.'

'You're thinking about what happened four years ago, aren't you?'

'Yes, I can't help it. I've been trying to remember what the other members of their group looked like.'

'And?'

'As I said to Brian on Saturday, there were four of them: Johnnie and two other guys and the girl. You and I haven't seen Felicity Carter yet,' he reminded her, 'although Brian seemed pretty certain it wasn't her.'

'What did she look like?'

'Young, early twenties, quite short, slim, with very long black hair; it was well below her shoulders I remember.'

'You'd know her again; do you think?'

'Perhaps, although it is possible she may have changed her image, but then perhaps not.'

'What about the two men? Would you recognise them?'

'I think I would,' Simon answered slowly, thinking back to that evening and trying to remember anything he may have missed, 'one of them would have been about the same age as Johnnie Baker, about twenty-four or twenty-five and had a thin face, sharp-featured, fairish hair, not the sort of face which would actually have stood out in a crowd, if you know what I mean, but the other man; he was quite a bit older, a good ten years I would have said, he was different. He was tall, extremely thin, also he had a beard.'

'He could have shaved it off.' Eliza, ever practical, suggested.

'True, darling,' he grinned at her, 'he could have shaved it off.'

'You're laughing at me!'

'No I'm not. Honestly.'

'Fibber!' she laughed, prodding him gently in the midriff, 'You shouldn't mock the afflicted, Simon!'

'You two sound very jolly this evening; you must have had a good day.' Brian said, coming over to them.

'I suppose we have,' Simon smiled at him, 'tiring, but then London is and as always, we are very glad to get back, aren't we, Eliza?'

'How right you are! Every time I go there these days I wonder how I ever managed to cope with all that dashing about.'

'Like a headless chicken!'

'I couldn't have put it better, Brian!' she laughed.

'By the way, Simon,' Brian said, 'you know we were talking about the rock band who were in here that night years ago?'

'Yes?'

'Well, I have a photograph of someone who may have been with them. I've had a good look at it, but I can't say I recognise him at all. He just looks like any other young man dressed in jeans and a black roll-neck sweater, trying to look like one of the Beatles.'

'Where did you get the photograph?'

'Ian Ash was in here earlier; apparently, they are re-opening the file on the Tilsly estate robbery and wanted to know whether this chap was with the rock band.'

'How on earth did he tie them up with that?'

'He'd remembered the robbery and on Saturday evening when he overheard us talking about Johnnie Baker, also the break-in at the Manor he began putting two and two together. Don't ask me how he managed to get hold of the photograph, though, I've no idea.'

'Once a policeman, always a policeman, eh?'

'Too true, Simon; anyway,' he went on, taking the photograph from his shirt pocket and handing it over to him, 'see what you think.'

Simon took the photograph from him and studied it closely. As Brian had said, he did look like any other young man of that build and colouring, also the clothes. Around about the time the photograph must have been taken, many young men around that age had adopted the same look.

'Do you recognise him, Simon?'

'I believe so. He's much younger in this picture, but his features are the same and his eyes as well. I can remember thinking at the time the unusual way they slanted; slightly downwards, a little eastern looking. Yes, Brian, I think he was with them that night.' He said, handing back the photograph.

'So, what do you think?'

'I really don't know what to think.'

'Incidentally,' Brian said, lowering his voice and leaning further across the bar towards them, 'have you heard about those two robberies in

Stockbridge?'

'Yes, Melissa has just told us.' Simon answered, unable to keep the smile from his face; there were times when his old friend could be so obvious, 'Where are you coming from, Brian?'

'Okay,' Brian grinned widely, 'here we go once again; trying to solve the mysteries of Meadowbank!'

'I really think it might be best, actually, to drop this speculation, you know, Brian. And, before you say anything, I can guess what you're thinking and, believe me, I don't blame you because I'm thinking along the same lines myself, but why don't we leave it to the police to solve? That is what they're paid for after all.'

'Alright, Simon,' he agreed, 'I hear what you say and you're right, of course, but between you and me,' he added, 'there is something decidedly shifty about that guy. I thought so as soon as he walked in here on Friday.'

'Johnnie Baker?'

'Who else? Look, he came here four years ago with his rock group, had a few beers, then spent the night goodness knows where and the next morning we hear about the break-in at Major Tilsly's place and, here he is again and what happens almost immediately?'

'I know,' Simon said, but not wanting to tell him he'd seen Johnnie Baker on Saturday night and grateful for Eliza's understanding; as usual she sensed exactly what he was thinking, 'you and I don't altogether trust the man, but I still think we should keep our suspicions to ourselves. For all we know, the police may be wondering about him also and, presumably, you'll be telling Ian Ash I recognised one of them who were in here that night?'

'Sure, if that's okay with you and you're sure he is the same one.'

'It's fine by me,' Simon said, 'and I'm sure alright, so, there you are then; that should be a lead for them. It is up to them to either prove one way or another if these two had anything to do with that old robbery and then they just might start putting two and two together about these latest incidents, that is, if they haven't already.'

'True,' Brian agreed, his expression suddenly thoughtful, 'I'll tell you one thing, Simon.'

'What's that?'

'Once Brenda Masters gets her teeth into all of this, you can be sure she won't let go until she gets right to the bottom of it.'

They were interrupted by the arrival of Martin Frame, the manager of Town & Country. Simon and Eliza had hardly spoken to him since he moved into the town to replace poor old Rodney Blake and looking at him now as he ordered a double whisky from Brian, Simon couldn't help comparing him with his predecessor. Where Rodney had been outgoing, often outrageously so, he had been a likeable kind of guy, but this Martin Frame, a totally different personality, was irritatingly pompous which Simon found off-putting and he wondered how long he would stay in Meadowbank.

'A very nasty accident on the Winchester Road, Brian,' he was saying, before taking a long sip of his whisky, 'police crawling all over the place; I was held up for more than twenty minutes.'

'Did you see how it happened?' Brian asked, a look of sympathy immediately replacing his habitual cheerful expression.

'Not really, except it looked as though the car must have gone out of control and careered into the side of a truck coming towards the town. The truck appeared to have emerged unscathed, but the car's a total wreck. What a mess! In fact, it's the worst I've ever seen.'

'Not much chance for the driver then?'

'Nobody could have survived that, Brian. Impossible. Probably driving too fast, I would say.' he added, moving away to speak to a couple at the other end of the bar.

'Not good.' Brian said quietly, giving the bar a wipe, 'Not good at all.'

'It's dreadful when something like that happens.' Eliza said, 'I always think it could happen to anyone; one minute, you're driving along the road and the next – well, nothing.'

'You're right, Eliza,' Brian smiled sadly, 'then there is nothing. It does make you think, doesn't it?'

*

Katie Brownlea dialled the number on her mobile, one she had once known off by heart. One minute, two minutes, and then she heard the familiar voice which took her back to what she considered now to be another lifetime.

'Hi! It's me.'

'Katie! How good to hear your voice. I knew you would phone, of course.'

'You know about Mark?'

'Yes, I had a call from an officer in the Hampshire constabulary this afternoon; apparently, it had taken them most of the day to find me.'

'I didn't know you'd moved.'

'Oh, yes, a couple of years ago, in fact.'

'It's awful about Mark, isn't it? I couldn't believe it when I heard, such a terrible shock. I wonder what really happened,' she went on, 'they seem to be saying he was murdered.'

'It looks like that, but,' he hesitated for a fraction of a second, and she could hear him take a deep intake of breath before he went on, 'Mark lived a pretty precarious life. He could never have gone straight, you know, Katie. It was not in his make-up; excitement and taking risks were paramount to him, they were part of his life; he would never have changed, even if he had wanted to.'

'And have you changed, Danny?' she asked softly, saying his name for the first time and discovering it didn't hurt anymore. She had been in love with Danny Howarth from the first day she had met him, only months after leaving school. He was years older than her and she had adored him even although she had known right from the beginning what he was like, never stopping to question the wisdom of the relationship as the months went by and having neither the wish nor the mental energy to think about leaving him and in the end, it was Danny who had left her. They had been crazy, irresponsible days and after they had split up and she had stopped feeling sorry for herself, she had vowed she would never so much as think about those times again, but now, hearing about Mark and what may have happened to him – well, she was finding she had no control over those old emotions; the memories, many of them painful, even disturbing; they were all flooding back and she was powerless to stop them.

'A good question, Katie.' he answered at last, 'Does anyone? I would like to hope that I have changed, but perhaps if I was going to be entirely honest, doubt it. Mind you,' he gave a dry chuckle, which she remembered so well, 'I'm older and I should be one hell of a lot wiser, but what about you, Katie? Are you still in Manchester?'

'I'm still here, yes. I'm married now, Danny; have been for almost two years now.'

'Really? And your husband, does he –'

'– does he know about my past?' she finished for him, just as she used to do.

'Sorry,' he said, 'I shouldn't have asked. It's none of my business. I just wondered, that was all.'

'I haven't told him everything; only about our rock group and how we used to spend each summer touring; all of that, but nothing else.'

'Perhaps you should have, Katie.'

'Because of Mark, you mean?'

'Indirectly, yes; somehow, the police have found out about the group, that we were all in it, I mean; they didn't enlighten me.'

'It's funny that, don't you think?' Katie asked him, wondering why she hadn't picked up on it earlier.

'What do you mean?'

'Mark had been living in Manchester, so why is Hampshire involved. The call I got was from there as well, probably the same police officer who spoke to you.'

'That had occurred to me when I got the call, but I put it down to them having difficulty in finding me, but, as you say, why Hampshire. In fact, Katie,' he went on, 'although I did spend some time in Southampton when I left the north, it wasn't for long before I moved to where I am now, in London, but you saying your call wasn't from Manchester, considering you are still living there, is strange.'

'Perhaps it was because he came from Winchester.'

'It still doesn't make sense, though. Surely his death would be investigated by the Manchester police.'

'You would have thought so,' Katie agreed, a sudden thought occurring to her which could just explain at least something, 'it could have been Johnnie who told them about our group.'

'I suppose so; it's a possibility, but it still doesn't explain any connection with the Hampshire authorities. Also, I don't think he kept in touch with Mark after the group broke up, but he may have done. They did live fairly close to each other though, come to think about it.'

'I don't think Johnnie is living there anymore.'

'Why do you say that?'

'Well, I can't be certain, but do you remember a girl called Felicity Carter; she was about my age and used to go to the same club as us; it was around about the time we were getting the group together.'

'Vaguely, why?'

'I bumped into her the other day; I hadn't see her for ages and she told me she and her boyfriend were going down south to live.'

'You're not thinking he was Johnnie, are you?'

'He was called Johnnie, actually. We had quite a long chat and she mentioned the name a couple of times.'

'It might not be the same one, though. Did she say whereabouts in the south?'

'No, she didn't and it never occurred to me to ask. I wish I had now.'

'You're not worried about any of this, are you, Katie?' he asked her, 'Because if you are, I don't think there is any need to be. From what I did manage to glean from the few questions the officer asked me, they were only trying to find out about Mark's background, who his friends were and when he had last seen them, that sort of thing. He was a loner, remember; he didn't even have a girlfriend, at least as far as I knew. I don't think it is a good idea to dwell on it, you know,' he added, 'if you do, it will only do your head in.'

'You're not saying he was gay, are you?'

'No – no,' he paused, 'that hadn't crossed my mind, but he could have been. What do you think?'

'Like you, I've not thought about it, but who knows, not that it matters now; he's dead.'

'Yes, poor sod!'

'Going back to what you were saying, Danny, I must admit I am a bit worried; the last thing I ever expected was a call from the police; it just brought everything back. Oh, I don't know what I mean really, except that it's made me a bit jittery. In a way, it's like being on a roller-coaster; the past is doing its best to catch up with me.'

Chapter Six

Jack Wilson, standing outside on his patio and waiting for Christine, heard the crash from the road, the force of the impact causing the framework on his patio doors to vibrate. He had lived in the house for a number of years and had lost count of the accidents there had been on that stretch of road in front of his property. Jack, together with his neighbours, had, on more than one occasion, drawn up petitions in an attempt to persuade the authorities to enforce a speed limit, but each time they had come back with the unarguable fact there already was a speed limit, and one which was clearly sign-posted from the outskirts of Meadowbank right up to where the road prepared to join the M27. While theoretically correct, this didn't take into account, at least as far as the protagonists were concerned, that many motorists were under the illusion they were already on the motorway. But, Jack was certain the accident this evening was a bad one, and going back inside the house and closing the patio doors his heart sank, as it always did when he thought about the inevitable aftermath when people were injured, sometimes fatally and their lives had come to an abrupt end.

At eight-thirty, when Christine had still not arrived and he knew, having heard the police and ambulance sirens come and go, that the road would now be clear, he began to become concerned. If she had been delayed she would have rung him he was sure, but there had been no call. He walked over to the sideboard and poured himself a small measure of whisky from the crystal decanter and took the glass with him, not through to the lounge where he spent most of his evenings, but into the kitchen. He needed to think and he didn't want those thoughts to be interrupted by the television. He had to concentrate on the call he'd had from her, not so much her actual words, those he could recall perfectly, but what had been behind them. Christine Saunders was a level-headed young woman, even when she had started working for the pharmacy. She had still been in her teens then and he couldn't remember her ever becoming flustered or upset and certainly not prone to making any rash judgements. She must be in her thirties now, he thought and as far as he knew she hadn't married. She may have done, but somehow he didn't think so. Surely, he reasoned, a husband would have been the first person she would have turned to for advice, not a man she had once worked for some years ago. It was possible whatever was troubling her had something to do with her work at the pharmacy; Jack couldn't think of anything else which he would be able to help her with. It wasn't as though they had kept in touch; they had seldom met, only in the street or the mini-market, but never in the pharmacy. He had not been able to explain to himself why, even from the first day of his retirement, he had not gone in there, choosing instead, White's the Chemist. It could have had something to do with his initial reaction towards his successor, putting it down at the time as purely chemical. He had only met Victor York twice; the first time when he had viewed the premises and then in the lawyer's office on completion of the sale, but he hadn't taken to the man. Even after all this time he had been unable to fathom out why; not that it was all that important. Christine, presumably, must get on with him; otherwise she wouldn't still be working there.

Annoyed by the circuitous route his thoughts were taking, at the same time realising he had to do something; he had to find out if she was alright. It was now two hours since she had called, too long he decided, taking out his old address book from the drawer in the hall table. He had her number here somewhere and if he was remembering right, it was for her mobile; she had given it to him a couple of years ago, telling him to phone her if he ever wanted a chat. It had been shortly after his wife had died and he had thought it a sweet gesture, but then Christine is like that he thought; always having time for people.

Jack found the page where he had jotted down her number and dialled, waiting for her to answer. After several minutes the line went dead on him; he had been disconnected. Odd he thought, the silent receiver still in his hand and then tried again, but this time there was not even a dialling tone. Of course there could be any number of reasons why he hadn't been able to get through he tried to rationalise, going back to the kitchen, but he didn't like it and had no idea of how he was going to be able to get in touch with her. He could be worrying needlessly, but deep down, he didn't think so. What was wrong with him he thought irritably; the plain facts were there, staring him in the face: Christine, a woman who used to work for him had rung him up, sounding extremely worried and asking if she could see him as she wanted his advice. On what? And then he'd asked her whether there was something wrong and she had said, and these had been her words exactly: "I believe there is, Jack, and I think you are the only person I can talk to." That was what she had said; she needed some advice. Had she perhaps thought better of it, deciding she had been over-reacting, not wanting to inflict her problems on to him? No, Jack dismissed the explanation instantly; that would have been out of character. She wouldn't have changed her mind and if she had, all she had to do was phone him again, but she hadn't. Christine would never have kept him waiting, thinking she was going to turn up at any moment. And then, as though he had known all along and had been putting the awful thought to the back of his mind, he knew what must have happened. It had been Christine in that accident out there. From when she had rung off it would have taken her only ten minutes at the very most to have reached that same spot in the road at the time of the crash, the sound of which eerily echoed and re-echoed in his brain. He didn't stop to reconsider, to think there could be another explanation; instead he went back to the hall, picked up the receiver again and telephoned the police station in Meadowbank.

The desk sergeant, cordially polite, but unable to give him any information, was quick to put him through to Inspector Ash. Jack knew him fairly well, but it didn't make it any easier in trying to explain his concern, and as he did so, wondering whether it wouldn't have been wiser to have waited until the following morning.

'Good evening, Mr Wilson,' the inspector said as soon as Jack had introduced himself, 'the desk sergeant said you were phoning about the accident earlier this evening on the Winchester Road.'

'Yes, that's right, I was,' Jack said, 'I realise how irregular this is, Inspector, but I have been waiting for a friend of mine to arrive and when she didn't and I had received no call from her, well, naturally I began to worry. I live on the Winchester Road, you understand, and I heard the crash earlier and as no doubt you've realised I am thinking the worse.'

'That's quite understandable, sir.'

'Can you tell me who was involved in the accident, Inspector Ash?'

'I'm afraid I can't,' he said quietly, 'not until the next of kin are informed. I'm sorry, but it's a formality.' he added.

'Next of kin?' Jack repeated under his breath, 'And,' he hesitated, 'was it a woman who was killed?'

'It was, yes.' but taking several seconds to reply; time which gave the impression of stretching out endlessly as Jack waited, but he knew in any case. It was Christine. He was sure of it.'

'How very, very sad.'

'She had no chance, sir, no chance at all. I do realise how frustrating this must be for you, but we're not at liberty to give you her name.'

'Can you suggest how I would be able to find out?'

'Presumably you have tried phoning your friend, sir?'

'I have, yes, but there was no answer.'

'I see. Mr Wilson,' he went on, 'would you be prepared to identify the deceased? Because, if you are, that can be arranged.'

'I would be.' Jack agreed, again without any hesitation in making such a decision and not even questioning why he should feel so strongly about a woman he hardly knew, but the thought occurring to him, it would seem they had not been able to locate anyone else who had known her.

'She was taken to Winchester, sir,' he said, 'and if it isn't too late for you we can take you there this evening.'

*

It was after ten when Ian, having taken Jack Wilson home, arrived back in Meadowbank. Brenda was still in her office and he went straight there rather than to his own. While the identification had not been as harrowing as some he had attended, he felt unutterably weary, wanting more than anything to call in at The Market Inn for a beer before they closed, but it probably wouldn't happen. There were many days like these he thought, walking along the corridor, stopping at the coffee dispenser and filling two plastic mugs, when they gave the impression of never coming to an end, especially at the start of an enquiry when the various loose ends started to appear, very often leading nowhere, except as a pile of notes on his desk.

'Coffee, ma'am,' Ian said, handing one of the mugs over to her, sure she wouldn't have had a break since tea-time and even then it would have lasted no more than twenty minutes, 'I thought you might be ready for one.'

'That was thoughtful of you, Ian. Thanks.' she smiled up at him.

'You were right,' Ian said, sitting down opposite to her, 'the woman was Miss Saunders.'

'I couldn't be certain, you know,' Brenda explained slowly, 'Christine Saunders didn't live in Meadowbank, but in a village a few miles north of Stockbridge and, although she had worked for the pharmacy for years, which is only a hundred yards or so from the Station, I hardly ever went in there and when I did I was more often than not served by Victor York. In fact,' she added, 'I can't remember when I last saw her.'

'Neither can I,' Ian said, 'and until tonight I didn't even know her name.'

'A very nasty accident, Ian,' Brenda said, her normal briskness returning, 'and we don't know how it happened; not yet, that is. The only witness we have is the truck driver and he's insistent her car went out of control; one minute she was driving normally, not fast, so he says, and the next, she'd slapped into the side of him. Well,' she went on, 'you've seen the skid marks yourself, but we will have to wait for the two reports before we learn anything more positive.'

'Two?'

'Yes, the one on the car and then there's the post mortem. As young as she was, she may have had a heart attack.'

'Of course,' Ian nodded; it's normal procedure he thought; he should have realised. 'Mr Wilson said something coming back in the car which, quite frankly, I think we should look into, ma'am.'

'Yes?'

'He called her by her Christian name, by the way, and told me she had worked for him for ten years, up to the time he took his retirement and, although hadn't known her all that well, he had liked her, trusted her judgement and when she phoned him earlier this evening, he didn't dismiss the fact that she sounded, while not exactly distraught, but extremely worried.'

'Did he say why this was?'

'He didn't know. All she said was that she needed to talk to him; that there was something wrong and she wanted his advice.'

'So, that was why she was on her way to see him?'

'That's right and well, you know the rest, ma'am; when she didn't turn up around the time he expected and he heard the crash which wasn't all that far away from where he lives, he told me he began to think the worst.'

'Curious.'

'I thought so.'

'She wasn't married; I checked that out while you were away,' Brenda told him, 'and didn't appear to have a boyfriend; at least not a regular one and she lived on her own. I've only been able to make some cursory enquiries, of course; we'll be able to find out more tomorrow. But, what I am wondering is, and I have no doubt it will have occurred to you as well, Ian, why should she have turned to man she had only really known as her employer, her ex-employer, in fact?'

'It might have been something to do with her work.' Ian suggested.

'I think you must be right there, also, I am no doubt being over-sensitive,' Brenda smiled wryly, 'but I don't like it, Ian. I think it's this pharmacy thing cropping up again. And,' she paused for a second, 'you know how much I dislike coincidences, but whatever it was she wanted to discuss with Jack Wilson must have been serious, so much so it couldn't wait until tomorrow. She had to see him this evening.'

'But she didn't make it.'

'True. Well, I think we've talked enough for today, Ian; it's late. We'll try and find time tomorrow, in the afternoon with luck and meanwhile I am going to make sure they do a thorough job in checking Christine Saunders' car and once we get that report we will have a better idea of the best way to take this enquiry; whether it was a straightforward fatal car crash or one with sinister connotations.'

There was still half an hour before closing time when Ian reached The Market Inn. There were only a few customers in the bar; presumably, this was normal for a Monday night he thought, ordering the beer he had been looking forward to for the last couple of hours.

'You're working late, Ian.' Melissa said, reaching up to take a glass from the shelf above her head.

'It's becoming a habit, I'm afraid, Melissa.'

'We heard about Christine Saunders.' she said quietly, 'What a dreadful thing to happen.'

'You knew it was her?' he asked, surprised but then why should he be? He had lived in Meadowbank all his life and was well used to how quickly news travelled, although he had not yet been able to find out how this actually came about. So much for trying to keep information confidential; it was virtually impossible.

'Yes,' she said, 'the driver of the truck came in here later. He was still pretty shaken, actually, but apart from that he seemed to be alright. He lives in Meadowbank and he recognised her when -'

'It's alright, Melissa,' Ian interrupted her, 'there's no need to tell me anymore; it's too distressing for you.'

'No, Ian, I'm okay, but he told us it was when they were carrying her to the ambulance. He said it took him several minutes, not until he was able to drive on into Meadowbank, that he remembered seeing her a couple of times when he'd been in the pharmacy.'

That would explain why this wasn't mentioned in the statement he made Ian concluded. This wasn't the first time a witness, especially one who had been involved in an accident of this nature, had experienced a temporary loss of memory. Ian had known quite a number since joining the force and no doubt he wouldn't be the last he thought with sad resignation, wondering, although not seriously, why he hadn't chosen a less stressful career.

*

Victor didn't hear about Christine's death until he arrived for work the following morning. The telephone was ringing when he opened the front door of the pharmacy and, hurrying through to the dispensary, he picked up the receiver.

'Good morning; Meadowbank Pharmacy.' he said automatically.

'Mr York?'

'Yes.'

'This is the Meadowbank Police Station, sir, would you mind waiting while I put you through to Inspector Ash.'

Victor was not kept waiting for long and within minutes he was talking to the inspector, who wasted no time in coming to the point, telling him Christine had been killed the previous evening in a car crash.

'Christine! She's dead!' he gasped, his breath catching painfully at the back of his throat as the finality of what he was hearing penetrated his brain, 'I had no idea! I've only just arrived for work; Christine is nearly always here before me, but she wasn't this morning. I assumed she could have been held up in the traffic.'

'The accident occurred last evening, sir,' Inspector Ash reminded him, 'at approximately nineteen ten hours.'

'Yes, yes,' Victor replied vaguely, 'nineteen ten, you say; that's ten minutes past seven.'

'That's correct, sir.'

'Where did the accident happen, Inspector? I'm wondering why I hadn't heard.'

'On the Winchester road;' the inspector answered, 'a mile and a half outside Meadowbank.'

'But, but,' he repeated, trying to stop himself stammering in such a foolish way, 'Christine lives – I mean, lived in a completely different direction.'

'We do realise where Miss Saunders lived, sir, but we are experiencing some difficulty in locating her next of kin. Perhaps you will be able to assist us.'

'I will, of course; if I can, but I don't see how.' Victor said, hoping this didn't mean he was going to ask him to identify her. That would be just too much!

'Miss Saunders had been working for you for some time, we believe?'

'Yes, she had; five years, in fact.'

'So you would know whether she had any family?'

'I don't think she did; both her parents died virtually within months of each other about four or five years ago. I remember her telling me that and she didn't have any brothers or sisters.'

'And she lived on her own?'

'As far as I know. The relationship between Christine and myself was purely professional and most of the conversations we had concerned the pharmacy.'

'I see,' he said, 'so you wouldn't have heard of a gentleman she knew called Matthew Richards then?'

'Never heard of him.'

'Mr Richard's name was in Miss Saunders' passport as her next of kin, but we haven't been able to get in touch with him yet, either at the address or the telephone number she had written down for him.'

'Well, I'm sorry, Inspector, I can't help you.' Victor said, wanting to bring the call to a close and glancing at his watch; almost nine-thirty and soon he would have to open up the pharmacy. Having no assistant was going to prove extremely difficult, plus the tedious and time-consuming task of finding a replacement. Very difficult indeed. Also, there was something at the back of his mind which had been niggling away for the last five minutes or so, but he couldn't think what it was. It had been something Inspector Ash had said, but frustratingly, whatever it had been, refused to surface.

'Very well, sir,' the inspector was saying, 'if Mr Richards should telephone or even call into the pharmacy, perhaps you would let us know. He may not be aware of what has happened to Miss Saunders.'

By the end of the morning Victor was beginning to think it would have been better to have closed the pharmacy for the whole day. Apart from coping single-handedly with a busier than normal stream of customers, many of them mentioning Christine and saying how sorry they were and what a loss she would be to the business, he wondered how he could possibly get through the remainder of the day. Usually, the pharmacy remained open during the lunchtime; Christine and him taking a different hour for their break, but, for the first time, he made an exception to this rule; at one o'clock precisely, Victor locked up and walked across the road to The Market Inn for a sandwich and half a lager, another unprecedented move, hoping he could find a quiet corner where he wouldn't be disturbed.

He only recognised a few people, but after ordering his beer and a ham and cheese sandwich, adroitly managed to avoid getting into conversation with any of them. He had brought a copy of that morning's newspaper with him, but more as a shield than to read about what had been happening in the rest of the world. From where he was sitting, next to one of the windows and facing up the length of the square and unable to see the pharmacy, not wanting to witness anyone turn away in disappointment when they discovered the door was locked, he tried to empty his mind. A bus had just pulled away from the stop outside the restaurant and he watched idly as it drew level with the window on its way to Winchester. That was it! The memory which had been lying sluggishly in his brain had returned to him. Christine had driven out that way yesterday evening, towards Winchester. That was the connection! Winchester Road. She hadn't been going to Winchester, but to visit someone who lived in Winchester Road! Victor only knew one person who lived in one of those houses on the straggling outskirts of the town. Jack Wilson, his predecessor! She had been going to see *him*. Inspector Ash had told him the accident had happened at ten minutes past seven and he distinctly remembered it was a couple of minutes after six-thirty when she had left the pharmacy. She must have gone somewhere first; a cafe perhaps, or she may even have come in here, to telephone Jack Wilson. It all added up, Victor thought, stifling a groan as he realised what this could mean. She had found out that he'd been fudging the figures; also that he'd been on to her. And what better person than Jack Wilson to turn to for advice. She hadn't known what to do with the knowledge she had and being the type of woman she was, she wouldn't have let the matter rest. Well, he concluded, taking a grateful sip of his lager, he could soon sort that out and the quicker the better.

Feeling considerably better having reached a decision he was now ready to solve his next problem and that was to phone his sister. Monica would help him out. He had no doubts about that. Like him, she had trained as a pharmacist and had often complained each time she had been on the phone to him how stymied she felt since her retirement. He'd give her a call as soon as he got back to the pharmacy and provided she wasn't planning on an early summer holiday she should be able to be here within the next couple of days. She would also be invaluable in helping him find another assistant; if anything, far better than he would be. It wouldn't take long he thought confidently until he had life back on an even keel and running exactly as how he wanted it to be.

*

Danny Howarth waited until Tuesday to phone Johnnie. Talking to Katie had made him think; he wanted to know whether it had been Johnnie who had given their names to the police, but equally important, and the more he puzzled over it, the more anxious he became, was why the call had been from the Hampshire constabulary and not from Manchester. As far as he was concerned he could just about understand why, but not in Katie's case. Nothing altered the fact that she had not moved away and had continued to live in the same town as Mark Astley. It didn't make a lot of sense and, as he dialled the number he had kept for Johnnie's mobile, he was hoping Johnnie could come up with some credible answers. Katie had told him Johnnie and his girlfriend were coming down south to live, it could have been Hampshire, but this was something else he could find out.

'Hi, Johnnie.'

'Danny? This is a surprise; I never expected to hear from you again.'

'Well, you know what they say about bad pennies, don't you?'

'Still the joker.'

'Not so much these days, Johnnie, especially at the moment after hearing about Mark.'

'Mark, yes.' Johnnie said, 'They're still not saying much about how it happened; at least I haven't seen anything more in the papers since Sunday.'

'No, neither have I. What do you reckon, then?'

'What do you mean?'

'Do *you* think he was murdered?'

'Don't ask me, Danny. Your guess is as good as mine.'

'Mark wasn't into heavy drugs; you know that, so this drug overdose thing doesn't gel with me.'

'Who knows,' Johnnie said, 'perhaps we'll never know.'

'Well, someone must.'

'What?'

'If he was murdered, there will be at least one person, I mean the killer.'

'I would drop it, if I were you, Danny.'

'Easy to say, Johnnie.' he said and not missing the slight change in his voice. Johnnie Baker was warning him off, but this was, until he could think it through properly, only an impression. 'Anyway,' Danny went on, 'the reason I'm phoning you is I had a call from the police asking me about Mark.'

'Ah.'

'Did you give them my name?'

'I did, yes. You see, they asked me whether Mark and I had ever worked together and I mentioned the rock group and, of course, they wanted to know who else had been in it.'

'Oh, I see; that explains it then. Katie phoned me yesterday; they'd been in touch with her also.'

'I guess they had to; police routine and all that.'

'I suppose so, but why the Hampshire constabulary; how come we didn't hear from the Manchester lot?'

'I have no idea.'

'Katie seemed to think you were planning to move south, by the way.' trying to find out in a roundabout way just where he was living without coming out with a direct question.

'What made her think that?'

'She bumped into your girlfriend and she told her.'

'I see.'

Is that all he can say Danny thought. Johnnie was being cagey. He had never known anyone, apart from Mark, that is, who could clam up the way he could.

'So,' Danny went on, deciding he would have to ask him outright after all, noticing the silences at the other end of the line were growing more pronounced. The last thing he wanted was for Johnnie to bring the call to an abrupt end, something he knew he was quite capable of doing, 'where are you living, Johnnie?'

'In Meadowbank, Felicity and I have rented a house there; it's not far from Winchester.'

'I know exactly where Meadowbank is. We were all there once, remember?'

'Of course I remember.'

'Why Meadowbank? Taking a risk aren't you?'

'Am I?'

'I would say so; someone could recognise you. Did that never occur to you?'

'Not really. Who could have? Both pubs were packed that night and it was a few years ago.'

'Anyway,' Danny went on, 'going back to the fact the Hampshire police appear to be involved in looking into Mark's death and you are actually living in the same county does strike me as puzzling.'

'As I've already said, Danny, I don't know why that was. Perhaps, as they spoke to me first and I was already down here, they passed it to the

Meadowbank police to deal with. I don't know.'

'You're not still working for Charlie East, are you?'

'Of course not.' the reply coming too quickly. He was lying.

'He's bad news, Johnnie.' Danny said to him, although realising he was wasting his breath in trying to warn him; Johnnie, again like Mark, always knew best.'

'That's ancient history, Danny.'

'What about Mark, then?'

'What about him?'

'Was he still with Charlie?'

'As to that,' he replied, impatience now creeping into his voice, 'again, I don't know.'

'Incidentally,' Danny said, veering away from saying anything further about one of the most ruthless men he had ever had the misfortune to meet; even thinking about him now, so many years later, sent shivers down his spine. Johnnie knew the rules and so had Mark if, as he was now beginning to suspect, he had been working for Charlie, 'How did the police know you were in Meadowbank and, another thing, how did they link your name with Mark's?'

'Because they read a text message on Mark's mobile to me, that's why.'

'I didn't know you two had kept in touch?' he asked him, by now more confused than ever. Johnnie was holding something back, but what it was, he knew he wasn't about to find out, certainly not from him.

'Now and again we met up,' and Danny recognised the contrived casualness in his voice; here come the lies he thought and waited for what he was going to come out with next; how he was going to extricate himself from the verbal corner Danny had done his best to put him in, 'we had a drink together some weeks ago and I told him Felicity and I were leaving Manchester and he said he'd keep in touch.'

What a load of eyewash! Keep in touch! Mark never kept in touch with anyone! Once anyone faded from the scene, as had happened when the rock group broke up, Mark didn't want to know them anymore. That was his way, but then he was no longer around to tell him he'd just been fed a pack of lies; dead men can't talk he thought bitterly.

Chapter Seven

Matthew Richards' flight from Zambia arrived at Heathrow Airport on time and, for once, his travel bag was among the first to appear on the carousel. By three o'clock he had checked through immigration and collected his hire car. He tried to get in touch with Christine as soon as he reached Arrivals, but couldn't get through. He tried again before leaving the airport, but still nothing. Either she had her mobile on charge or there was some problem with it he decided, pulling out of the car park and taking the junction which would take him on to the M3 heading west. He wasn't unduly concerned; in less than a couple of hours he could be in Meadowbank and he would go straight to the pharmacy. Matthew hadn't spoken to her for almost a week; his work as a geologist attached to the copper mines in Zambia had meant having to spend several days in the bush, where any form of communication had not been possible. He wished now he had rung her before leaving Lusaka, but reaching the airport in time to catch his plane had been one hectic rush; he hadn't had time.

Once on the motorway and, becoming more accustomed to the feel of the Honda, he was able to maintain a steady speed and shortly before five on that Tuesday afternoon he had left the M3 and on the last fifteen miles or so on the A3057 which would take him into Meadowbank. He was looking forward to the next three weeks' leave, especially to being with Christine again. To some, he knew their relationship was considered an unusual one, but it had, over the last three years suited them both fairly well. The money he was earning in Zambia would be hard to find in England and he enjoyed spending a good part of each year in Africa. Christine had never complained or said she should give up her job with the pharmacy and join him out there and, perhaps realising the lifestyle of an expatriate wouldn't really suit her, he had never suggested it. Besides, the conditions of his contract were excellent, enabling him to take these trips back to England every three months.

Matthew parked the Honda in the same car park Christine used at the rear of The Bridge Cafe. He couldn't see her car, but he didn't put any importance on that, assuming she hadn't been able to find a space when she arrived for work that morning.

Crossing the square to the Meadowbank Pharmacy, he opened the door and went in. There was a man behind the counter and he assumed this must be Victor York, Christine's boss. He tried to see into the room beyond him, which looked as though it might be the dispensary, expecting Christine to be in there, but she wasn't.

'Good afternoon, can I help you?'

'Er –' Matthew hesitated, 'I was hoping to see Miss Saunders –' stopping abruptly at the change in the man's manner; what had been an automatic and polite greeting had turned into something quite different; Victor York, if it was him, was giving every impression of someone in utter confusion. Also, the colour had drained from what had been a ruddy complexion and he appeared to be finding it difficult to look at him directly.

'You are?' he asked, leaning forward slightly and resting both hands on the counter.

'I'm Matthew Richards,' he explained, 'a friend of Miss Saunders.'

'Oh dear, you don't know do you? I am very sorry to tell you, Mr Richards,' he said, his voice by this time far from steady, 'but Christine was involved in an accident last evening and –'

'– and what?' Matthew interrupted him, resisting the urge to shake him, but it was clear he was in a state of shock, finding it impossible to go on, 'Where is Christine? Is she in hospital?'

'No, no, she isn't. I'm sorry,' he said for the second time and Matthew felt the blood leave his own face as he stared at him, waiting for him to tell him what had happened, 'but she didn't survive.'

'No!' Matthew staggered against the counter, having to put out a hand to steady himself, as the full force of those words literally hammered into his brain.

'Perhaps you would like to come into the dispensary and sit down, Mr Richards?'

'No, I'll be alright. Just tell me what happened.'

'I don't know the details, not the full details, that is, but it would seem her car went out of control when she was driving along the Winchester Road and hit a truck coming in the other direction and she died instantly.'

'When did this happen; you said it was in the evening?' scarcely recognising his own voice.

'Just after seven.'

'Was she actually going to Winchester, do you know?' Matthew asked him, wondering why Christine should have been breaking her normal routine.

'I don't know, Mr Richards.'

'I'm finding this so difficult to take in.' Matthew said, taking a deep breath, not knowing what he should do next. Obviously nothing for Christine; the woman he had known for three years and had loved dearly. They had suited each other so much, and now she had gone. Just like that.

'I'm sure you are; in fact, everybody who knew her were very shocked when they heard about the accident.'

'Have you any idea where they have –' pausing to take another deep and steadying breath before going on, '- where they have taken her?'

'I expect it would have been to Winchester, but I'm not sure.' he answered, 'The police will be able to tell you, though. They already knew you were a friend of hers.' he added.

'How did they know that?'

'When they phoned me this morning, they asked me if I had ever heard her mentioning you because they'd seen your name in her passport as her next-of-kin.'

'Oh, God!' Matthew groaned, 'They've been trying to get hold of me, haven't they? And, I wasn't here; I wasn't even in England! How dreadful. I'd better get in touch with them straight away. You say you had a call from them; was this from Meadowbank police station or Winchester?'

'He was from our police station,' he said, 'Inspector Ash.'

'Where is the police station; I don't remember seeing one?'

'It's very close in fact,' he said, making no attempt to hide his relief that he was going, 'just walk across the square and turn left, you can't miss it; it's the large red-brick building.'

Thanking him, Matthew left the pharmacy and, as he had explained, it wasn't far away, the short walk giving him no time to pull himself together. The shock had been tremendous, numbing, like nothing he had ever experienced before.

The desk sergeant smiled at him sympathetically when he gave him his name and after buzzing through on one of the telephones on the desk, escorted him along the corridor into the main part of the building. Tapping on a door further down on the left-hand side, Matthew just had time to read the plaque: "Chief Inspector Brenda Masters" before being shown into the room and introduced to the woman sitting behind the desk.

'It's good of you to call into the Station, sir,' she said, standing up and shaking hands with him, 'we had been trying to get in touch with you.'

'I went to the pharmacy hoping to see Christine, and –' he faltered, wondering if he was going to be able to finish what he wanted to say, 'and,' he continued, 'I heard about her. I had no idea. No idea at all. I've been out of the country and I only got back this afternoon.'

'That explains it, then.' she said and gestured for him to sit down, 'First of all, Mr Richards, we offer our condolences; it must have been a shock to hear the news the way you did.'

'I can't describe how much.'

'How well did you know Miss Saunders?'

'We met three years ago,' Matthew said slowly; even thinking of Christine hurt like hell, 'we were lovers.' he added quietly, not trusting his voice.

'There is something else you need to know, Mr Richards.'

'Yes?'

'This afternoon, we received a report on the check which was carried out on Miss Saunders' car; this has revealed there is strong evidence that it may have been tampered with prior to the accident.'

'I don't understand.'

'I'll try to explain.' she said, 'At the moment of impact, the steering column snapped; we've been told this shouldn't have occurred with an accident of this nature as both the vehicles were travelling at relatively low speeds at the time. A further and more detailed check was then made when a number of components appeared to have been removed, each of them relevant to the functioning of the steering column.'

'Removed!' Matthew gasped, 'You mean deliberately?'

'They must have been; the mechanics could find no trace of them either inside the vehicle or at the site of the accident.' she said, and even in his distress, Matthew wondered how she could remain so calm, so much in control, both in the way she was talking to him and in her expression, but then, this was part of her job: breaking bad news to people; she had to remain dispassionate. 'Also,' she went on, 'whenever this was done, it must have been between the time Miss Saunders parked the car before arriving at the pharmacy in the morning and to when she left to drive towards Winchester shortly after seven that evening. In other words, with defective steering, an accident could have happened at any moment after she left the car park.'

'I can't believe this, Chief Inspector, I can't!'

'I'm sorry, sir; I realise this must come as an additional blow to you, but there appears to be no room for any doubt in the report, leaving us no alternative now, but to treat Miss Saunders' death as one of murder.'

'Murder!' Matthew whispered the word, putting both hands up to his head, instinctively wanting to blot out what she had said. Christine had been murdered? Why? Why?

'Are you alright, sir?'

'Sorry.' ashamed to have lost control, 'Sorry,' he repeated, 'I'm finding it so difficult to take all of this in.'

'It's understandable, sir.' and for the first time since he came into her office he heard a trace of sympathy in her voice.

'What I can't understand, that is if you are right, Chief Inspector, why Christine? To me, because I knew her so well, I guess I find it too incredible to accept. Who would have wanted to have gone to such lengths?'

'You can rest assured, Mr Richards, we will do everything in our power to find who was responsible. You say you've been out of the country; when did you last see Miss Saunders?'

'I was back in England at the end of March,' he told her, trying to distance himself mentally from that time; the memory was too painful, and surprised by the abrupt way she had moved away from what they were talking about, 'and, as I always did, I stayed with Christine.'

'I see,' she nodded, 'and the last time you spoke to her; this would have been?'

'Last Wednesday evening,' he said, 'I'm working in Zambia and usually phoned her every second day, but I was out of contact almost up until the time I left last night.'

'And how did she sound on Wednesday?'

'Fine,' Matthew said, 'she was absolutely fine; she told me how much she was looking forward to – to –' but unable to go any further. What he was feeling was affecting him physically, reducing his normal practical personality to a crumbling mess. He had to be alone; he couldn't afford to crack up. There was too much to do; the funeral to arrange and everything else it would involve and then he would be able to leave England and try somehow to get his life back together again.

'I do understand how you must be feeling, sir, but I have a reason for asking this.'

'Why?' taking a deep gulp of air.

'Because, we have been told that on Monday evening Miss Saunders was sufficiently concerned to phone someone she used to work for to tell him she needed to talk to him about something which was worrying her.'

'Do you mean Jack Wilson?'

'You know him?'

'Christine once introduced him to me; so, Chief Inspector, what you're saying is that she phoned him up because she was worried.'

'That's right and whatever it was, must have occurred after she spoke to you and before she phoned Jack Wilson.'

'It must have had something to do with her work. It must have been.'

'We don't know that, sir.'

'But why else?'

'Mr Richards,' she said patiently, 'you are under considerable stress at the moment and it is all too easy to jump to conclusions, whether rightly or wrongly, but we will find out, we'll get to the bottom of the truth.'

'You sound very confident.' Matthew said, by now running out of steam. The whole situation was, in his opinion, unsolvable. If Christine hadn't given Jack Wilson any details of what was causing her so much concern, how the hell could the police find out? It was impossible. Utterly tragic and impossible.

'Quite frankly, sir, we *have* to be confident. Only in this way can we get to the root of the problem and with hard work and diligence we will.'

Leaving the police station and standing for a moment on the top step, Matthew felt he had emerged from a long dark tunnel; in the relatively short time he had spent in the chief inspector's office he had completely forgotten about the real world. There were people out there he thought, looking down into the square, who lived, at least on the surface, perfectly ordinary, everyday lives. Murder was alien to them; the nearest they would ever get to it would be by watching television; an episode of Inspector Barnaby, perhaps, where throughout the series a seemingly large number of victims came to a violent end. But this was the first time he had been shown that sudden and unexpected death wasn't something you watched in a film or, as all too often, on the news in a part of the world where you were very unlikely ever to visit, and quickly dismissed as having nothing to do with you, but when it did, became more than real, but very, very personal. Losing Christine felt to him at that moment like being suffocated in a thick heavy blanket; he wanted to push his way out, but he couldn't and the more he tried, the tighter the grip became. There was no way, he decided, stepping down on to the pavement, he would go to her house this evening. He simply wasn't up to it; tomorrow would be soon enough.

The main door of The Market Inn was open and without hesitating he went inside. He had been there a number of times when he had met Christine after work and they'd had a couple of drinks before going for a meal. Also, he remembered they had rooms; perhaps it would be a good idea if he stayed in Meadowbank for the night.

There were half a dozen customers at the bar and only a few of the tables were occupied, but, apart from that, it wasn't too busy. Brian Morrison smiled a welcome and then he must have recognised him because it instantly changed to one of concern. I suppose everyone in the town must know about Christine by now, Matthew thought, perhaps it might have been wiser to have driven into Stockbridge where he didn't know anyone, but it was too late, he was in and couldn't merely turn on his heels and walk out of the pub.

'Hello, Matthew,' Brian said, 'I take it you've just got back?'

'Hello, Brian, that's right; this afternoon.'

'And by the look of you, mate, I would say you've only just heard the news.'

Matthew could only nod his head; the tightness in his throat making it impossible for him to utter a word.

'Terrible about Christine; we're all so sad about it, Matthew.'

'Thanks, Brian.' he managed, and for the second time that afternoon finding it difficult to trust his voice.

'Look, if there's anything Melissa and I can do, you only have to say.'

'Thanks. I'm sorry, I must sound a right inarticulate ass, but I simply can't get it into my head that she's gone.'

'If you want to stay on later after we're closed and if it will help to talk, well, we'll be here.'

'I don't know what to say. Actually, I was wondering if you had a spare room; I don't want to go back to Christine's house, not tonight; it would be too much.'

'That's no problem and,' he went on, 'we'll do better than that. Why not eat with us later this evening; I don't expect you've had much today.'

'Only the stuff they served up on the plane.'

'Say no more;' Brian smiled, 'now, what are you going to have to drink? You look as if you're in need of one.'

Matthew ordered a whisky, but only a single. Brian had been right; he hadn't had anything substantial to eat all day; in fact, he hadn't had much the day before either, when most of the time had been taken up driving the hundred miles or so to Lusaka Airport. Lusaka, Zambia, Africa, all seemed a million miles away; another world he thought, taking the first sip of his whisky, appreciating the smoothing warmth as he swallowed. He *would* get through this. It would take time, but once he had managed to come to terms with her death, he was beginning to feel it might be possible, although still a long way to go before he reached that stage of being at peace with himself and with his loss. Being here, in Brian and Melissa's pub did help and, somehow, in a way, it was bringing Christine closer to him. The open and unconditional friendliness Brian had offered him had been overwhelmingly comforting. He was a good guy, remembering Christine had told him he and Melissa were getting married, last Friday it would have been and he hadn't even congratulated him he thought, but he would; later that evening.

As though sensing he wanted to be on his own for a while, Brian had moved to the other end of the bar. From where he was standing, Matthew had a clear view of the pharmacy. He couldn't make up his mind about Victor York; a dried up sort of man and, although not all that old, had an old-fashioned manner about him. Christine had never talked about him much. He had always got the impression she hadn't particularly liked him, not that she had ever said so. Thinking about him, reminded Matthew of his predecessor. The one time when he had met Jack Wilson, he had decided instantly he was a straight-down-the-middle sort of man. Christine had told him in the early days when they had first met, that Jack had taken early retirement; something she had thought to do with his wife who had been ill for a number of years. Yes, Matthew thought, he would have been the kind of person she would have turned to for advice, although Matthew couldn't help feeling, as he'd said to the chief inspector, that whatever had been troubling her must have had something to do with her work.

'Are you alright, Matthew?' Melissa broke into his thoughts, resting a hand lightly on his arm, 'I'm terribly sorry about Christine.'

'Thank you, Melissa.'

'Here's the key to your room,' she said, smiling gently at him, and he was grateful for her tactfulness in not saying anything further about Christine; there was a limit to how long he could maintain control on his emotions, even although slightly fortified by the whisky, 'and Brian says you'll be eating with us. How does Beef Strogonov sound?'

'It sounds good,' he smiled for the first time that day, 'and I believe I'll be able to work up an appetite for that.'

*

The lounge bar of The Royal Oak was busy; Ted, the barman, fully occupied with taking the order from a party of half a dozen newcomers when Johnnie arrived. Charlie East was already there, waiting for him, at one of the tables in the far corner of the room and Johnnie walked over, pulling out a chair and placing the briefcase he had brought with him on the floor between them and next to the one which was already there.

'Good evening, Johnnie.'

'Good evening, Mr East.'

'What would you like to drink, Johnnie; I'll try and catch Ted's attention?' Charlie asked, once the brief and formal greeting had been made.

Johnnie asked for a lager and they waited until Ted had brought it over before either of them said anything further. Charlie East was looking as suave as ever he thought, taking in the perfectly tailored navy blazer and the open-necked blue and white striped shirt; the plain blue silk cravat adding a silent gesture of flamboyancy or, more likely, the cynical thought occurring, a rather obvious statement of his undoubtable wealth. Johnnie had known him for years and in all that time he had always looked the same and, strangely, hadn't appeared to have aged. He had no idea how old he would be; in his fifties, perhaps even more he reckoned, raising his glass to him before taking a sip of his lager.

'Everything alright then, Johnnie?'

'As far as I know, yes, except I had a visit from an Inspector Ash on Sunday after I phoned you.'

'Oh, yes?'

Johnnie then told him about the police finding the text message on Mark's mobile; the one he had sent last Thursday, also about mentioning the rock group. Johnnie had learned very early on in his relationship with Charlie to hold nothing back. It was better that way. He knew Charlie trusted him, at least as far as a man like Charlie East would ever trust anyone.

'Nothing to worry about there, I'm sure.' Charlie said, picking up his own glass.

'I don't think so, not from the police anyway.'

'What do you mean?'

'I had a phone call from Danny Howarth on Tuesday.'

'Did you, now?'

'Yes, you see the inspector asked me who else had been in the group and naturally I had to give him Danny's name, also Katie's.

'Naturally. So, why the worried frown, Johnnie?'

'Well, I'm not sure really, but there was something in Danny's manner which struck me as being more than a little – inquisitive; for want of a better word, I suppose.'

'Too many questions, you mean?'

'That's right,' Johnnie nodded, 'he kept harping on about why the police in Hampshire were investigating Mark's death and not Manchester. Also, and I didn't like the way he said this, but he asked whether I was still working for you.'

'Tried to warn you off, I suppose?'

'How did you guess?'

'Easy, Johnnie. Danny appears to have forgotten a few things. You could say he's also forgotten his roots. Not good, that. He's bent, Johnnie, and now it would appear he has decided to, how shall I put it, turn over a new leaf and conduct his life along more honest lines, rather than close that particular door on his past life he is trying to make waves and, quite frankly, not to put too fine a point on it, that is unacceptable.'

'Why would that be, do you think?'

'Well, you probably never knew this,' Charlie went on, 'but he and Mark were related, although only through marriage.'

'Really?'

'Yes, they weren't even half-brothers. A complicated story as it happens, but both Cyril and Angela Howarth had been married before; Danny being the product of his father's short-lived liaison with an Italian chorus girl who, incidentally, quite literally left him 'holding the baby', while Mark was Angela's son from an equally brief marriage.'

'So, how close was the bond?'

'Surprisingly, very close although there was more than ten years difference in their ages. They were a pair those two; a couple of young tearaways. Well, you probably know about Mark's background, but, Danny's on the other hand was more or less the same, although in his case he left home long before Mark did and ventured further afield.'

'Complicated.'

'Very. However, when Danny decided to sever his ties with me, it was far from amicable. He doesn't like me, Johnnie, and from what I'm reading between the lines it would seem he still doesn't. No doubt, in his somewhat befuddled brain he's thinking I had something to do with Mark's untimely end.'

How much he would have liked to ask him, come right out with it and ask him whether he did or not, but to ask that would surely have added the final nail to his own coffin. Johnnie was no fool; he recognised dangerous ground when he came close to it and as always in his life, he intended to look after his own skin. Whoever killed Mark had nothing to do with him and whether Charlie East had a hand in it or not, well, he didn't want to know. Time to change the subject he decided, finishing off his drink.

'Did Danny tell you what he was doing now?' Charlie asked him.

'No, he didn't, only that he's living in London now. Don't ask me where exactly, Mr East, because I didn't think to ask him. I reckoned it might have sounded suspicious to him if I had.'

'No, no, Johnnie,' he was quick to reassure him, 'you did right. What about Katie Brownlea; is she still with him?'

'No, I'm sure they're not. He told me that Katie had phoned him to say she'd had a call from the police as well.'

'Presumably, she's still up north.'

'I would say so, but I don't know for sure.'

'Alright, Johnnie,' he said, 'I'd suggest you put all of this out of your head. At the end of the day, Danny Howarth is small fry. We'll have another drink and I can give you the details of your next assignment, which will be this Saturday. Is that alright with you?'

'Fine; no problem.'

'Good, and I've got a fellow lined up to cover for you on this one.'

'That's a relief; so, when do I meet him?'

'He'll be in Meadowbank on Friday evening and I've asked him to be in The Bridge Inn at seven-thirty; being a Friday, the place should be packed.'

'That sounds okay.'

'I won't be there, Johnnie, for obvious reasons.'

'Did you hear about the accident last night?' Johnnie asked him as they waited for their drinks and wanting to change the subject. He was very much aware of the possibility of being overheard. It didn't matter that he didn't recognise anyone in the bar, but it didn't necessarily mean he hadn't been recognised. It was second nature to him to be constantly on alert; watching his back at all times had become the norm.

'No. Where was this?'

'Just outside the town, on the Winchester Road; a pretty bad crash from what I've heard and the driver of the car, well, she was killed outright.'

'Tut, tut, driving too fast, I expect. Was she from Meadowbank, do you know?'

'She didn't live here, but she worked for one of the pharmacies; the one practically next door to us in fact.'

'Poor woman; tragic, eh?'

'These things happen.'
'Too true, Johnnie; all too often, I'm sorry to say.'

Chapter Eight

Brenda walked across the square to the Meadowbank Pharmacy. There was no sign of Victor York, but the plump grey-haired woman who bore a remarkable likeness to him, stepped briskly up to the counter to serve her, her smile instantly evaporating when Brenda introduced herself.

'Oh! Chief Inspector Masters! Yes, well, I'll just get my brother; he's in the dispensary.'

Brenda waited while the woman retreated into the room at the back of the pharmacy, re-emerging immediately followed by Victor.

'Chief Inspector.' he said, shaking her hand.

'Only a few words, sir,' Brenda said, looking beyond him to the open door of the dispensary and Victor, perhaps taking the hint, gestured for her to follow him back in there.

'This is my sister, Chief Inspector.' he turned round belatedly to introduce her, 'Monica has very kindly agreed to help me out over the next few weeks until I can find a replacement for Miss Saunders.'

'That's fortunate for you, sir,' she said, 'to have someone who could come here at such short notice.'

'I certainly am,' he agreed, smiling at his sister, 'Monica, like myself, is a qualified pharmacist and since her retirement has more free time on her hands.'

Going with him into the dispensary, Brenda marvelled there were still people in this new century who managed to exist in what, to her, seemed to be another era entirely. She had never noticed it before, but this morning, his rather stilted and quaint way of talking definitely suggested he was a product of the old school.

'Well, Chief Inspector,' he said, waiting until she was seated, 'it is obvious to me you must be here with regard to the death of Miss Saunders?'

'That's right, sir,' trying to ignore the pompousness in his tone, finding it jarring as well as slightly patronising, 'I'm not only following up on the telephone call you had from Inspector Ash yesterday, but since then, what previously had given every appearance of being a straightforward road accident, is now being treated as a murder enquiry.'

'What?'

'I apologise for having to break this to you in such an abrupt way,' Brenda said, 'but the check made on Miss Saunders' car has revealed a number of serious defects which must have been carried out deliberately.'

'I – I,' he blustered, sitting down heavily in the chair at the other side of the desk, 'I don't know what you mean. What sort of defects and you say they were made deliberately; this is all very hard to believe.'

'The evidence is irrefutable;' she said and going on to explain, 'integral components of the steering column had been removed and this caused the accident.'

'But – but –' once again, he faltered, 'who could have done this?'

'As to that, sir, at the moment we don't know, but given some time, we will; you can be sure of that.'

'I hope so, Chief Inspector; I really hope so. For this to happen to a young woman like Miss Saunders is unthinkable!'

'I agree,' Brenda said quietly, 'unthinkable, but, yet, it happened. However,' she went on, 'there are a number of questions I would like to ask which may help us with our enquiry.'

'Such as? I don't see how anything I can say could possibly help in any way. In fact –'

'- Sir,' she interrupted before he had any time to say anything further, 'allow me to continue.'

'Of course,' he said, lowering his voice and looking towards the pharmacy where by now there were a number of customers waiting to be served, 'this whole – this whole business is frightful and so disruptive to the business.' he added, petulance creeping into his voice. Victor York, she decided, didn't like his daily routine disturbed and the loss of his assistant would certainly have meant that. From what Brenda had heard about Christine Saunders since Monday had been quite telling. She had been considered, by more than one person she had spoken to, as having been an asset to the pharmacy with her tactful and helpful manner; people had genuinely liked her.

'I am sure it is, sir.' Brenda said, hoping he wouldn't recognise the insincerity in her voice, but she didn't think so. At that precise moment he looked as if he had been quite literally punched in the solar plexus, 'But, if we could continue and I will try to make this as brief as possible.'

'I would appreciate that, Chief Inspector.'

'First of all,' Brenda said, 'I would like you to describe to me what Miss Saunders' manner had been like on Monday.'

'Her manner?'

'Yes, did she look worried or pre-occupied in any way, or was she as she always appeared?'

'She seemed to me to be exactly the same, Chief Inspector.' he answered.

'You're sure?'

'Of course I am. We didn't have much time to spend talking, but, then, Mondays are always like that; people do seem, for some unfathomable reason, to converge on the pharmacy as soon as we open.'

'Who arrived first; you or Miss Saunders?'

'Christine was already here when I arrived.'

'Was this unusual?'

'Not at all.'

'You remain open during lunchtime, I believe?'

'That's right we do. We take, sorry, I mean, we took turns to have our break.'

'And Miss Saunders; do you know where she went for lunch?'

'The same place as I do, every day, in fact; The Bridge Cafe.'

'On Monday, have you any idea whether she went there?'

'I don't know for sure, of course, but I would say she did.'

'I see,' Brenda nodded, 'and, at the end of the day, what time did you close?'

'Unless it is one of our days for late night closing, it's seven, but this Monday, I didn't actually lock up until well after that time.'

'And Miss Saunders?'

'Christine left at six-thirty, as usual.'

'On Monday, when she went out, where were you; in here or in the pharmacy?'

'I was in here.' he answered, a puzzled frown creasing his forehead, 'I was on the phone as a matter of fact.'

'Therefore,' Brenda said, 'you probably didn't see where she went?'

'Sorry,' again, the frown appeared, 'I don't understand.'

'What I meant, sir, the direction she took, whether it was to the left or the right.'

'Oh, I see. No, I've no idea. Why do you ask?'

'It's a small point,' Brenda said, 'but we know Miss Saunders made a telephone call around seven which, according to what you've told me, would have been after she left the pharmacy and we were wondering where she was during that time up to when she drove out of Meadowbank.'

'Presumably, she would have been using her mobile, Chief Inspector?'

'She was, yes.'

'Well, she wouldn't have needed to go anywhere to do this, would she?'

'What you're saying is correct, sir,' Brenda said, 'and as I said, it is only a small point, but it is also a missing link which does need to be clarified. However,' she went on, by now choosing her words carefully, wanting to make sure he fully understood the implication of what she was saying, 'the person Miss Saunders phoned, has informed us that she sounded extremely worried, therefore, if, as you say, she appeared to be the same as usual that day, we would like to know what had occurred in less than half an hour to have caused her so much distress.'

'I really have no idea, Chief Inspector.' he shrugged, and Brenda could tell he wanted the interview to come to an end; he'd had enough, but she wasn't quite finished. 'This –' he hesitated, obviously trying to decide whether to ask the question or not; his reluctance to say anymore could have been out of an inbuilt politeness not to appear over-curious, but perhaps not, '- this person Christine called; I was just wondering who it may have been. None of my business, of course, I realise that.' he added quickly.

'I'm afraid we are not at liberty to divulge the name, sir.'

'Oh, I see.'

'Finally,' Brenda said making to stand up and catching a fleeting expression of relief on his face, 'could you give me an outline of Miss Saunders' responsibilities?'

'Responsibilities?' he asked, and she was sure his jaw dropped; his whole demeanour immediately replacing any former sign of looking forward to a speedy respite from her questioning.

'Yes, sir,' she said, 'responsibilities; for instance, apart from dealing with the customers and everything else which that would inevitably involve, did she have any further duties?'

'Not really; you must understand, Chief Inspector, Christine was not *qualified* in any way in respect to the pharmacy profession. She came here straight from school, in fact, and I suppose you could say she learned various aspects of the business as she went along. Don't get me wrong,' he stressed, 'she was excellent at her job. I couldn't fault her; totally conscientious at all times.'

Trying to decipher the real meaning behind his convoluted explanation was not easy; he was so incredibly pedantic Brenda thought and not sure where this particular line of questioning was going to lead, if anywhere.

'Let me put it this way,' she said, deciding on a different direction, 'was Miss Saunders computer literate?'

'Well, now you come to mention it, yes, she was. She'd been on a course; it must have been about eight years ago, which meant she was able to assist me on the accounting side of the business.'

'Accounting side,' she repeated, 'perhaps you could be more explicit?'

'Nothing too complicated,' he went on and she inwardly cringed when she heard again that patronising tone in his voice, 'relatively fundamental really; it was in respect to our stock system.' he explained quickly, almost dismissively, as though he had no real interest in such a mundane matter, 'Each time we received deliveries from our suppliers she would key the products into the system.'

'I see,' Brenda commented, 'and the sales? Was she responsible for the recording of them also?'

'No, she wasn't; this is our main computer, Chief Inspector,' he said, pointing to the computer on the desk, the blank screen telling her it had not yet been switched on that morning, 'those entries you're referring to are keyed-in at the point of sale and at the close of business they are then transferred automatically to this computer, all of which enabled me to see at a glance what our stock levels were.'

'And was the re-ordering carried out by you, sir?'

'Oh, yes, Chief Inspector. As I'm sure you will appreciate, in a business of this nature accuracy in re-ordering drugs and pharmaceuticals is of paramount importance and,' he continued to pontificate, 'in my professional opinion should never be delegated.'

'Quite.' Brenda said, 'And, did you take care of the other accounting entries?'

'Oh, no,' he smiled, 'I simply don't have the time. At the end of each month we hand all our paperwork to our accountants and they take over from there.'

'Plus the discs.'

'The discs?'

'Yes, sir, presumably they would have needed these to substantiate those deliveries, also the sales and stock levels?'

'Oh, yes, of course. Of course.'

'Are your accountants in Meadowbank?'

'They are yes; a small family firm, Wilcox & Wilcox, in Bridge Street, but may I ask, Chief Inspector, why you are going along these lines? I hope you are not suggesting there have been any discrepancies in my pharmacy, because if that is the case -'

'- Please, sir,' Brenda interrupted the flow, 'I'm not suggesting anything, but the fact remains that there has to be a reason for Miss Saunders' death and this is what we are trying to establish.'

'Christine was an honest woman, Chief Inspector.'

'All the more reason to make absolutely sure she may not have in some way, perhaps unwittingly, placed herself in a vulnerable position. We have to look at every possibility, sir; only this way can we start eliminating. I do hope you understand what I'm saying?'

'I'm not sure I do.'

'I'll put it in plain words,' she said, 'your pharmacy, any pharmacy if it comes to that, carries a stock of drugs, a good proportion of which, if falling into the wrong hands, could yield a lucrative return for anyone sufficiently unscrupulous.'

'Oh, dear me!' he gasped, 'But nothing like that has happened in my pharmacy; I would have known about it, Chief Inspector.'

'It is to be hoped you would, sir,' she said, 'but these are possibilities I have to mention to you.'

'All of this is quite beyond me.' Victor said, putting a hand up to his brow and for a second closing his eyes as though in pain, 'Totally beyond me!'

'Incidentally, sir,' Brenda said, standing up from the table, 'do you know where Miss Saunders normally parked her car?'

'Always in the same place,' he replied, looking surprised at the question, 'in the car park at the back of the mini-market and The Bridge Cafe.'

'As no doubt you do yourself, Mr York?' Brenda asked him, bringing the interview to an end.

'When I have the car, yes, but when the weather is fine as it is at the moment, I walk to work.'

'As you did on Monday?'

'Yes, that's correct, Chief Inspector; I find it is good exercise and not too far from where I live in Meadowbank.'

It was like a breath of fresh air Brenda thought, finally emerging from the pharmacy, all too aware of the bewildered expression on Victor York's face as she left. What she had to do now was to try and find out whether Christine Saunders spoke to anyone before she phoned Jack Wilson and, if that had been the case, she could have met them on her way to her car. There had been no record of any calls having been received on her mobile and the only out-going one had been the call to Jack Wilson shortly before seven that evening. Either, Brenda thought, waiting at the kerb to cross the square, Victor York wasn't all that observant or he hadn't been telling the truth. As to that possibility, she was reluctant to pursue for the moment; time enough later, she decided, reaching the pavement at last and walking, not back to the Station, but in the other direction, the one Christine would have taken to reach the car park at the rear of The Bridge Cafe. Victor York had told her she had left at six-thirty and Brenda remembered Ian saying that Brian always opened up the pub punctually each day at that time. Was it possible, she wondered, approaching the door of The Market Inn which, as it was now, would have been open on Monday. Had Christine decided on the spur of the moment to go in? Or, had she made an arrangement to meet someone there? There was only one way to find out she thought and that was to go in and ask.

Brian was behind the bar and as soon as he saw her he looked across and smiled, immediately taking her back years; to when they had been no more than teenagers, to a time when she had never imagined she would join the force. He really didn't look all that much different; a bit more stout than he had been, but he had managed, in spite of the various problems he'd had to contend with since then, to hold on to his boyish outgoing disposition. She hadn't seen him for a few weeks, which reminded her guiltily she hadn't yet congratulated him on his marriage to Melissa.

'Hello, Brenda,' he said, once he had finished serving the handful of customers in front of her, 'how are you?'

'Not too bad,' she smiled at him, 'and what about you? And Melissa?'

'We're fine, thanks.'

'I take it you weren't able to get away for a honeymoon, then?'

'Chance would be a fine thing,' he grinned, 'but, as you know, we're coming up to our busy time; perhaps later in the year.'

'Anyway, Brian,' she said, 'congratulations; to you both and I hope you'll be very happy.'

'Thank you very much,' he acknowledged, 'now, what would you like to drink, Brenda?'

'As much as I would like a glass of wine, I'd better not, thanks.'

'On duty, eh?'

'On duty,' she repeated ruefully, 'but I'll have a coffee.'

'Espresso, or would you prefer a cappuccino?'

'Cappuccino, please; I need an injection of energy to take me through the rest of the day.'

'Not good?'

'I don't know,' she shrugged, 'I've known better.'

'Matthew Richards was in here last evening, Brenda,' he said, lowering his voice, his expression becoming serious, 'in fact, he spent the night here; he couldn't face going back to Christine's place, at least not last night.'

'So,' Brenda said, 'he told you, then?'

'That it wasn't an accident? Yes, he told us. He's pretty cut up about it all; it's going to take him some time to come to terms with losing her. It's really tragic.' he added.

'I know. Brian?'

'Yes?'

'On Monday, when Christine finished work which, I've been told was at half-past six, did she, by any chance, come in here?'

'She did, actually.'

'Were you surprised to see her?'

'I was, now you come to mention it,' he replied, 'I don't know how well you knew Christine, but she kept herself very much to herself; quite a shy woman really. The only time she did come in was when she was with Matthew; hardly ever on her own.'

'How did she seem to you, Brian?'

'In a nutshell, not too happy.' he said, without any hesitation, 'I could tell there was something on her mind.'

'But she didn't say anything to you?'

'Oh, no, that wasn't Christine's way. I got the distinct impression she wanted to be on her own; there was definitely something troubling her.'

'Did she stay at the bar, then?'

'No, she took her drink over to one of the tables.'

'Which one?'

'That one over there.' he said, pointing to a table in the corner of the room.

'She wasn't meeting anyone?'

'No, she wasn't; she just sat there on her own. She only had the one drink and before she finished it, she rang someone on her mobile and then she left –' leaving the sentence in the air, no doubt thinking of what happened to her shortly afterwards.

'I see.' Brenda nodded, his words confirming already what she had been thinking; whatever had been worrying Christine Saunders hadn't just occurred; it had been something which had probably been simmering in her mind all day, or, even the day before that, for all she knew. And Victor York hadn't noticed?

*

Wilcox & Wilcox, Chartered Accountants, established since nineteen sixty, were on the first two floors of the building next to The Bridge Cafe, the notice on the glass-fronted door also announcing they closed for lunch between midday and two o'clock. Although not quite two, the door was open and, turning the handle, Brenda walked inside; the room, not that it could ever be described as such, was little more than a narrow vestibule and the only redeeming feature was the pretty dark-haired girl sitting behind one of the smallest desks Brenda had ever seen, and who smiled up at her, not quite disguising her surprise they could possibly have a client. The place wasn't exactly buzzing with activity Brenda thought, walking towards the desk and taking in the depressingly untidy stack of out-of-date magazines on a low table placed alongside a row of uncomfortable looking chairs whose faded chintz covering had seen better days. It was like stepping back in time she decided, introducing herself to the girl, and for the second time that day she was discovering there remained pockets in Meadowbank which had scarcely changed over the years, certainly this one had barely moved into the twenty-first century, and wondering whether either of the Wilcox partners would be replicas of Victor York. She hoped not.

Less than five minutes later, a door to the right of the desk opened and one of the partners came in, walking briskly across the short distance to her, one hand stretched out in readiness to greet her: 'Good afternoon, Chief Inspector.'

'Good afternoon, sir; it's good of you to spare me some time.'

'Not at all; not at all,' he repeated, 'this is one of our quieter times of the year.' he added, 'We'll go into my office, shall we? Perhaps you would like a coffee?'

Brenda declined and followed him up another flight of stairs; these much worn and creaking alarmingly as they reached the landing. He stopped at the first door they came to; a tarnished brass plaque impressively explaining to anyone who didn't know already that this was the office of Ronald C Wilcox, ACA. ACCA.

'Now, Chief Inspector,' Ronald Wilcox said, once he had positioned his tall angular frame on to the swivel chair on the other side of the desk; this one in darkly polished oak and taking up a good part of the room, 'how can I help you?'

'First of all, sir,' Brenda said, trying to make herself comfortable in the high-backed chair which surely must have been manufactured long before they opened their office in nineteen sixty, 'are you aware of the recent death of Miss Christine Saunders?'

'Ah, yes, indeed; a sad business. Poor woman.'

'We are treating Miss Saunders' death as murder, Mr Wilcox –'

'Good Lord!' he gasped, putting a hand up to his mouth; the eyes behind the silver frames of his glasses, staring at her.

'When the accident happened,' Brenda explained, 'there was nothing to suggest that that was what it was, but since then it has been revealed that it had been engineered; Miss Saunders' car had been severely tampered with, therefore we've no alternative, but to treat her death quite differently.'

'This is shocking, quite shocking!'

'Murder is, sir, and it is for this very reason we have to do everything in our power to find the perpetrator.'

'But,' he hesitated, obviously puzzled; Ronald Wilcox was no actor; she was sure his various expressions portrayed exactly what he was feeling, 'how can we possibly be of any help?'

'It's early days yet,' she told him, 'and we still have a great deal of work to do; in fact, our enquiries have hardly begun, but,' she went on, 'without going into unnecessary details, also not to take up too much of your time, our first task is to eliminate various and rather obvious possibilities of why Miss Saunders should have been killed.'

'Yes?'

'On the day of the accident,' Brenda said, 'only minutes before it, we understand Miss Saunders was extremely worried about something, sufficiently so, to make her approach someone for advice and this advice, we believe, was most probably of a professional nature. Regrettably, she was on her way to meet this person on Monday evening.'

'Dear me; how dreadful. You used the word 'professional', Chief Inspector, do you mean in connection with her work at the pharmacy?'

'This is a possibility and for that reason we are reluctant to be categorical; on the other hand, we can't rule it out completely without further investigation.'

'Do you think *drugs* had something to do with her death, Chief Inspector?'

'I expect you mean because of where she works?'

'Well, yes, I suppose I do,' he said slowly, deliberately, and she could tell he was trying to assimilate in his mind what she had said so far, 'it would be the most obvious suggestion, but, I've known Christine Saunders for a number of years and I would have vouched for her honesty at any time.'

'You're not the first person I've talked to in the last couple of days who has spoken highly of her, sir, but I'm sure you will appreciate that in our capacity as police officers we have to remain completely neutral; we can only deal with hard proven facts.'

'I understand. Of course, I do, but I still cannot believe Christine would have gone down that particular path; it would have been alien to her nature, so, if I can be of any help in trying to exonerate her, I most certainly will.'

'Thank you, sir. What I would like you to do is to give me a summary, if I could describe it in such a way,' Brenda said, 'of the accounting services you provide for the Meadowbank Pharmacy. I have already spoken to Mr York and he's explained to me how their stock system is operated, but perhaps you could qualify this, together with the other accounting procedures provided by your firm.

'That will be a relatively simple matter, Chief Inspector,' he said, sitting more upright and pressing his palms together, presumably adopting his business mode, 'the service we provide for the pharmacy is two-fold, you understand; a book-keeping one and an accounting one.'

'I see,' Brenda nodded, 'Mr York did tell me they handed over the relevant paperwork, together with the computer discs, at the end of each month.'

'That is correct, but not the discs; the data on those are for the control of stock, so there is no necessity for us to use them. Our software is customised for the accountancy profession and we key-in the purchase invoices in total, not as Christine did, item by item, and as for the sales, the print-out from the two cash registers are handed in here, along with everything else we need to complete the monthly figures.'

'That all sounds straight forward enough.' Brenda said.

'Oh, it is, Chief Inspector; believe me.'

'At the end of the year, sir,' she put in quickly before he had a chance to elaborate on their system of computer accounting, 'there will be a physical stock-taking, won't there?'

'Oh, yes, of course.'

'And this is carried out by yourselves?'

'No, this was done by Mr York and Christine.'

'Is this normal practice, sir?' she asked him, 'I mean, I always thought this was part of the accounting procedure.'

'For limited companies, yes, it would be, but the Meadowbank Pharmacy isn't a company, therefore the Inland Revenue requirements are a little less rigid.'

'And, have you, yourself, always been satisfied with the way the final accounts appear? I'm sorry, I'm putting it badly, but not having any accounting background, I'm not familiar with the correct terminology.'

'Not at all, Chief Inspector, there's no need to apologise. We, the profession, that is, are inclined to be somewhat hidebound in the use of what many of the younger generation describe as technical jargon, but I understand exactly what you mean. But, to answer your question, we have always been entirely satisfied, as have both the Inland Revenue and the periodic checks carried out by Customs and Excise.'

'Well, thank you, sir,' Brenda said, standing up, 'also for giving me so much of your time.'

'All I can say, Chief Inspector is if I have been any assistance in helping you resolve this dreadful business, well,' raising both hands in front of him, 'that can only be a good thing.'

Chapter Nine

He was out there again; standing with his back to the new housing development and staring across the road seemingly at nothing in particular; at least that was how it seemed to Isobel Gallier as she opened the door of The Bridge Inn at six-thirty that Wednesday evening. There was something vaguely familiar about the man, but if she had seen him before, it must have been a while ago, but, then, quite a number of tourists did return to the town she thought, going back inside, although she had to admit, continuing to wonder about him, he didn't look much like a holidaymaker; there was nothing remotely casual about his manner; either in the way he was dressed in a rather expensively-cut linen suit and a black cotton roll-neck, or how he had given her the distinct impression of having no real interest in his surroundings; if so, why didn't he wait for them inside the pub, not just stand out there, making himself conspicuous, as he had done at lunchtime?

Isobel's first regulars were beginning to arrive and for the next half an hour she was fully occupied, having no time to give the man another thought until, looking towards the open door, she saw him again. This time he was coming in and he wasn't on his own. Charlie East, a newcomer to Meadowbank and becoming a frequent customer, was with him. It was Charlie who came up to the bar to order their drinks, while he walked across to one of the tables.

It was while she was pouring the beers she remembered when she had seen him and she had been right; it was some time ago, four years in fact. Michel had still been here then and she could recall exactly when it had been. It was seldom these days Isobel thought about her late-husband and certainly not the manner of his death, but it had been Michel who had served him. It had been a Saturday night and, for once, he had been around to help her behind the bar and by the following weekend Michel had gone. She could even pin-point the date in April.

The man's hair had been longer then and he had reminded her of the singer, Gilbert O'Sullivan and, ironically, what had stuck in her mind, he had been in a group, also, although he'd spent most of the time at the bar, the others had been sitting at one of the tables at the far end of the room. She couldn't remember what they had looked like, except for the girl, who appeared to have been his girlfriend; a lot younger than him, with long straight black hair with a thick fringe which had practically covered her eyes, also how annoyed she had been with him for not sitting down with them. On looking across at him now, Isobel could even remember his name; they had called him Danny. That was it; Danny.

'What about you, Isobel,' Charlie asked her, 'would you like a drink?'

'No thanks, Charlie.' she smiled, wondering how long it would be before he learned she never drank while on duty. This was a rule she had made for herself when she first started in the business and she had never once deviated; there was time enough later, when everybody had gone and they were closed, to relax and enjoy one, especially if Terry was with her, as he should be later on this evening. His new job in London meant he didn't get back to Meadowbank until at least seven each evening, but he had stressed at the time he accepted the contract he didn't mind; that it was worth it to be with her and she had felt gladdened by that. Terry Simpson was a good man and hardly a day went by when she didn't think that. He had been through a great deal in his life and had, a bit like herself really, picked up the pieces and, as the song went, started all over again. Last week, he had asked her to marry him, but typically he hadn't put any pressure on her to give him an immediate answer. She did want to marry him, but a small part of her was holding back, preventing her making that final commitment. She hoped, when she told him this, he would understand. She wasn't all that sure she fully understood herself; perhaps it had something to do with having had to work so hard these last few years after Michel had gone, she had grown used to her independence, also, hearing about his death earlier in the year, exactly four years from that time when she had always believed he had walked out on her, was still too raw. She still needed some more time.

'If you're sure, Isobel.' Charlie East said; exactly as he always did.

'I recognised your friend, Charlie;' she said to him, 'it's taken me several minutes, but he was in here a few years ago.'

'Really?' a look of surprise on his face, 'I don't think so.'

'Perhaps I was mistaken,' Isobel admitted slowly, looking across again at the man who now had his profile turned to her, and becoming more convinced than ever it was him alright, 'but he does look like him. He reminded me then of Gilbert O'Sullivan and he still does.'

'The singer?'

'Yes.'

'I'll tell him, Isobel;' he smiled, picking up the two glasses from the bar, 'he'll be flattered.'

How odd, she thought, watching him walk over to their table. Why should he have been so quick to say what he did? Anyway, she decided, giving the top of the bar a wipe, it's none of my business, and turned away to serve some customers who had come in.

'You're looking very thoughtful this evening, Isobel.' Terry said to her soon after he arrived.

'Am I?'

'Yes, what's on your mind?'

How well this man knew her she thought; she couldn't hide anything from him, but he was right, as he so often was where she was concerned, she was pre-occupied. Also, she was *right*; the man with Charlie had been in here before. She was positive. So, why should he have denied it? What on earth was it to do with him? Charlie East had only been in Meadowbank for a month, having bought one of the town houses on the Stockbridge Road. He was friendly enough, although the snippets of conversation she had overheard when he'd been standing at the bar had only been of a superficial every-day kind, nothing too serious. Politics didn't appear to hold any interest for him, neither did sport; a favourite topic with many of her customers, also, she had quickly discovered, he hardly ever talked about himself and about all anyone had learned about him was that he had spent several years working overseas; at what, they had no idea, and that he had moved here from London and, once again, exactly where in London, no-one knew. And, here he was this evening, deep in conversation with a man some years younger than himself and who had, it would seem, been waiting for a good part of the day for him to turn up.

'It's nothing really, Terry,' Isobel said, 'just something which is niggling me slightly.' and then going on to tell him.

'We don't know the relationship Charlie has with this chap, though, do we?'

'What do you mean?'

'Well,' Terry said, 'for all we know the pair of them could be related and then I suppose Charlie would have known, or perhaps your Gilbert O'Sullivan lookalike may have told him he had never been here before.'

'True,' she said thoughtfully, 'I hadn't thought that, but it's possible, although,' she went on, 'if it is, Terry, why tell him that?'

'I don't know,' he smiled, 'it was only a suggestion. You say he was part of a rock group?'

'That's right, he was. There were four of them; I think they were just passing through Meadowbank that evening.'

'Passing through?'

'That's what I heard, yes. You seem surprised?'

'Well, I was thinking; Meadowbank is a little bit off the beaten track to be 'passing through', wouldn't you say?'

'I suppose it is; oh, I don't know, Terry,' she sighed, 'I'm probably making too much out of nothing.'

*

'You may or may not be interested to learn that our good landlady recognised you, Danny.' Charlie East said, bringing their beers over to the table.

'So?'

'So?' Charlie repeated, raising his glass to his lips, 'shouldn't you be a trifle concerned?'

'I don't see why?' Danny said quietly, not wanting their conversation to be overheard, 'I have nothing to hide.'

'That's rot and you know it!'

'Okay,' Danny said, continuing to keep his voice down and wishing Charlie would do the same, but he had no intention of saying so, 'I was here with the group four years ago; we had a few drinks in the only two decent pubs in the town and kipped down in a field for the night before driving on to Bournemouth the following day.'

'I don't think it is quite as simple as that.'

'Isn't it?'

'As I was nowhere near at that particular time, I, personally, have nothing which need concern me. Do I have to spell it out to you, Danny?'

'Perhaps you will have to, Charlie.'

'I hope you are as brave as your words sound.'

'What's that supposed to mean?'

'That Tilsly case remains open, you know. Also, it wouldn't take much to persuade the authorities to start up their investigations again.'

'And who is going to do this *persuading*? You?'

'Not directly, no.'

'Alright,' Danny sighed, 'I recognise a threat when I hear one; I know when I'm being told to back off, Charlie. This is all because of Mark, isn't it?'

'I have no idea what you're talking about.'

'What happened to him, Charlie?'

'As to that, you know as much as anyone else who reads the newspapers.'

'The police are treating his death as murder; I know that much, so what happened to him? I want to know.'

'Perhaps Mark was foolish enough to overstretch himself. Perhaps he got too smart or too greedy. Take your pick, Danny; there's a wide choice of reasons.'

'I intend to find out,' Danny said, 'it's important to me.'

'So, that's why you've gone to the trouble of coming down here? Just how long have you been hanging around, drawing attention to yourself, Danny, waiting for me to turn up. And, incidentally, how did you know I would?'

'Simple logic,' Danny replied, 'you are a creature of habit and I already knew where the pubs were, so it was only a matter of time before you would come to one or the other.'

'Well, well, all I can say is, you've had a wasted journey. You won't get any answers from me; at least not the ones you obviously want.'

'Mark was still working for you, wasn't he?'

'No comment. As a matter of interest,' Charlie went on, 'how did you know I was in Meadowbank?'

'I was wondering when you would ask me;' Danny smiled, leaning back in his chair, pretending an indifference he didn't feel. Charlie East was a big man and not only in build; he'd been in the business for a very long time and Danny knew all too well he didn't suffer fools gladly, also, he had the money and the power to deal with people and situations he didn't like, 'you can call it a hunch if you like, but one which paid off and even surprised me.'

'Go on; I'm listening.'

'It was Johnnie, without even realising it, who gave me the idea. You see, I had already discovered you were no longer at your Chelsea address and I heard Johnnie had recently come to Meadowbank; it was then I started to put two and two together. I couldn't understand why he should have chosen this town of all places, putting himself in a potentially vulnerable position when he might be recognised.'

'Like you have been?' Charlie reminded him unnecessarily.

'True, but then I'll be returning to London tonight while Johnnie appears to be staying here. And,' Danny continued, 'he was most emphatic when I asked him that he no longer worked for you. In fact, so much so, he may as well have said he was. And, from that moment, I did some serious thinking; I had already read about the pharmacy robberies in this part of England which, according to the press, are being so cleverly carried out that the police are baffled and I thought, only thought, mind you, there could be a connection between, not only you and Johnnie, but with Mark as well.'

'An interesting deduction, Danny; perhaps you chose the wrong vocation.'

'Am I right, then?'

'Do you really expect me to answer that? Are you so naive? If I said, no you were wrong, what would your reaction be? And, if I said, you were spot on, what then? What would you do then, Danny; without dropping yourself right in it, head first?'

'That would be for me to decide.' Danny said and meaning it, but he had no idea; he hadn't thought it through that far. He hadn't thought beyond establishing whether this man sitting opposite to him right this minute in a typically English country pub, was responsible for Mark's death or not. To drive down to Meadowbank this morning had been a spur of the moment decision and one which he hoped he wasn't going to regret, realising, looking at the grim expression on Charlie East's face, he wasn't handling this conversation at all well. But, he did owe Mark something. Not vengeance for his murder; he was incapable of that, but at least to do his best to get to the truth. Although they hadn't been brothers, not even half-brothers, the bond between them had been a strong one. They had spent more years apart than together and in recent years, since the break-up of the group, those times when they had met had been few, but it hadn't made any difference. When he had read about his death, then later learning the police were treating it as murder, he instinctively felt he had to do something.

'So, Danny,' Charlie said, leaning forward and breaking into his thoughts, 'what are you doing these days?'

'I'm still in the music business; promoting groups, that sort of thing,' he answered, 'and most of them with a hell of a lot more talent than we ever had.'

'Ah, Danny, Danny.' Charlie smiled, immediately reminding him of the old days: when Charlie East moved his lips in that particular way in the formation of what he believed to be a smile. He was a sadistic bastard; something Danny had always known. He was a manipulator; a controller of people. God knows, he had done his best right from the moment he had found him out for what he was, to delve back into his past trying to dig up what lay hidden behind that false exterior, but he hadn't succeeded. Charlie had perfected his past, his background; he'd made sure no-one would ever be able to find out too much about him. One day, Danny thought, watching him now; the super-confident way he had of now and again looking around the bar. "I'm the King of the Castle", he seemed to be saying, and "catch me if you can – or, if you dare!" Oh, yes, he truly considered himself to be above the law, but eventually he would be caught; there would come a time when he would quite literally have his back to the wall and then what? How would he extricate himself from that, Danny wondered.

'You don't change; do you, Danny,' he was saying now, 'always the dreamer, always the guy who believed he could put the rest of the world to rights. But,' he added, leaning towards him, the half-empty glass in his hand, 'you're not going to win this one. You're crooked, Danny Howarth; in the same way as Mark was, absolutely crooked!'

'And you're squeaky clean, I suppose?'

'I'm completely neutral my friend; completely neutral and also, if you would only face facts, untouchable.'

'I don't think so for one minute, Charlie,' Danny said, 'no-one is; especially if they operate on the other side of the law. You are a crook,

Charlie East!'

'Am I?'

'You know damn right you are; and I'll tell you something else, bearing in mind what you know about me, it takes a crook to catch a crook!'

*

The call from Victor York the following morning was recorded by the desk sergeant at precisely nine-fifteen and put through to Ian Ash's office immediately. In essence, and in his usual precise way, Victor informed him that he and his sister, on arriving at the pharmacy shortly after nine, had discovered there had been a break-in at some time during the night. Ian, accompanied by a fellow officer, wasted no time in walking across the road to the pharmacy. A distraught looking Monica York was waiting for them at the open door and quickly ushered them inside.

'It's good of you to come so quickly, Inspector. My brother is in the dispensary; that's where most of the damage has been done, as you will be able to see for yourselves.'

'Ah, Inspector Ash,' Victor York, framed in the doorway to the dispensary, called out to them, 'as my sister has said, it is indeed good of you to get here as promptly as you have. This has been quite a shock to us both; the last thing one would expect.'

'Alright, sir,' Ian said, cutting him short and introducing Sergeant Alan Williams, 'we'll have a look and see how, first of all, they managed to enter the building.'

'Oh, that's quite obvious, Inspector,' Victor put in sharply, 'by the back door, through here,' and leading them into the dispensary, 'the lock has been forced and not without considerable damage to the door, I might add.'

As he had said, the damage was severe; not only was the wood at the edge of the door badly splintered, but the lock had been almost levered completely away from its casing. The glass on the front of one of the cabinets had also been smashed; several shards of it scattered on the floor at their feet.

'It's terrible, isn't it?' Monica York said from where she was standing, having only taken a couple of steps into the dispensary.

'Indeed it is, madam,' Ian said, turning back briefly to look at her, 'I think it might be a good idea if you delay your opening this morning until we are able to assess the situation.'

'Of course,' she agreed, stepping back, 'I'll go and make sure the front door is locked.'

'You do that, Monica.' Victor said, obviously asserting his superiority, at the same time reminding Ian of who really was in charge of the pharmacy.

'Now, sir,' Ian said, turning again to face him, 'first of all, we will have to check for fingerprints; after that, you will be free to do your assessment and see what is missing. We will need to take your fingerprints and those of Miss York; for elimination purposes.'

'Of course, Inspector; I'm sure that is normal procedure.'

'Have you discovered any further damage?' Ian asked him.

'No, only in here; the back door, as you've seen for yourself, and this cabinet.'

'Which contained, sir?'

'Prescribed drugs, Inspector. It is kept securely locked at all times, not that that has been a deterrent to whoever broke in here last night.'

'We'll try to get as close as we can to that time. You don't appear to have any alarm system?'

'No, we don't.'

'Perhaps it might be a good idea to consider having one installed.' Ian suggested, somewhat surprised his insurance company hadn't insisted on this, considering the prevalence of robberies in recent months.

'Oh, I will.'

'What time did you close the pharmacy last evening?'

'Seven, as I usually do on a Wednesday.'

'And did you both leave at the same time?'

'Yes.'

'After we have finished in here, Mr York, we will need to check outside, but all in all, it shouldn't take more than thirty minutes to complete. And,' Ian went on, 'when you have compiled your list of all the missing items we would like a copy. You will, presumably, need to have one for insurance purposes.'

'Of course, Inspector, I understand. Hopefully, it won't take me long, although at the moment I have no idea what has been stolen; no idea at all.' he repeated, standing in the middle of the dispensary, a bewildered expression on his face as he swivelled round on his heels to look at the remaining contents in the cabinet, most of which had been pushed to one side while others had fallen to join the broken glass on the tiled floor.

Ten was striking from the church clock in the square as Ian and Sergeant Williams retraced their steps back to the Station.

'A very clumsy break-in, sir.' Alan Williams commented.

'That's exactly what I was thinking, Alan.'

'They seemed to know what they were looking for though.'

'Why do you say that?'

'Well,' Alan hesitated for a moment, obviously thinking it through, but Ian already had a good idea where he was coming from and waited for him to elaborate, 'why didn't they clear the whole of the drugs cabinet; they seem to have been fairly selective.'

'You're right, of course. But,' Ian said, 'usually in break-ins of this nature, at pharmacies, for instance, certain drugs will sell on the street quicker than others, but as you say, they could have taken everything and sorted out what they wanted later; it would have reduced the time they were in there.'

'Yes, it would and although it will get dark at the back of the building; I didn't see any lamps along that path, they wouldn't have had all that long, given the actual hours of darkness we have at this time of the year.'

'I suggest you add it to the report, Alan,' Ian said, pushing open the main doors of the Station, 'and we'll speak again later today.'

Ian passed Brenda's office on the way along the corridor to his own and, seeing him, she called out: 'Have you a minute, Ian?'

'Of course, ma'am,' he said, stopping in the open doorway, 'I've just come from the pharmacy across the road.'

'I heard you'd been called over there.'

'Yes,' he said, walking into the room, 'and to quote Alan Williams, who was with me, it was a clumsy break-in.'

'In what way?'

'Well, I couldn't help comparing it with the descriptions we've had of the others,' he explained, 'when each of them, without exception, gave every appearance of being carried out by professionals; leaving no trace behind them, but this was quite different.' And going on to describe the scene which had confronted them both when they'd arrived at the pharmacy.

'I see what you mean,' Brenda said when he'd finished, 'all a bit too obvious, perhaps?'

'That's right,' he said, 'unless it was a deliberate ploy to take the focus away from themselves, to make us concentrate instead on a bunch of amateurs.'

'Could be,' she agreed, her expression thoughtful, 'but there is something you've told me which, quite frankly, I'm finding disturbing, Ian.'

'Yes?'

'The fact the entire contents of the drugs cabinet hadn't been taken sounds very much to me that, whoever was responsible, had taken the time to be selective; they knew what they were looking for.'

'I know; I've asked Victor York to let us have a list of everything that's missing.'

'That should prove interesting. I haven't had a chance to tell you I had a word with his accountant yesterday, who was able to explain to me the extent of the services they provide the pharmacy and something surprising emerged; they left the end of year stock-taking to Victor.'

'Trusting of them.'

'I would say so, however, one important point came out of all of this and that was that Victor York lied to me. He told me he always handed over to them the computer discs containing the data Christine keyed into their stock system; this was done at the end of every month, but when I mentioned this to Ronald Wilcox, he said there was never any need for them to have the discs.'

'So, he lied.'

'Yes, Ian, and we have to find out why. I do feel this is crucial to the case.'

'We go back again, don't we,' Ian said slowly, trying to pull together far too many loose ends and the more he tried, the more tangled they became, 'to why Christine Saunders was so worried and I think we're both agreed this must have had been to do with her work?'

'I'm sure of it, Ian.'

'It could have been something she had discovered in this stock system of theirs, some anomaly, perhaps.'

'It's possible.'

'He could have been fudging the figures, ma'am.' he suggested, although tentatively, not quite knowing how she would react to this suggestion.

'I have been wondering about that, especially with this latest development.'

'The break-in?'

'Yes, but think about it, Ian; how can we be sure there had been a break-in?'

'Certainly,' he said, 'there were no other fingerprints found; only those of Victor York and his sister, but of course they could have been wearing gloves.'

'That's true, but whichever way you look at all of this, I think we'll have to take a close look at those figures.'

'It will alert him, of course.'

'I realise that,' she said, 'but it can't be helped; if we don't, this whole case, and I mean the murder enquiry, may very well collapse. We simply have to move forward, even if it means upsetting a few people, namely Victor York.'

'You're right and if he's nothing to hide, he shouldn't be too concerned.'

'If we are thinking along the correct lines,' Brenda continued, 'and any alterations had been made to, let us say, Christine's input of figures which, according to Ronald Wilcox, were from the purchase invoices and he had been siphoning off certain drugs, he would have to make up the deficit if there was any chance we were to insist on a physical stock-take.'

'Hence last night's break-in which could have been orchestrated by him.' Ian finished for her.

'That's right, Ian, so what do you think?'

'It does seem a feasible possibility, but if we are wrong in our suspicions –' but leaving his sentence unfinished. Brenda knew what he was thinking; he could read her expression plainly enough.

'– "Warrior" Bill will be, not to put too fine a point on it, not too pleased, but I'll take that risk, Ian; just as I have done before and no doubt will do so a few more times.'

"Warrior" Bill, their illustrious superintendant; seldom seen, but his presence always felt, especially at times like these, Ian thought, hoping this wasn't going to be one of them.

'Do you want me to carry out the check, ma'am?'

'I'd prefer it if you would, Ian; your computer expertise is far better than mine. Meanwhile, before you go, I received a profile report on Charlie East while you were out and it makes interesting reading.'

'I look forward to reading it,' he said, standing up and making towards the door.

'I'll get a copy run off for you and put it on your desk;' she said, 'now that Mark Astley's murder has been officially confirmed, I don't think we should overlook there could be a possible link between Charlie East and those members of the rock group, and, Ian,' she smiled, 'after you've read the profile, I'm sure you will agree with me.'

*

'The reason I'm phoning, Victor, is because I want you to hold on to those items for a few more days.'

'Why, Charlie? That's not what we agreed.'

'I know what we agreed,' Charlie East said impatiently, 'but the situation has changed.'

'Must you talk in riddles? *Things* are difficult enough at the moment without this setback.' Victor complained.

'I'm sure they are, and it's for this reason I've decided it might be better if you and I were a little bit more circumspect, in other words, we shouldn't be seen together.'

'Better for whom? As if I didn't know! Listen, Charlie, I want those packets off these premises!' making an effort to keep his voice down; Monica was only a matter of a few feet away in the pharmacy; fortunately, since Charlie rang, she had been kept busy with a steady stream of customers, with a couple still waiting to be served.

'No,' Charlie put in, his voice sharp, 'you listen to me! People are talking, Victor, and I don't like what I'm hearing.'

'What are they saying?' curbing the rising panic.

'Well, it appears to be common knowledge around the town that Christine Saunders was murdered, also that she appeared to be extremely worried about something shortly before her death. You know even better than I do, Victor, how rumours are rife here; how long will it be before these armchair detectives will come up with the name of the person responsible?'

'You really surprise me, Charlie, you really do,' Victor said quietly, 'I thought you had more to do than listen to idle gossip.'

'I wouldn't call it idle exactly.'

'Well, I would!'

'Anyway,' Charlie continued, 'getting back to the purpose behind this call –'

' – I meant what I said,' Victor interrupted, 'I want rid of the stuff and as speedily as possible.'

'Why the panic?'

'I'm not panicking.'

'It sounds very much like it to me. What's wrong, Victor, or perhaps I shouldn't ask?'

'I've already had three calls from the police; the first two asking me about Christine and then, this morning, about the break-in.'

'Break-in?'

That made him sit up, Victor thought, but there was no satisfaction in knowing he had penetrated his hard core of contrived impregnability, no satisfaction whatsoever. He didn't really know why he mentioned the break-in; perhaps simply for that reason. It seemed to Victor that he had spent these last days trying single-handedly to deal with problems, which, if Charlie East had been a different sort of man, he would have shown some consideration; he could have offered some help, advice even, but characteristically, he hadn't.

'Someone broke into the dispensary last night,' he told him, 'and naturally, I had to report it.'

'Do you think you could manage to be more explicit, Victor, if it isn't too much trouble?' he asked him, his voice heavy with sarcasm.

'There's not a great deal more to say, except that a number of drugs were stolen.'

'Don't take me for a bloody fool!'

'What do you mean, Charlie?'

'You know damn well what I mean. There was no break-in last night.'

'Well, all I can say,' Victor answered, with a calmness he wasn't feeling, 'the evidence was there when Monica and I arrived at the pharmacy this morning.'

'Ah, you have your sister there; to help out, I suppose?'

'Yes, that's right; I can't possibly manage the business on my own.'

'No, I don't expect you can, especially when you appear to be so busy with other matters.'

'Look, Charlie,' Victor said, deciding to ignore the jibe, 'I'll have to ring off; I've a lot to do.'

'I dare say you have,' Charlie said, 'and with this latest development, it is even more vital we don't meet up for a while, until the situation has simmered down somewhat. All I will say, though, is that the timing of your so-called robbery wasn't too clever.'

He was startled to notice how his hand was shaking when he finally replaced the receiver. Talking to Charlie, especially lately, was always stressful, but up to now, he had been able to control his nervousness. This whole business was turning into a nightmare he thought; first the problem over Christine followed by the necessity to put right the short-fall in the stock levels and now, these blasted packages. He had to find a more secure place for them.

'Victor,' Monica called out to him from the pharmacy; he was relieved to see that for the first time since they had opened that morning there were no customers, 'he's coming back.'

'Who is?' frowning and walking through to the pharmacy.

'Inspector Ash; he's just this minute passed the window.' and as she spoke, the door opened and the inspector walked into the pharmacy for the second time that morning.

'I apologise for disturbing you, Mr York,' Ian said, 'but could we have a word please; in the dispensary, if you don't mind?' and Monica, Victor noticed, immediately taking the hint, busied herself rearranging a new supply of toiletries on one of the shelves at the other end of the pharmacy.

'Of course, Inspector.' he said, once again, taking him into the dispensary, 'What can I do for you?'

'I'm here in respect to your accounting system, namely your method of controlling the stock. We have already spoken to your accountants,

Wilcox & Wilcox, who confirmed what you had told Chief Inspector Masters yesterday, except for one point.'

'One point, Inspector?' and knowing exactly what was coming next, but playing for time. This was another blow Victor thought; it had not occurred to him they would have doubted what he'd said yesterday. In hindsight, he realised now, he should have done, especially when the chief inspector had wanted to know how Christine had been on the Monday, at the same time remembering Charlie had stressed how people were talking and reaching their own conclusions about her death.

'Yes, sir,' the inspector was saying, and he waited for him to spell it out, 'you informed Chief Inspector Masters you always included a computer disc with the paperwork for your accountants each month, but Mr Wilcox has told us this wasn't so, therefore, we now consider it necessary for us to examine your method of controlling the stock levels.'

'I can give you a perfectly simple explanation about those discs, Inspector. I'm afraid it was a slight misunderstanding on my part; as I, incidentally, explained to the Chief Inspector, I left that side of the business entirely in Christine's hands and she was the one who put the various papers together for the accountants and, well,' he went on, deliberately looking at the inspector directly, willing him to believe what he was telling him, 'I assumed, wrongly as it has turned out, that the disc would be in the same box file.'

'I see,' Ian said slowly, and Victor found it impossible to read his expression, although he could tell by the slight tightening around the man's jaw line that he hadn't believed one word of his quickly cobbled together spiel, 'and when the file was returned to you once the accountants had completed their work, did you never see the contents, check, perhaps, to see that everything was in order?'

'No, I didn't. Christine did that; it was part of her duties, Inspector and it certainly didn't require both of us.'

'And you trusted her?'

'Implicitly.' realising as soon as he had spoken that, here, there could be a way out of this mire; he would have to be careful, of course; watch what he said and guard every nuance which might alert the inspector and, ultimately, his superior, Chief Inspector Masters. He didn't underestimate either of them, having recognised their intelligence, together with their trained abilities. They would, he felt certain, not rest until they reached the hub of their enquiries and he, Victor York, had to be one hell of a lot smarter. Up to now, they probably suspected him of manipulating the accounts, but why should they not, instead, turn their energies on to Christine? If they did, he reasoned, they may then change their tack which would take the heat off him, give him the necessary time to work out some kind of strategy.

'I never had any reason to question Miss Saunders' integrity.' he said, but stopping there; that was enough he decided, he mustn't overdo it.

'From what we have heard about Miss Saunders,' Ian replied, 'neither have we. However, we still require a check to be made of the system.' he finished enigmatically, immediately dashing any hopes Victor may have had had, but for the time being he would have to go along with them. The man was a police officer, for goodness sake, not exactly a computer technician; those figures were fine, he'd made sure of that and there was no way Inspector Ash would see anything amiss.

'Very well, Inspector,' he said, 'I'll leave you to it. As you can see, the computer is already switched on and I'll just show you how to access the stock control files.'

'Thank you, sir,' Ian said, going round to the other side of the desk and pulling the chair closer to the computer screen, 'I don't intend to spend too much time here; all I want to do is run through various entries, that sort of thing, and then, if you could give me, shall we say, the last twelve months' purchase invoices, together with the relevant discs, I'll take them back to the Station with me and complete the check.'

'Oh,' stymied for a second; he hadn't expected that, 'I suppose that's alright, then. I'll get the discs for you; Christine always kept them in a separate cupboard from our other records; for security reasons, you understand.'

'Very wise,' Ian nodded, his eyes now focused on the screen, 'by the way,' he added, 'have you had time to compile a list of those missing items yet?'

'I have, but it's only hand-written, Inspector. I was going to ask my sister to type it out for me, but she has been so busy this morning.'

'That's alright, sir.' Ian said, taking the sheet of paper from him.

Victor didn't stay in the dispensary, but left the inspector in there by now firmly ensconced in front of the computer and already, after only a few minutes, giving every indication of being completely familiar, not only with computers, but with the pharmacy's own particular software.

'Everything alright, Victor?' Monica asked him.

'Why shouldn't it be?' unable to keep the sharpness from his voice; he had never known his nerves to be so much on edge.

'Sorry, dear,' she said, 'I was only asking; he did seem to be with you for rather a long time.'

'Routine, Monica,' he said, 'they have their job to do and I have no choice but to go along with them. At the moment,' he said, knowing he would have to make some sort of plausible explanation to her, 'he's going through our system on the computer.'

'You're not worried, are you, Victor?'

'Me? Worried? Of course not, Monica. There is absolutely no reason why I should be.'

Chapter Ten

Felicity had only been gone five minutes; the front door closing behind her, when Johnnie's mobile rang. Leaning across the table and pushing the remains of their late breakfast to one side, he picked it up, pressing the on-switch.

'Johnnie? Is that you?'

'Katie,' recognising her voice instantly, but the last person he expected to hear from, 'how are you?'

'Not too great, Johnnie,' Katie Brownlea replied, sounding out of breath, as though she had been running, 'I'm desperately worried.'

'What's wrong?' he asked, at the same time bracing himself for whatever she had to say and having a pretty good idea what it was going to be. He hadn't spoken to her for more than four years, not since they had all gone their separate ways; it wasn't as if Katie and he had been all that close: she was Danny's girl; at least she had been back then.

'I've been trying to get hold of Danny since yesterday,' she explained and he could hear the breath catching in her throat, 'all day, in fact, and then again this morning, but for some reason, he's not answering his mobile.'

'I'm sorry, Katie,' he said slowly, wondering how he was going to deal with this latest intrusion, because that was what it seemed like to him. First, the call from Danny, which had been disturbing enough, reminding him of a time he would much prefer to forget, and now this one, from Katie, 'I don't see how I can be of any help.'

'I – I just thought you might have seen him, perhaps know where he could be, that's all.'

'Why should I?' his voice much sharper than he intended, but he couldn't help it. He didn't need this; he really did not.

'I know he was in touch with you, Johnnie, because he rang me afterwards; also I was aware of how concerned he was over Mark's death.'

'He was, that's right enough, but, tragic although that is, Katie, once again, as I told Danny, I can't do anything. I know absolutely nothing about what happened to Mark.'

'You do know he was murdered, don't you? You do know that much?'

'Yes, I did hear,' keeping his tone as neutral as possible, which wasn't easy, when part of his brain was literally racing full speed ahead, wondering and speculating exactly what Danny must have said to her.

'Are you telling me you didn't see Danny on Wednesday?'

'Of course I didn't,' surprised by the question, 'why should I?'

'Because he rang me early that morning to tell me he was on his way down to Meadowbank.'

'Well, that's news to me. Why should he have been?'

'He was trying to find Mr East.'

Those were the words he wished he had not heard; Danny, foolish, impetuous Danny, had, if what he was beginning to think, taken it upon himself to confront Charlie East for some cock-eyed reason, presumably to do with Mark, and with that realisation feeling an overwhelming hopelessness for his old friend. Nobody could dislike Danny Howarth; it just wasn't possible. Okay, deep down, he was no different from the rest of them, willing to take risks, calculated although they were, anything to make a quick buck, but Johnnie had always thought that one day, Danny, being so much older than the rest of them, would decide to go straight and become a respectable honest citizen, marry, settle down and put his shady past well and truly behind him. And, perhaps he had, but it would seem the unusual bond he had with Mark was getting in the way.

'I really don't know what to say, Katie.'

'You must help, Johnnie! You must be able to! Danny was determined to find out what happened to Mark and he truly believed Mr East had something to do with it.'

'He had no grounds for thinking that way; he was only assuming.'

'Perhaps he was, but it doesn't matter; Danny still wanted to see him.'

'I don't see what that would have achieved, you know,' Johnnie said, trying to get through to her mounting hysteria which seemed to him a bit over the top. Why should she be so concerned about an old boyfriend?

'You're still working for Mr East, aren't you, Johnnie?'

'Why do you think that?'

'Because Danny told me.' the answer coming immediately and with it he felt the first stab of annoyance.

'And I told him I wasn't. It sounds as though he's doing a lot of assuming.'

'You don't understand do you?' she was crying now, and he wondered how long it would be before she was unable to say anything and lost control completely. 'You just don't get it; do you, but then you only ever thought about yourself. You never gave a damn for the rest of us! Not once!'

'I honestly don't know why you're getting yourself into such a state,' deliberately keeping his voice level; nothing would be gained by losing his temper, 'Danny's probably decided to be out of contact for a few days; have you considered that?'

'If anything has happened to him, like it did with Mark -' and, this time, obviously finding it difficult to say what she wanted, '- if it has,' she managed at last, 'I'll never forgive myself!'

'You were right, Katie, I don't understand. What have you got to reproach yourself for? It's not as though you and Danny are still together; he told me you'd married, so what's your husband got to say about the way you're behaving; he can't have failed to notice, surely?'

'Ben isn't the observant type,' she answered without the slightest hesitation, dismissing a man he was never likely to meet, 'anyway,' she went on, 'he's away at the moment and he knows nothing about my time with Danny, not even all that much about the group, but it looks as if he's going to; that is, if I can't get in touch with Danny soon.'

'What do you mean?'

'When I report him as missing, that's how. I'll have to tell Ben; better coming from me than from the police.'

'Katie, am I hearing right?' Johnnie gasped, appalled at what she was planning to do, 'Why you?'

'Someone will have to, Johnnie.'

'Yes, but why should it have to be you?' he repeated.

'I can't really answer that,' she said, her voice calmer now, although he could hear the occasional sob, 'except that I don't think Danny has anyone else in his life right now; anyone who cares, I mean.'

'And you do?'

'I do, yes, even after all this time it matters to me what happens to him. We were together a long time before either of us met up with you, Johnnie, so you can't really know how strong our relationship was.'

'Have you thought what may happen if you did this? Really thought it through, I mean. The police already know about our rock group; they've already been asking the three of us about our friendship with Mark; they could start putting two and two together and may just come up with four.'

'That was ages ago, Johnnie.' waving aside any suggestion of his and, seemingly, having no inkling of where further questioning would lead.

'A period of four years ago isn't that long, Katie,' trying to make her see reason and understand all the implications, 'but that night in Meadowbank was only one of a number we spent touring that summer, as I'm sure you will remember, and back then, the police were trying to solve robberies, not a murder!'

'I know that.'

'In any case, if you were to contact them about Danny, what help would that be in finding him?'

'I can see I'm not going to get any support from you, Johnnie; I should have realised. And you are quite wrong, you know, I have given this a lot of thought. If I can't get hold of Danny by tomorrow, I *will* phone the police. Can't you understand; I owe it to him. As I said, Danny phoned me before he left London; he told me where he was going, so he must have wanted me to know, otherwise why tell me? Have you thought of that?'

After Katie had rung off, he sat for a while, in exactly the same position, oblivious to the unwashed cereal bowls and coffee mugs. They didn't matter, but what she had said, most certainly did. Slowly and meticulously, he tried to rationalise. Normally, with a person reported as missing, an adult that is, the police didn't immediately send out a search party. At least he knew that much, but there was nothing remotely normal about this business. It wouldn't matter whether Katie contacted the police in Manchester or the inspector she had already spoken to in Meadowbank; in either case they would be alerted and Danny's disappearance would automatically be linked to their current enquiries into Mark's murder. Johnnie hadn't asked her what she planned to say to them; the truth was he didn't want to know; he didn't want to know any more; he'd heard enough. In fact, groaning out loud, he'd heard too damned much! And if she decided to mention Charlie East's name, well, if she did that, it didn't bear thinking about. Of course she had to be prevented and the sheer responsibility and inevitability of everything was too much. He shouldn't have to make decisions of this nature; why the hell had she phoned him? Why hadn't she tried to find Charlie without involving him? Questions. Questions. And far too many of them, but he knew one thing; he would have to let Charlie know and with a dreadful sinking feeling at the pit of his stomach, he dialled Charlie East's number.

*

Katie Brownlea was no fool; she was also a realist. Although she had never met Charlie East, Danny had told her plenty; enough to make her realise that he was ruthless with, apparently, sufficient expertise and money, to avoid the law. For a long time she had thought that Charlie East made up his own laws and if anybody had the temerity to break any of them, they would have to bear the consequences of his wrath. There were no doubts in her mind now that he was implicated in Mark's murder. And this brought her full circle back to Danny. Where was he? He hadn't told her much when he rang; only that he was going to Meadowbank as he wanted to find Charlie. He hadn't said he was going there to speak to Johnnie Baker. It had been Charlie he'd wanted to see, not Johnnie. He hadn't even told her that Charlie was living in Meadowbank, but he must be, the thought occurring to her for the first time. She regretted now phoning Johnnie; that had been a mistake. And, of *course* he was still with Charlie. Danny had thought so and the fact that Johnnie was denying it meant absolutely nothing at all. Katie had always had reservations about him, nothing specific, but she had treated him warily, never really trusting him. Oh, they'd had some laughs; the four of them, especially after they had finished a concert, winding down and reducing the flow of adrenalin which was always high after the last chord had been played. And the robberies? They had acted as another level of excitement. Of course, she had been stupid to have been involved, but she had gone along with Danny as she always had done in those days, but now, well, she was ashamed of that part of her past, but none of this made any difference to wanting to make sure that Danny was okay. As she had said to Johnnie, she felt she owed it to him. For old times' sake; or did it go deeper than that? Did she still love him? She didn't know, but what she did know was, that each time she had spoken to him this week, she had been transported back to those days, irresponsible though they had been, but at the same time they reminded her of how humdrum and predictable her life had become. She shouldn't be thinking like this; it wasn't right and Ben really did deserve more from her. She had never compared him with Danny, not for one minute; what would have been the point? It had been a joint and amicable decision for them to end their relationship; it would never have worked in any case. She realised that, but there had been times during the last couple of years when she found Ben's serious attitude towards life more than a little tedious, if not downright boring, but what the hell did she want? A good, steady and law-abiding husband or a man with a totally different set of values; a man, handsome in a rakish sexy sort of way, who metaphorically put two fingers up to what he used to describe as 'the establishment'? At that precise moment she really didn't know.

How much longer should she wait before contacting the police? She had said to Johnnie if she hadn't heard from Danny by tomorrow, she would do it then, but by that time it could very well be too late. If only she had not been so impulsive; phoning Johnnie had been stupid, but there was no point harping on about it; just sitting there, staring out of the window and wishing she had acted differently. But, she thought impatiently, getting to her feet and walking across the room and into the kitchen, she had to do something. But what? It was hopeless. She hadn't mentioned to Johnnie that Danny had promised to ring her when he got back to London; at least she'd had some sense, not that it made a great deal of difference now. Right this very minute Johnnie would, she was absolutely certain, be talking to Charlie. Perhaps Charlie would dismiss her as being unimportant; a hysterical female waiting for her old boyfriend to call her, something like that, but Katie didn't really think so. Although she hadn't said she would mention Charlie East's name to the police, both he and Johnnie couldn't afford to take that risk. They had too much to lose, especially Charlie, who had always managed to stay in the background, never being around at the time one of his assignments was being carried out. He never put himself in a vulnerable position; he was far too smart for that. Perhaps Danny had been able to outwit him; he may have done, but he hadn't phoned and it was for this reason she was fearing the worst.

Filling the coffee pot and taking a mug from the cupboard above the worktop, and a carton of milk from the fridge; all automatic actions, at the same time doing her utmost to remain calm, while every instinct was telling her to leave; run, just get away from where he would be able to find her. To do that she decided, would be even more foolish than that phone call to Johnnie. Neither of them knew where she lived anyway, also they didn't even know her married name, nor did they have her phone number; only Danny had, so, for the moment she did have an advantage which she must use to think through carefully what she should do next. It would be easy to pick up the receiver and dial the number Inspector Ash had given her, but was she ready for the possible consequences? What if, for some perfectly innocent reason, Danny had been prevented from getting in touch with her and he phoned her later? How would she feel then? No. Surely there was something else she could do. There had to be. There was a thought lodged at the back of her brain; something Danny had said. It was when he had phoned on Tuesday, shortly after he'd spoken to Johnnie, but, elusively, whatever it was refused to surface. She would remember she was sure, pouring coffee into the mug and going back to what he had said. Mostly, it had been about Mark, but there had been something else. And, then, she remembered; almost word for word: "I never told you this before, Katie,' he had said, "but Mark and I grew up together, although I left home when I was still in my teens and, of course, as you know, I was quite a few years older than him. I suppose you could say ours was a rather complicated sort of relationship, when, after the divorce, my father married Mark's mother. Takes a bit of working out, wouldn't you say?"

Danny had then gone on to say he hardly ever saw his father, although he kept in touch from time to time, even although he was now living in London and not all that far away from where they were in Winchester. That was all he had said and she hadn't asked any questions. His father would have his London address, feeling sure Danny would have given it to him when he moved down south.

It would be another week before Ben would be back home. She was free to go away for a few days if she wanted to, there was nothing to stop her and, dialling Directory of Enquiries, she asked for the telephone number of Mr and Mrs Howarth, explaining she didn't have their full address, only that they lived in Winchester. There was no problem; she was given the number and within minutes she was talking to Danny's father.

*

"Profile on Charles (Charlie) East:

Born:	3rd January 1950
Educated:	Junior/Secondary School: Peckham Rye, North London: 1955-1966
Further Education:	Catering College: Bloomsbury, London: 1966-1968
	Bruce's Business College: New Oxford Street, London: 1969-1971
Married Status:	Married Muriel Cheung: 1976
	Divorced: 1979

Moved to Hong Kong in December 1971, worked for merchant bankers in Hong Kong and Kowloon, prior to setting up his own financial consultancy business in 1976. At the time of a corruption scandal involving a casino in Macau, of which he was on the board of directors, he resigned in 1987 and left the Far East. There was no evidence to prove he may have been involved, although there were strong rumours at the time to the contrary, both in Macau and Hong Kong Island.

Settled in the south of France in 1987, where, during the following ten years, owned a string of restaurants along the Cote d'Azur, in partnership with an ex-college friend, Walter Prescott. The latter was charged with fraud and embezzlement in 1992; again, Charlie East's name was linked and although charged along with Walter Prescott, there was insufficient evidence against him and all charges were subsequently dropped. Walter Prescott served five years, committing suicide shortly after his release in 1997.

Arriving in England and purchasing a property in Chelsea in late 1997, he formed Aztec Investments Limited, taking early retirement in 2005 although remaining on the Board, and moving out of London, purchasing his current property: Number Four, The Mews, Stockbridge Road, Meadowbank, Hampshire."

'Rather a colourful background, wouldn't you say, Ian?'

'I would say so,'' he agreed, 'he certainly made up from a fairly ordinary start in life. The report doesn't say anything about qualifications though.'

'Perhaps he didn't have any,' Brenda said, 'but it would appear he seems to be rather adept at ducking and diving.'

'He does, doesn't he? It doesn't tell us a great deal though about these last eight years, once he returned to England.'

'No, that's true, but somehow I don't believe Charlie East has been exactly idle.'

'Leopards don't change their spots, you mean?'

'Something like that, yes.' she smiled at him. 'But,' she went on, 'having said that, I think we'll have to do considerably more spade-work to find what makes our man tick!'

'So far,' Ian said, 'apart from the fact he was with Johnnie Baker last Saturday evening, someone we believe had something to do with the earlier robberies, we have no reason to suspect him of having any connection.'

'Not sufficient to bring him in for questioning, no, you're right, but at least with this report,' she said, pointing to the sheet of paper in front of them, 'it does give us a background to his character and one we should be aware of.'

'What do you suggest we do for the moment?' he asked her.

'There's not a great deal we *can* do,' Brenda emphasised, 'more is the pity; what we need now is some input from another source and, Ian, I'm confident we'll get it. There is a pattern beginning to unfold here, I'm sure of it, and I've been saying not long after we received the report from New Scotland Yard about these current pharmacy robberies, that there is a connection and, by that I mean, one with Charlie East.'

'You're thinking about Johnnie Baker?'

'I am for the moment,' she said, 'but I'm not discarding the other members of their group, but first, Johnnie Baker, Ian. You say he's renting the house in the square?'

'Apparently; that's what he told Brian Morrison.'

'This is only a hunch, Ian,' she said slowly, 'but I would very much like to know who bought Alison Moore's house? In other words, who is Johnnie Baker renting it from and how did he find out about the property in the first place? And,' Brenda added, 'why is he here in Meadowbank:

some distance from Manchester? If he and his girlfriend wanted to come south why pick a relatively unknown market town in the depths of Hampshire; why didn't they go to London? These are the questions we should be asking ourselves.'

'It shouldn't be all that difficult to find out who bought the house, ma'am;' he said, 'we know Alison moved to London, but I would have thought she would have put it on the market with Town & Country; they were virtually on her doorstep, after all.'

'That's true,' she agreed, 'perhaps you could have a word with Jacqueline Wellings.'

'Of course,' he agreed, 'I'll do that. Meanwhile, ma'am,' he went on, 'there's Christine Saunders' murder.'

'I know,' she sighed, 'yes, that as well, not forgetting the latest development.'

'The break-in, you mean?'

'Exactly, Ian; so were you able to find out anything this morning?'

'I did and it looks very much as though those figures had been altered.'

'And not by Christine Saunders?'

'No, that would have been impossible, ma'am. I've been through six months' purchase invoices, primarily those from the drug suppliers and a number of the entries had been changed shortly after the initial entries and then changed back again; this being done on Wednesday.'

'So, it has to be Victor York?'

'I don't see who else it could have been. And,' he continued, pulling a sheet of paper from his folder, 'I found this inside the file.' handing it over to her.

'I see she's written her name on the top of it.'

'Yes, also Monday's date.'

'Yes,' Brenda nodded, scanning down the hand-written notes, 'it would appear she had been going through a number of the invoices and listing the changes which needed to be made.'

'That's right and you'll see she's put a tick beside each one of them and they tally with those figures on the corresponding purchase invoices.'

'So, that's what was worrying her. She'd found these discrepancies and was planning either to report them or change them herself, Ian.'

'There's a bit more, ma'am.'

'Yes?'

'The shortfall in the records were for two specific drugs; two cartons of amphetamine and one of morphine and on the list Victor York gave me of those items which had been stolen from last night's break-in they were for the same two drugs and no others.'

'Not too clever, Ian.'

'You would have thought he could have been more imaginative.'

'You would, wouldn't you?' she agreed, 'they all do it, you know, Ian?'

'What, ma'am?'

'Over-step the mark; get too damn smart, or as my mother would have said, "too big for their boots", so whichever way you look at it, this is pretty damning for Victor York.' she said, looking directly at him, feeling at the same time the familiar stirring of excitement when an enquiry was reaching what she always described to herself, as the point of no return. Victor York was as guilty as hell; for forging the accounts, but the big question was, did he murder Christine Saunders?

*

Town & Country were on the point of closing when Ian arrived there shortly after six-thirty. There was no-one in the front office, but as soon as he went in, Jacqueline came through to meet him.

'Ian.' she said, the blue-grey eyes not quite concealing her surprise at seeing him; he was probably the last person she expected to walk into their agency at that time of the evening, but in her professional way, she quickly recovered and shaking hands, took him into her office.

'I'm sorry,' he apologised, 'I should have come earlier in the day.'

'No, it's no problem.' she assured him and he was reminded once again the strength of her personality; she'd been through a considerable amount of stress these last few months following the murder of Rodney Blake, but she still managed to give every appearance of being in control of what could not have been easy; being left with the responsibility of running the agency virtually on her own and waiting for Rodney's successor to arrive. Ian had yet to meet him, but from what he had picked up, not intentionally, but living in a town like Meadowbank, pieces of information, gossip really, literally fell into his lap, that so far Martin Frame had said or done nothing to exactly endear himself to those who had met him. Even although he had spent all his life in Meadowbank, it didn't mean he was unaware of the reception any newcomer was faced with, which meant he could sympathise with him; it was no easy feat to convince the 'fully paid-up' residents that you really were quite a nice guy.

'You may think what I'm going to ask you, Jacqueline, somewhat unorthodox,' he said, once they were both seated, 'but it's regarding Alison Moore's old house in the square, which we understand has now been sold.'

'Number twenty-eight? That's right, it has.'

'And did your office handle the sale?'

'No, unfortunately we missed out on that one,' she answered, 'although Alison did place the property with us shortly before she left Meadowbank, it was actually our head office in London who carried out the sale.'

'That was too bad.'

'It was, but it happens and very often it can work the other way, you know. Being networked the way we are does have its advantages and it means there is a better chance of moving the properties; having them on our books for any length of time is not good for our image.'

'I can understand that; progress, eh?'

'As you say, progress,' she smiled at him, immediately looking years younger, reminding him again of the extra responsibility she'd had to deal with in what he knew was a busy agency; perhaps too much for one person to carry.

'Are you able to give me the name of the purchaser of number twenty-eight, Jacqueline?'

'Of course, that's no problem,' she said, repositioning the screen of her computer and scrolling down until she found the line of text she was looking for, 'here we are. The completion date was the third of April this year and the purchasers were Aztec Investments Limited of Regent Street, London W.1.'

'Not an individual buyer, then? Was this unusual?' scarcely believing what he had heard. Aztec Investments Limited. Well, all he could say, Brenda Masters is one clever lady. A hunch it may have been, but once again, she had been right, so here was another connection between Charlie East and Johnnie Baker.

'Not all that unusual,' she smiled again, 'we're finding that more and more properties are being bought by companies; it's a lot to do with the market, both the property and the financial markets, I mean. With the current economical climate people are finding it difficult to borrow, existing house-owners have taken the step of selling up and deciding instead to rent while they wait for an improvement in interest rates and in the hope that property prices may come down.'

'I see,' Ian said, 'complicated.'

'Not really,' she said, 'and I suppose it does make sense and means we continue to sell, so, really, these companies and, incidentally, individual people also, are helping us. It also means the rental side of our business has picked up quite considerably.'

'And are you handling the rental of number twenty-eight?'

'No, we're not.'

'A pity.'

'All too often the purchasers will handle this themselves.'

'More economical?'

'In one respect, yes, but they still have to comply with the strict rental laws and to make sure this is done correctly, also to cover each party they will have to consult a lawyer.'

'I'm very grateful for your help, Jacqueline,' Ian said, 'not only have you answered my question, but I have learned something about the property business. Incidentally,' he added, 'we would appreciate it if you were to treat this conversation as confidential.'

'Of course I will, Ian.'

*

It was another warm evening and Matthew Richards, once he had left the A390, drove the remainder of the way to Meadowbank with the window wound right down. He could have gone instead to Christine's house, but the thought of spending another night there with only the television for company, was more than he could stand; instead, he had packed his bag when he had left the house that morning, intending to book once more into the pub. He needed to be with people; not necessarily to talk to them, but to feel part of the community.

It had been a long day; starting with a meeting with Christine's bank and building society, then there had been the funeral in the afternoon, followed by more meetings, the last one with her lawyer in Winchester. All her affairs were in order; there were no complications. The one surprise he had was when he was told she had made out a will, although she had never said anything to him, and had left all she had to him. It was at that point, in the lawyer's office, after he had finished reading out the full contents of the will, when he had almost broken down. He had been unable to say anything; even to nod his understanding had taken all of his effort. He couldn't fault the lawyer; he had been openly sympathetic and had quietly left him on his own for ten minutes or so and it had given him the chance to compose himself. Soon, he would be able to leave England and had already booked a flight for Sunday morning and, tomorrow, he would make the arrangements with the estate agents in Meadowbank to put Christine's house on the market; he had been able to find a local firm to deal with the contents and then, that would be that, he thought, sighing deeply and pulling up outside The Market Inn.

Before going inside, Matthew unbuttoned the top button of his shirt and pulled off the black tie he had been wearing for most of this awful day, rolling it up and putting it on the shelf below the dashboard. He never wanted to wear it again. If he did, it would remind him of her, remind him of how she had died, and the mystery surrounding that death. He would much prefer to remember the times he had spent with her; they were worth remembering, nothing else.

The pub was packed and he was thankful for that. This was exactly what he wanted and pushed his way towards the bar. Brian was the first person he recognised and as soon as Brian spotted him he smiled his welcome: 'Hello, Matthew; it's good to see you. I won't ask how you are; I don't need to.' he added.

'Thanks, Brian.'

Matthew ordered a beer, as much as he would have liked a whisky, but thought better of it. There was still a lot to be done and now only one day to get everything completed; he needed a clear head, also he must have something to eat, having had nothing substantial for the last couple of days.

'We have a room available, if you want to stay the night, Matthew.' Brian said, passing the beer across to him.

'What are you, Brian Morrison,' Matthew smiled, 'psychic?'

'Perhaps.' Brian grinned.

'I would, please, and for tomorrow night also, if that's alright. I'll be leaving on Sunday.' he added.

'We'll miss you, mate,' he said, 'but it's probably for the best. There's nothing like work to concentrate the mind.'

'I hope you're right. I will come back to Meadowbank, but not for a while. It's going to take some time to get myself back on an even keel.'

'That's understandable and you know you'll always be welcome here.'

Matthew took his beer over to the only empty table and, pulling out a chair, sat down.'

'I hope I'm not intruding?'

He had been so engrossed in his thoughts he hadn't noticed Jack Wilson; Christine's old boss, although as he looked at him, he didn't seem all that old; years younger in fact to that dried up old stick, Victor York, 'Not in the least, Mr Wilson,' Matthew said to him, 'but you haven't a drink, what can I get for you?'

'No, really,' Jack Wilson said, 'it's just that I saw you sitting here and I wanted to say how very sad I was about Christine. I don't think,' he went on, sitting down opposite to him, 'there is anything else I *can* say. I am sorry, Matthew; I truly am very, very sorry.'

'Thank you.' Matthew said, standing up, 'I would like you to have a drink with me, please.' he added, and without giving him the opportunity to protest any further, Matthew walked across to the bar for another beer. Derek served him and a few minutes later he was back and, sitting down again, raised his glass: 'You're good health, Mr Wilson.'

'And yours, Matthew,' Jack Wilson responded, 'and when did you get back to England?'

'On Tuesday.' Matthew answered slowly; the memories of those first few hours running kaleidoscope-like through his brain, 'I came straight to Meadowbank as I hadn't been able to contact Christine.'

'Oh, dear,' Jack shook his head, placing his glass back down on the table, 'and you wouldn't have known about what had happened? What a dreadful shock that must have been for you when you found out?'

'It was, yes, but somehow, I've managed to get through these last few days. There's been such a lot to do which I guess has helped a little. I should have been in touch with you, Mr Wilson –'

'- Jack,' he smiled across at him, the brown eyes reflecting his sorrow, 'please call me Jack. But, Matthew, I wouldn't have expected to have heard from you.'

'Perhaps not, but I still think I should have been in touch, especially as the police told me Christine had been on her way to see you that evening.'

'Yes, poor girl, she was quite distressed when she phoned me, but I expect they told you?'

'They did, yes. It was Chief Inspector Masters I spoke to; she did strike me as an extremely capable person and I got the impression they were doing their best to get to the bottom of it all.'

'You're right; they will,' Jack said, 'Brenda Masters is an excellent officer; we are very lucky to have her in Meadowbank, in fact, she's a credit to the force. Clever, Matthew, as well as being capable.'

'What about yourself, Jack,' Matthew said, 'have you any ideas why Christine was killed?'

'Not really.' he answered, 'Like you have probably been, Matthew, I've been racking my brains, but apart from the fact that whatever was worrying her must have concerned her work in some way, I haven't been able to come up with anything.'

'It's all – all so sinister.'

'Indeed it is,' he agreed, 'and it is too easy to jump to conclusions. Probably best to leave it to the authorities to solve; it will drive you mad otherwise. You need the next few weeks to try and come to terms with losing Christine and puzzling over why and who could have possibly been responsible won't help you.'

'Sound advice.' Matthew said, realising what he had said did make sense.

'Good; we'll have another beer, shall we, or would you prefer something stronger, a whisky, perhaps?'

'No, thank you,' Matthew smiled his gratitude; talking about Christine, especially to someone who had known her personally and for a such a long time had not been so bad; at least it had eased the crushing feeling of despair he'd been carrying around with him since he'd heard the news, 'a beer will be fine.'

'Hello, Jack. It's Matthew, isn't it; I thought I recognised you;' a short, blonde-haired woman who looked vaguely familiar to him, came up to their table, 'Christine's friend?'

'That's right,' Matthew answered, shaking her hand and then recalling who she was. Mary, he never did know her surname and she owned The Bridge Cafe on the corner of the square. Christine had taken him there one lunchtime, although it must have been several months ago, back in the winter sometime.

'I was terribly sorry about what happened to her, Matthew. In fact, I believe I can speak for everyone else in the town who knew Christine. She was a lovely woman.'

'Thank you, Mary. It's kind of you to say that.'

'It's quite true; she's going to be missed so much. She came into the cafe nearly every day for her lunch, but I expect you already knew that? Victor York as well,' she went on before he was able to answer, 'at different times of course because of the pharmacy.'

'You would have seen her on Monday, then?' Matthew asked, more for something to say, than to know whether Christine had been in there or not.

'Oh, yes, poor love; little did I know it would be the last time I would see her. She was a bit subdued though, but I daresay she'd had a busy morning. She'd told me often enough that Mondays were their busiest days.'

'And I expect Victor York was his normal dour self, Mary?' Jack asked.

'He probably was,' giving him a quick, spontaneous smile, 'but he didn't come into the cafe that day. Mind you, it did surprise me a little, but then I saw him from our kitchen window; he was walking across the car park, so I assumed he had to go somewhere else that lunchtime.'

'Perhaps he wanted a change?' Jack suggested mildly, 'Anyway, Matthew,' he went on, picking up their empty glasses, 'I'll get us those drinks. What about you, Mary? Would you like one?'

'Oh, no thank you, Jack,' she said, 'I have one already. My husband will be wondering where I've got to, so I'll say goodbye now. And, Matthew,' turning to look at him closely, 'once again, my deepest condolences.'

And, for the second time, he thanked her and watched as she walked away to join a group of people at the far end of the bar.

'You think Victor York had something to do with Christine's death, don't you, Jack?' Matthew asked him when he came back, placing their beers on the table. In spite of what he had said earlier, Jack Wilson did have his suspicions; he'd had his reasons for asking Mary what he had. He had wanted to know where Victor York had been during his lunch break, although all they did know was that he didn't spend it as he usually did in The Bridge Cafe.

'I'm no detective, Matthew,' Jack said, a rueful smile hovering on his lips, 'and I would be the last person to point a finger at anyone unless I had some positive proof to substantiate such an accusation.' he finished; both of them aware he hadn't answered Matthew's question. Okay, Matthew decided, he wouldn't press him, but he would try another approach: 'How well do you know Victor York?' he asked him.

'Hardly at all,' he answered, 'I've never seen him in here, or in The Bridge if it comes to that. I don't think he's all that sociable. I've only been in his company a couple of times and this was when I was selling the business; hardly long enough to get to know him, but I have to say, Matthew, I didn't take to the man; a bit too po-faced for my liking, lacking in any degree of empathy whatsoever. I'll put it this way; he knew why I had decided to sell up a good ten or fifteen years before I would have normally, but my wife was dying, Matthew. I had been told she had, at the most, only another year to live, although as it happened, she went beyond that by a further three and I wanted to spend as much time with her as possible. When I explained to him why I was taking early retirement, there was no change in his expression; I may just as well have said I was about to lose my pet rabbit.'

'That's truly sad,' Matthew murmured, now understanding a lot more than he had an hour ago, 'but what do we have to go on?'

'Not a great deal, I'm afraid. Probably nothing.'

'So,' Matthew insisted, 'where was he during his lunch break on Monday, if he wasn't in the cafe?'

'That, Matthew,' Jack Wilson said, his voice sombre, 'is perhaps something you and I will never know.'

Chapter Eleven

Katie arrived in London in the middle of the afternoon, having driven down from Manchester earlier in the day. The first thing she had to do was find a place where she could leave the car; during the time she was going to be in London it would be more of a hindrance than any real use to her. She remembered there was a multi-storey car park opposite the Royal National Hotel in Bloomsbury; an area she knew well. That would be fine she decided; expensive, but the way she was feeling right now, that was the very least of her worries. She had lost count of the times she had tried to phone Danny and then, shortly before she had left Manchester this morning, she had dialled again and this time the line was dead. Either he was out of range, but surely that was unlikely, or his mobile needed to be put on charge.

She had slept badly the night before; tossing and turning until well after midnight, her brain refusing to switch off and before it was light she'd had enough. The sooner she was on the road, the better. At least then, she would be doing something positive. The talk she'd had with Danny's father had further disturbed her and long after he had rung off, the possible impact of what he'd said, didn't let up and continued its relentless circuit in her head. He had also been trying to get in touch with Danny for the last couple of days and, like her, without any success. He had wanted to know whether Danny would be going to Mark's funeral which was this afternoon. He hadn't sounded all that concerned about not being able to get hold of Danny and she hadn't said anything. This was her problem; it didn't belong to anyone else and she certainly had no intention of burdening him with her worst imaginings. As Katie turned into the entrance to the car park, waiting in the queue to drive up the ramp, she wondered whether this decision, impetuously made after talking to Johnnie yesterday, was such a good idea after all, but she was here now. She had written Danny's address down on a piece of paper, which was tucked into a side pocket of her bag, although she had no idea what she would do should he not be there. She hadn't thought beyond the moment when she finally reached his house. She hadn't made any plans. Perhaps try and find someone who knew him; one of his neighbours, or at the nearest pub. Further than that, she had a complete mental block. Danny could not simply have disappeared off the face of the earth she thought, disgusted by her pathetic attitude. Where had all that adventurous spirit, that craving for excitement, gone? She wasn't even thirty yet, for God's sake! Far too young to be thinking in this indecisive middle-aged way.

They had a room available at The Royal National, which she guessed they would. She had stayed there many times in the past; one of London's largest hotels and didn't charge an arm and a leg either she thought, squeezing into one of the lifts, balancing her travel bag between two giant-sized rucksacks and then, when the lift reached her floor, having to manoeuvre herself out on to the corridor.

Half an hour later, after a shower and a change of clothes, she was back down in the lobby and feeling considerably better; more like her old self. Danny lived in Buckingham Street and she knew more or less where that was; one of the roads off the Strand on the way towards Trafalgar Square. Surprising herself by remembering the number of the bus she should take and, after purchasing her ticket at the machine next to the bus stop, she waited with all the rest of London's home-going commuters for the number ninety-one bus to appear. She didn't have long to wait and within minutes, or so it seemed to her, they had turned into the Strand and she could see Nelson's Column ahead and then, on the left-hand side, the familiar dark paintwork of Waterstones Book Shop. This was her stop and pressing the bell, waited for the bus to come to a standstill.

Buckingham Street led off from Craven Passage but before turning left she noticed the Ship & Shovell; the pub uniquely positioned on either side of the narrow road, which was really no more than an alley. This could be Danny's local; it was more than likely Katie thought, walking past the open doors of the pub on her way into the road where he lived. His house was a hundred yards further along, sandwiched between a firm of solicitors and a dietician. It was a neat building; stone-faced and painted cream and, like its neighbours, with window boxes filled with early summer geraniums outside the ground floor windows. Here we go she thought, taking a deep breath and ringing the bell. She could hear it echoing from inside and even as she waited for the door to open it had a hollow sound to her ears. He wasn't there. Danny wasn't in there. She waited a few seconds and tried again, but it was like those telephone calls she had been trying to make: no response. The house was empty; beyond that, she refused to think. She had to keep her head; she had come this far and there was no way, absolutely no way, she was going to give up now.

Katie chose the larger part of the Ship & Shovell, the one on the right-hand side, judging that Danny would be more likely to drink in there. Although not yet six, already the pub was beginning to fill up with several of the customers standing outside on the cobbled walkway with their drinks and soaking up what was left of the sun. Inside, it took some minutes for her eyes to readjust to the dimness, but it looked inviting; a long dark-oak bar curving round on the left; highly polished optics and shelves of shining glasses; high-backed stools and against the windows, low tables and comfortable-looking seats with chintzy coverings to match the curtains.

'Hello, darling,' the barmaid, about her own age, Katie reckoned, smiled a spontaneous welcome, 'what can I get you?'

'A glass of white wine, please.'

'Any preference? Chardonnay, Muscadet or, we have a nice selection of Italian wines?'

Katie asked for the Chardonnay and watched while she poured it. Most of the customers were sitting down, with only a handful standing next to her at the bar, including an elderly gentleman who gave every appearance of being the pub's regular; he had that particular look about him, as though he came in every day and took up the same position, with a pint of Guinness clutched firmly in his hand. Every pub has one she thought; the mainstay of the traditional English pub, also they never missed a trick. If Danny did use this pub, he would know just how often and probably would remember the last time, but before approaching him, she decided to have a word with the barmaid.

'I'm looking for a friend of mine,' Katie began, having made up her mind to come straight out with it, rather than skirting around the edges of what she wanted to find out, 'I've been trying to get in touch with him and I wondered if he'd been in recently. Danny Howarth, he's called.' she added.

'Danny Howarth? You're a friend of Danny's?' she asked, pushing her thick blonde hair back from her forehead.

'Yes; I haven't seen him for a while and I thought as I was in London I would look him up.'

'Oh, I see,' she nodded, 'I didn't think I'd seen you before.'

'Has he been in recently?'

'Come to think of it, darling,' she answered, 'I haven't seen him since – er – when was Danny last in, Frank?' she called over to the old man who was avidly listening to every word they were saying and not making the slightest pretence to hide his interest.

'Tuesday evening, Polly.' the prompt reply given without any hesitation.

'You're sure, Frank?'

'Of course I am!' indignation evident in the withering look he gave her and, making no further comment, returned to his Guinness.

'Sorry,' Polly smiled across the bar at her, 'not much help, are we? It's funny, though,' she went on, 'Danny is in here most evenings. I hadn't realised it had been so long since we saw him.'

'He was around the following evening.' Frank piped up; his drink for the moment forgotten as, once again, he took centre-stage; the focus of their attention.

'Oh, was he?' Polly asked, a puzzled frown on her face and it was apparent this was exactly what the old man wanted; he had his audience and Katie stifled a groan as she waited for him to elaborate, 'It's just that you didn't say, Frank.' she added.

'Well,' he said and Katie was sure that the smile which hovered for a couple of seconds was one of delight, 'you only asked when he'd been in here, didn't you?'

Polly's expression told her everything; she was used to him and expected no less. He was in his element and, if the situation hadn't been so worrying, Katie may have been amused, but all she could think about was Danny and why he hadn't been in touch.

'I was on my way home, you see,' Frank spoke to her for the first time, ignoring Polly, 'and Danny was getting out of his car; I live across the road from him and by the time I'd let myself into the house he'd gone.'

'What do you mean; he'd gone, Frank?' Polly echoed exactly what she had been about to say, 'Do you mean he went inside his house or what?'

'I don't know, do I?' his voice querulous now, apparently running out of steam, and Katie expected he didn't know any more than what he'd told them. 'I suppose he must have done; his car was still there, but when

I looked across later, it was getting dark by then, he hadn't switched on any lights in the house.' he finished, his expression unreadable as he looked at her. The first thoughts which came into Katie's mind were that he was deliberately making a mystery out of nothing and, whatever she did, she shouldn't believe there was anything strange in what he'd said. Quite simply, he had seen Danny; presumably shortly after he had returned from Meadowbank, that's if he had gone there on Wednesday and by the time he got home, being tired had gone straight to bed. Logical although that may sound, it still didn't explain why he hadn't phoned; it hadn't been all that late. This was now Saturday, so where was he? She would go back to his house again before returning to the hotel; one last try and then she would have to seriously consider what she should do next.

'You're not worried about Danny, are you?' Polly asked her.

'I don't know whether I should be or not; what I can't understand is why he hasn't been answering his mobile.'

'Don't get me wrong,' Frank butted in, 'but could be he's had it stolen. It's happening all the time, you know; people leave their mobiles on the bar and next minute, they've gone.'

'You could be right,' Katie said, wanting to believe him, 'I hadn't thought of that.'

'There you are then,' he nodded, obviously pleased with himself for solving her problem; if only it could be as easy as that she thought, 'that's probably what happened.'

The pub was becoming more crowded and Polly had to move away to serve more customers who had suddenly converged on the bar and thanking her and the old man, Katie finished the last of her wine and left, retracing her steps to Danny's house and ringing the bell and, as before there was no answer; the door didn't swing open and Danny wasn't standing there with a look of surprise on his face at seeing her. She was about to walk away when she remembered Frank mentioning that Danny had been driving and his car had still been there, outside the house. There were a number of cars parked alongside the kerb, but she had no idea whether any of them could be his or not. They appeared to be in their allotted spaces in front of each building; the official notice fixed to a lamp post stating that the area was reserved for residents only. She could return to the pub and ask Frank what kind of car Danny drove, but she didn't want to do that, even although Frank would be bound to know, probably also the registration number, but she realised by doing this he, Polly as well, would think her behaviour extreme, far in excess of a friend wanting to look him up while in London. She couldn't afford the luxury of sharing her concern for him, however tempting that might be. Again, applying logic, Katie looked at the cars, in particular, the one immediately in front of number thirty: a white Renault with a grey trim; a compact sort of car, easy to park and ideal for city life she thought. Was this his? And trying to decide what to do next. She had to find out and the only way was to ask his neighbours. Why was she dithering like this? Why couldn't she merely go up to the door of the dietician's for example and ring the bell; what was stopping her? And, then, as she was about do this, the door opened and a girl came out, walking down the short flight of steps to the pavement and going over to the Renault, at the same time fumbling in her bag for the keys.

'Oh, dear,' she said, appearing to notice Katie for the first time; the bunch of keys now in her hand, 'you live here, don't you and I've been taking up your parking space?'

'No -'

'Sorry,' she continued, without taking a breath and seeming not to have heard Katie, 'I only started working here this week and I was told the owner of number thirty was away, so I thought –'

'- It's alright,' Katie interrupted quickly, 'this isn't my house. Look,' Katie said, 'you seem to be in a hurry, but perhaps if you could tell me who told you the owner was away, I'd be grateful. I've been trying to get in touch with him.' she added.

'Oh, I see,' she said, bending down to insert the key into the lock, 'it was my boss, actually, Miss Middleton.'

'Is she in at the moment;' Katie asked her, 'she may be able to tell me where Danny has gone?'

'She is, yes,' the girl answered, looking at her watch, 'Sorry, but I have to go. Just ring the bell.'

Miss Middleton was a tall, slim woman; ultra-smart in navy and white linen and showed no surprise once Katie had explained why she was there. Instead, she opened the door wider and invited her in, Katie following her along a narrow passageway and into a small reception area.

'You say you're a friend of Danny's?'

'Yes, that's right; I used to know him quite well, but it was some time ago and I thought I would call and see how he was; I'm only in London for a few days.' telling her more or less the same as what she had said to Polly.

'When did you last speak to Danny?'

'On Wednesday morning,' surprised at the question. How well did she know him, Katie wondered. She didn't appear to be his type, but then who was she to judge. The woman was probably about the same age as him and she hadn't seen Danny since they had broken up almost four years ago; he could have changed quite a lot in that time. Goodness knows, she certainly had.

'Did he say anything to you about going away?'

'No –' unsure exactly how much she should say to her, 'only that he would be out of London for most of Wednesday and that he would phone me when he got home.'

'And, I take it, he didn't?'

'No.'

'Obviously, you've been trying to phone him?'

'Several times and then, the last time when I tried, the line was dead.'

'I've been trying to call him as well, Mrs -' apparently noticing her wedding ring and reminding her she hadn't introduced herself.

'I'm sorry,' Katie helped her out, 'my name is Katie; Katie Brownlea.' not knowing why she had used her maiden name.

'I'm Myra,' she smiled, formerly shaking her hand, 'and as I've finished work for the day, can I offer you a glass of wine?'

'That's very kind of you.'

'Not at all, Katie. Shall we go through to my office; it's far more comfortable in there.' she said, leading the way into a room at the rear of reception.

'As I was saying,' Myra Middleton said, pouring out their wine, 'I've been trying to call Danny; since Thursday morning, in fact. I arrived for work earlier than usual and had been surprised not to see his car parked outside and to be perfectly honest with you when during the day it still didn't appear I became more than a little worried about him, especially later in the day.'

'Why was that?'

'Because,' she said, lifting the glass to her lips, 'we had a dinner appointment for Thursday evening. He had told me he would be away on Wednesday and I hadn't expected to hear from him, but when he wasn't at the restaurant I did think it odd; not like him at all. I felt sure if he had been held up for some reason or other he would have been in touch.'

'I've just spoken to one of the customers in the Ship & Shovell pub and, apparently he saw Danny coming back here on Wednesday night.'

'Did he? That's interesting, so I wonder what happened; perhaps he was called away and forgot about our dinner.'

'It's possible, I suppose,' Katie said doubtfully, 'but I don't know how well you know Danny, Myra, but do you really think he would forget something like that?'

'No,' trying to smile, but didn't quite make it, 'I don't think he would.'

'What kind of car does he drive?' Katie asked her.

'A dark blue BMW.'

'There is no dark blue BMW parked outside, Myra.'

'I know that,' she agreed, 'therefore perhaps I am right and he had been called away. Indeed, what else can I think?'

'I don't know.' trying to keep the despondency from her voice, not wishing to further alarm her. Although Myra hadn't given her any hint of what sort of relationship she had with Danny, it was plain she was upset not to hear from him.

'Where are staying while you're in London?' she asked Katie.

'The Royal National in Bloomsbury.'

'The reason I'm asking is when Danny does turn up I'll be able to tell him you've been looking for him and he'll know where to find you.'

Waiting for the bus to take her back to Russell Square, Katie was glad she had decided to say as little as possible about Danny and hopefully had managed to convince Myra she wasn't all that concerned about not catching up with him. To do so she felt would not have been all that clever. If Myra got the slightest inkling Danny was in any danger, she may very well have insisted on calling the police. In the bus, Katie couldn't get the feeling she had missed something. Would Danny have confided in Myra, Katie wondered, and with this possibility she was reminded again she had no idea how close they were. If he had, then Myra may be thinking along the same lines as herself; that, like Mark, Danny had been killed. And, subconsciously, she was already assuming when she told the girl Danny was away that he wouldn't be coming back. Minutes before her bus pulled up at the stop outside the hotel, Katie had mentally ticked off what she had learned so far which was that Danny had been seen getting out of his car on Wednesday night and, although Frank hadn't noticed any lights being switched on inside the house, the car had not been there the following morning. When, Katie wondered, had it been driven away; later that night or early on the Thursday before Myra arrived for work, and who had been driving? Danny or someone else?

*

The next morning, Katie was no further forward in reaching any decision. She had managed to sleep, but those hours after midnight and before the light began to filter into the room, around six, had been disturbed by a series of dreams; most of them revolving around Danny, his voice clearly coming out to her right from the first moment she had met him in The Rose and Crown in Manchester, up to that night in Meadowbank when they'd parked outside the old manor house on the outskirts of the town and she had stayed in the car while Danny, along with Mark and Johnnie, had crept, keeping close together, as they had crossed the lawn, then reaching the French windows to the right of the building. Although it had been impossible for her to have seen anything more from where she was, but dreams, being what they were, she followed silently behind them, her footsteps as soundless as theirs and once she was inside the house, watching while they took down the four paintings, extracting the canvases from the frames and rolling them up, also, as Mark scooped up the silverware, placing all of it into the bag they had brought with them. They had then, without anything being said, or even so much as whispered, left the house as stealthily as they had entered it and, once again, she was behind them; completely invisible until they reached the car and Mark slid in behind the steering wheel and, letting out a whoop of excitement as he started the engine, he turned the car back towards Meadowbank and on towards the motorway: "Wake up, Katie!" he had said, "The deed is done! You should have been with us; it really was a piece of cake!"

A piece of cake! A piece of cake! It was those words, reverberating through her brain which had finally disturbed her and sitting upright she knew she would not be able to get back to sleep. She had had dreams before, some of them nightmares, but none had been as vivid as that one and, throwing back the duvet, she got out of bed, padding barefoot across to the window. It was almost six and the beginning of a new day had started to make its appearance; the pale sky streaked with deepening shades of peach and grey. What a mess, she thought, turning away from the window and switching on the coffee pot, what an absolute mess. How had she got herself into this situation? But, she knew the answer to that. Through her own stupidity and obsession with Danny, her first real boyfriend, any of the previous ones having instantly faded into oblivion as soon as she met him. And, now, she thought, where was he, but she believed she knew the answer to that also. Danny had gone and she would never see him again. Just like Mark.

She switched on the television after she'd had her shower and was brushing her hair when she heard Danny's name mentioned, her arm suspended in mid-air as she stared at the newsreader and listened to what she was saying in her dead-pan and disinterested voice: "The body of the man taken from the charred remains of a car found in a ravine at the Devil's Punch Bowl has now been identified as Daniel Howarth; thirty-eight years of age, a free-lance public relations officer in the music and entertainment business and living in the West End of London, his body having been spotted by construction workers from the nearby new motorway as they reported for duty on Thursday morning. The Surrey police are treating Mr Howarth's death as murder and are meanwhile continuing with their enquiries. The next of kin have been informed."

Katie sat down heavily on the edge of the bed and put her head in her hands, remaining like that for several minutes. So, she had been right all along. Danny had been murdered. And, it must have happened late on Wednesday night and it had taken all this time for the police to discover his identify. Poor Danny. Poor, poor Danny. She wanted to cry, but she couldn't. Who would she be crying for anyway, a grain of commonsense told her. For Danny? For herself? But, what she did know, she had to make that call to Inspector Ash. She didn't want to phone the Surrey police; it would be far too complicated to explain and, in any case, they would have to speak to Meadowbank, so she may as well either phone them, or alternatively, drive there and speak to the inspector face to face.

She picked up her bag from the dressing-table and was about to leave the room when the hotel phone rang: 'Katie? It's me, Myra; have you heard? About Danny?'

'A few minutes ago, Myra,' Katie said quietly, 'on the news.'

'Katie,' Myra said, her voice shaking, 'I must see you. I think we need to talk.'

As they had arranged, Katie met her in the hotel coffee shop and as soon as she saw the woman she knew Danny had meant a lot to her. Although she had put on some make-up, it didn't camouflage the paleness of her skin and it was evident by the slight puffiness around her eyes she had been crying.

'Myra,' she said gently, putting out a hand to her, 'please sit down. I've ordered a pot of coffee. Would you like something to eat, some toast perhaps?'

'No, thank you,' she said, her voice barely audible, 'I couldn't eat a thing.'

'When did you hear?'

'The same time as you, I think,' she answered, 'on the nine o'clock news.'

The coffee arrived and Katie, feeling so much stronger than her, leaned forward to fill both their cups. She was shocked at Myra's appearance, feeling she was on the verge of breaking down and wondering if she didn't have someone far more suited than herself to help her through this.

'I'll be alright,' Myra said and, like the previous evening, attempting to smile, but, as then, not succeeding, 'once I get over the shock, which was indescribable, Katie. I just couldn't believe what I was hearing.'

'I know. Drink your coffee; perhaps tea might have been better?' Katie said, pushing the cup towards her.

'No, this will be fine. What about you; how are you feeling?'

'I'm okay. Of course, hearing about Danny was dreadful and in such an impersonal way, but, well,' she shrugged, unable for the moment to go on; still not quite sure what she should or could say to her, but knowing there wasn't really anything she could think of which would help her;

Myra was grieving for him, that was obvious, 'I have to say,' she went on, 'I have been waiting for something to happen, not as awful of this, of course, but I have been fearing the worse.'

'Me to;' Myra said softly, 'me too.'

'I think this is all very difficult for you.' Katie said, conscious of the inadequacy of what she was saying.

'I'm sorry, Katie,' she said at last, putting her cup back on the saucer, 'this – losing someone who meant such a lot to me, well, I didn't realise I would ever react the way I am.'

'You loved him, didn't you?'

'I did, yes; very much.' Myra said softly, her eyes filling with tears, 'I'm sorry,' she repeated, taking a tissue from her bag, 'I didn't mean to be like this, I really didn't.'

'Listen, Myra, I do understand -' and prevented for saying anything more by her mobile ringing, '- damn!' she muttered, pressing the key and hearing Ben's voice: 'Hello, Katie, it's Ben; are you alright? You said you'd phone me yesterday and when you didn't, I began to worry about you.'

'I'm sorry, Ben,' she said, trying to think of what she could say to him. She had completely forgotten to call him as she'd promised. It was obvious she couldn't just come out with the truth and tell him why; she would need to side-track him somehow. 'I guess,' she began her hastily put-together explanation, 'because it's been such a quick week and then I got the hours mixed up and by then it was far too late to call you. What time is it with you now?'

'Twenty past five,' Ben said, 'I'm afraid I won't be back until the week after next, Katie,' he went on quickly, 'I have to fly on to Singapore this evening; some problem with the plant there.'

'That's too bad, Ben; I was so looking forward to seeing you. It seems an age since you left.' Katie said, making her best attempt to put the right amount of disappointment into her voice. Unwittingly, Ben was giving her the much needed time to do what she had to. Katie had no illusions; she knew that eventually she would have to tell him about Danny – and everything, but for the time being she had been given a respite and that was all that mattered to her.

'Can't be helped, darling,' he said, 'anyway, I'll make it up to you when I get home; perhaps we can have a short break somewhere, you'd like that, wouldn't you?'

Ben didn't stay on the line for much longer, saying he would phone again sometime during the week. Putting the mobile back into her bag she looked across the table at Myra, noticing she was looking a little better; at least there was more colour in her face.

'That was my husband,' she said, 'he's working out in the Far East at the moment.'

'I thought it might be,' Myra said, refilling their cups, 'I take it he's no idea you're in London?'

'No, he doesn't. Ben knows nothing about Danny; he's never shown much interest in any of the friends I had before we met.'

'He won't know about the rock group, then?' she asked, looking at her above the rim of her cup.

'I did tell him, actually,' she said, 'but he wasn't really interested.' pausing for a moment, sensing there was more to what Myra was asking and continuing to worry about how much she could divulge, 'What else did Danny tell you?'

'He told me about you, Katie; that you had been together for quite a while, also the names of the other two in the group.'

'Did he mention the touring we did during the summer months?'

'Yes, those as well. Please don't think I'm being judgemental, because I'm not, and I'm certainly not playing games, trying to find out more about that time in Danny's life. I'm not like that. As far as I'm concerned, the past is just that: the past, and that's where it should belong.'

'I agree, but there are times when it has a habit of returning.'

'I know; like now. Danny felt exactly the same. From the very beginning of our relationship, he told me about what he described as his misspent younger days and how much he regretted all of it. Those were his words, Katie; not mine. But, when Mark Astley was murdered, well, I believe that acted as a catalyst to him. You knew that Mark and Danny more or less grew up together?'

'Yes.'

'Well, although they were not related, nevertheless, the bond had been a rather special one. They could go for months, years even, not meeting up or even phoning each other, but Danny remained extraordinarily protective towards him and when Mark was killed, it hit him hard. Danny wanted to find out who was responsible.'

'He told me that as well, only the other day.' Katie said sadly, 'But, Myra, did he say who he thought it was?'

'Not his name, no. He said it was better for me not to know, only that he was positive it was the same man they all worked for, although Mark and the other man, Johnnie Baker, I believe he's called, had been with him for much longer than Danny; years earlier, in fact.'

'I know his name, Myra.'

'I thought you might,' she sighed, 'but, Katie, for God's sake, be careful.'

'I'm trying to be,' Katie said, 'but it's not easy.'

'I'm sure it isn't.'

'Also,' Katie put in, 'I think I know where he lives and, if I am right, it's where Danny told me he was going on Wednesday.'

'What do you plan to do now?'

'I'm not sure,' Katie said slowly, 'but I know what I should do.'

'Tell the police, you mean?'

'Yes; I think I have to, don't you?'

'I suppose so,' Myra agreed, but sounding doubtful, 'but I'm concerned for you. What happened to Danny –' stumbling over his name, and then taking a deep breath before continuing, '- was terrible! Just terrible! I can't bring myself to think what it must have been like for him; it's more than I can bear. Perhaps later, Katie, when I'm stronger. I hope so.'

'Do you know, Myra,' Katie said, 'I've reached the stage where I don't care whether I have to face questions over those robberies. At one point I did, especially at first, when I heard about Mark and then after the call from the inspector in Meadowbank, but now, I feel quite differently. I want, more than anything, for the person who did this to Danny to be exposed and punished.'

'I feel that way as well,' Myra said, her words no more than a whisper, 'and if I can help you in any way, Katie, believe me I will.'

'Thank you, Myra; that's sweet of you, but I don't see how you can, or anyone, if it comes to that. I think this is something I will have to face on my own.'

'Perhaps I might be able to, you know. Danny told me you never participated in what they were doing, that you only went along with them

_'

'- but, surely,' Katie interrupted, 'that makes me just as guilty?'

'I don't see it like that and, incidentally, neither did he, Katie. I am prepared to swear on oath that that was what Danny told me, if it should ever come to that.' she added.

'It happens to be the truth.' Katie said, for the moment touched by the sincerity in Myra's voice. She meant exactly what she said. At last, here was someone she could confide in; a friend. She knew, when the time came, which it would she was sure, and she had to tell everything to Ben, she couldn't possibly expect a favourable, or even loving, reaction from him. But, the future of her marriage, or really the strength of her marriage, was something which would eventually be tested and as she sat facing Myra at that moment, in the coffee shop in London on the Sunday morning when both of them had so recently learned about the death of someone they had both loved, there wasn't a great deal else which really mattered to her.

'I know it's the truth, Katie,' Myra said, 'Danny wasn't a liar.'

'No, I know he wasn't.'

'A minute ago you mentioned Meadowbank?'

'Yes?'

'Is that where Danny was going on Wednesday?'

'That's what he told me.'

'And he believed the man we've been talking about is living there?'

'He did.'

'Aren't you going to tell me his name?'

'It's Charlie East.'

Chapter Twelve

The Salmon's Rest opened at the same time as they always had on a Sunday morning; at fifteen minutes to eleven, coinciding with the church bells ringing out across the square, and reminding the people of Meadowbank they should spend the next hour in prayer, also in exercising their lungs in singing hymns selected by an enthusiastic new choirmaster, most of which they had never sung before and perhaps never would again.

Barbara, outside the restaurant, having unfastened the wooden shutters and still with plenty of time before they could expect their first luncheon customers, leaned against one of the window ledges and turned her face up towards the sun. May had been an extraordinarily warm month and the long-range forecast she had listened to earlier promised many more weeks of uninterrupted sunshine. Good for business she thought, although judging by the number of people who had made bookings well in advance, she was beginning to realise that the weather didn't make all that much difference to them. Buying the restaurant had been a gamble; both Harry and she had known that well enough, and it gave every indication that this one just might pay off. They liked the town and had made a few friends in the short time they had been there, not that there had been a great deal of time for them to do much socialising, but Harry had only said earlier that morning how much more relaxed he felt compared to what he had been like in London, even although, if anything, he was working longer hours and with more responsibility. She was pleased he was settling in so well, because she felt exactly the same. Long may it continue she thought, looking along the pavement and seeing Felicity walking towards her. It had been a lucky day for them when Felicity Carter had called into the restaurant looking for work; she was a hard worker and Barbara hoped she would stay in Meadowbank for a while, having already learned that good reliable staff wasn't exactly easy to find.

'Hello, Felicity,' she called out to her, 'it's a lovely morning, isn't it?'

'Hello, Barbara; yes, it is.' she agreed, but there was something lacking in her response. Felicity, she had been quick to discover, smiled easily and spontaneously, but this morning, although she did smile, it was automatic and didn't reach her eyes. Something was bothering her, but unsure whether she should say anything to her or not. Everybody was entitled to their off-days Barbara decided, so there was no reason why Felicity shouldn't also.

'Let's go inside, shall we,' Barbara suggested, 'I've made a pot of fresh coffee; we can have a cup before we need to start?'

As soon as they were in the restaurant and Barbara, turning round to look at her, she knew she would have to ask her what was wrong. The girl looked as if she was on the verge of tears.

'Do you want to tell me what's troubling you, Felicity?' she asked gently as they both walked through to the kitchen.

'Oh, dear,' she said quickly, 'I was hoping you wouldn't notice.'

'Whatever it is,' Barbara said, 'it doesn't do to bottle it up, you know.'

'I suppose you're right.'

'Is it something to do with Johnnie?'

'How did you guess?'

'It was presumptuous of me, I'm sorry; I was just jumping to conclusions.'

'Well, you're right as it happens, Barbara. He didn't come home last night and he hasn't phoned – or anything -'

'There could be a simple explanation, Felicity.'

'I've been trying to think of one, but I can't. Not one.'

'Well, it isn't midday yet and wherever he went last evening he may have decided to stop over and he could still be asleep. Have you thought of that?'

'It's possible, but I don't think so.'

'Have you tried ringing him?'

'Oh, no, Barbara, I wouldn't do that. You see, Johnnie wasn't out drinking last night; he was working.'

'I see; I hadn't realised.' embarrassed, and wishing now she hadn't made any suggestions. What sort of work did he do, she wondered, presumably he was on night-shift somewhere, having seen him a number of times in the square during the day, but for some reason she decided not to ask her. This reticence could have had something to do with the withdrawn look on Felicity's face. She didn't want to talk about him anymore, perhaps already regretting having said anything in the first place.

Fortuitously, the first customers started to arrive then, forcing them to cut short their conversation; Barbara to do the finishing touches to the choice of starters and to make sure Alistair, the young man she had taken on as a trainee chef had the main courses under control, and Felicity, by this time, Barbara was glad to see, had perked up a little, ready to greet the new arrivals and show them to their tables. Harry, no doubt diplomatically keeping out of their way during the time they were in the kitchen, was now behind the bar. Let the show begin, Barbara murmured under breath.

It was well after one and the four of them had been working non-stop without any let-up; all the remaining tables which hadn't been pre-booked, being taken up by a party of six who told them they were on holiday, when Felicity's mobile rang, the subdued strains of Freddie Mercury's 'Barcelona' emerging from her shoulder bag which she had slung over the back of one of the kitchen chairs. There was nothing Barbara could do about it and there was no way she would have taken the mobile out of the bag, and eventually it stopped ringing. A further half hour went by before she had the chance to mention it to Felicity and by the instant relief in her expression it was plainly evident she was certain it would have been Johnnie. At least he had tried to contact her Barbara thought, hoping he would have a good explanation and one which would satisfy her. Barbara had met him once but only briefly and had no idea what sort of person he was, but what she did know was, that Felicity adored him. Each time she mentioned his name, which was often, the way her eyes sparkled, even how her voice softened, were all self-explanatory; to Felicity, Johnnie could do no wrong. Barbara had kept these observations to herself, but such intensity of feeling, especially in someone as young as Felicity, was to her, unhealthy and she only hoped he wouldn't let her down. It wasn't only that her boyfriend was so many years older, but he had an over-confident way about him and, although she wouldn't have mentioned this to anyone, not even to Harry, there was a slyness in his expression which she didn't like and was certain she could never trust a man who looked like that. Perhaps she was being over-protective towards the girl; the daughter she and Harry never had? Could be, she sighed, but she was sure if they'd had a daughter she would not be at all happy about her having a boyfriend like Johnnie Baker.

The last customers left the restaurant shortly after two-thirty. Barbara re-loaded the dishwasher while Alistair cleaned the grill and the hotplates and wiped along all the working tops, in readiness for when they would be opening again at six-thirty. They'd only been in business for a week, but each one of them had their own allotted tasks and were, Barbara noted with satisfaction, working well together. Felicity had finished re-setting the tables for the evening; cutlery and glasses in their places, together with the dark green napkins, all neatly folded as Barbara had shown her, when her mobile rang again. This time she heard it and managed to get the phone out of her bag in time. Barbara made to move away, not wishing to overhear what she was saying, but the look on the girl's face stopped her. She had never in her life seen the colour drain from anyone's face so rapidly. From her normal peach complexion, Felicity had turned ashen. Alarmed, she moved quickly towards her.

'Felicity,' keeping her voice low, trying to transfer some of her calmness to her, 'who is it? Is it Johnnie?'

'No,' her voice no more than a whisper, 'it's the police, Barbara,' her whole body trembling now as she stared at Barbara, her eyes brimming with tears, 'they've taken him into custody.'

'Would you like me to speak to them?' Barbara asked; it was apparent Felicity was incapable; she could hardly stand and the hand holding the mobile was shaking uncontrollably.

Silently, Felicity passed the mobile to her and pulling the chair out from the table sat down and all this time not taking her eyes from Barbara's face.

'Hello,' Barbara said into the mouth piece, 'I'm Barbara Wood; Miss Carter works for me. She's had rather a shock.' she added somewhat unnecessarily and aware of Harry standing in the open doorway, his expression full of concern as he looked questioningly at her.

'Good afternoon, madam, I'm Chief Inspector Gerald Carpenter from Winchester Police headquarters. It's good Miss Carter isn't on her own at a time like this and I do regret having to break the news to her about Mr Baker in this impersonal way.'

'All Felicity was able to tell me, Chief Inspector,' Barbara said, 'was that her boyfriend had been taken into custody.' hearing Harry's quick intake of breath from where he remained standing, but looking now with concern at Felicity as by this time tears were streaming unchecked down her cheeks.

'That's right. I don't want to go into too many details, madam, except to say we received a call from someone shortly before midnight last night who had seen two men breaking into a pharmacy in the Winchester area. Our officers were successful in reaching the pharmacy before they were able to leave and immediately arrested the pair.'

'How dreadful!'

'Indeed it is,' he agreed and she liked the sound of his voice; mature with a faint west country accent, 'however,' he continued, 'Mr Baker will have to remain here at least until Monday; that's when he will be appearing at Winchester Assizes and what happens after then will depend on the court's decision.'

'Is there any chance Miss Carter can see him?'

'I wouldn't advise it, madam; coming here would, I believe, prove quite stressful for her, far better for her to wait until Monday.'

'I'm sure you're right,' Barbara said, 'she has been terribly worried about him when he didn't return home last night.'

'I've no doubt she was,' and she recognised the dryness in his voice; here was a man well accustomed to this kind of situation and knew exactly how to deal with the various reactions of those people affected, 'and this is why we've been trying to contact her today. Mr Baker was anxious to put her mind at rest,' he added, 'although under the circumstances, I dare say she is more worried now than she was before.'

'She's extremely distressed,' Barbara said, looking over at Felicity who hadn't moved, although she had stopped crying and making a poor effort to pull herself together. Harry, meanwhile, had done the sensible thing, as he always did in any emergency, by bringing her a small brandy and watching as she took a few tentative sips. Alistair had, by this time, finished his various chores and was obviously anxious to leave, but too shy to say anything to Harry, 'but if you could tell me the time the Assizes will be meeting on Monday, between then and now, we'll do our best to see she is alright.'

'Eleven o'clock,' he said, 'and I would say is she if able to be there about fifteen or twenty minutes before we will be able to arrange for her to see him before he is called.'

The Chief Inspector brought the call to a close and Barbara handed the mobile back to Felicity, telling her what he'd said. She had regained some of her colour and pushing her hair back from her face, stood up.

'Thank you very much, Barbara.' she said, 'I can't tell you how grateful I am. Also, I'm sorry to have inflicted all of this on to you, and to you, Harry. I feel – I feel,' she hesitated, looking at them both in turn, 'so ashamed.'

'Don't be, love.' Harry said immediately. 'It's not your fault.'

'Perhaps not,' she nodded, handing him back the glass, 'but that doesn't make much difference to me. I don't know what you must think.' she finished lamely.

'Listen, Felicity,' Barbara said quietly, 'your boyfriend, it would seem, had been doing something illegal and he was caught. You weren't there, so we don't view you any differently. Why should we?'

'I don't know whether you'll believe me, but I didn't know what Johnnie was doing, but I have to be honest with you both, I did realise, although he never told me, the work he was involved in was not exactly honest and apart from that, it's all I know and that is the truth.'

'You don't have to make any sort of explanation to us, Felicity,' Harry said to her, 'I would like to think that both Barbara and I are sufficiently worldly-wise to understand the situation. The bottom line seems to be that your boyfriend has been found out and will, no doubt, have to pay the price. These are hard facts, Felicity and I'm sorry if I'm sounding harsh, but it is the way I see it. If you step outside the law you should expect at some time or other, repercussions, which will not be at all pleasant.'

'I know.' Felicity said softly, 'You're right, Harry.'

'You'll want to go there on Monday, won't you?' Barbara asked her practically, feeling desperately sorry for the girl.

'I have to.'

'Of course,' Barbara agreed, 'it's only natural. Would you like me to come with you?'

'Barbara!'

'No, Harry,' she smiled across at him, 'it's alright, really. We're not open on Mondays; also I don't like the idea of Felicity going there on her own.'

'Then we'll both go.' he said firmly.

*

Victor had, in his opinion, waited long enough for Charlie to get in touch with him. The last time they had spoken had been on Thursday and it was now Sunday. He was beginning to get jittery and having Monica around all the time didn't help. She was constantly asking him if he was alright, as though she sensed in her sisterly and stifling way, that everything certainly was not alright. He had a couple of hours respite; Monica having decided to attend the morning service in Saint Stephen's and he intended to make full use of this. He tried both Charlie's home and mobile numbers, but there was no reply from either of them. There was nothing for it, he decided, picking up his car keys from the hall table, he would take the unprecedented step and go to his house. Charlie wouldn't like that, but too bad. He would have to lump it! Victor wanted to offload those packages and the sooner the better as far as he was concerned. He hadn't heard anything from the police since Thursday, but after Inspector Ash's second visit that morning which had unnerved him, he had been left with the distinct impression that the man was very close to discovering why those figures in the stock system didn't tally. Just how bright was he, Victor fretted? Was he mentally capable of reaching the right conclusions? Victor had a nasty feeling he was, and if not the inspector, certainly, from what he had heard about her, Chief Inspector Masters, once she started looking into it, was more than capable. It was time he started watching his back; nobody else was going to do it for him. Not Charlie East, that was for sure, and not even Monica; she'd be no help whatsoever. No, he was now facing the unpalatable truth; he was on his own in this whole unsavoury business.

Number Four, The Mews, on the Stockbridge Road, was the second of the two-storey mews houses and it didn't take Victor long to reach there. The gate was open and he drove into the driveway at the side of the house. There was no other car there and he noticed the garage doors were closed. Going up to the front door, Victor rang the bell. Once again, no response. And why am I surprised he asked himself cynically, at the same time alarmingly aware of his heartbeat quicken as he did all he could to curb his rising panic. It wasn't as though there were any of the immediate neighbours he could ask; the house next door was empty and had been for some months now, so that was hopeless. He could, he supposed, try further along. There was just an off-chance they may, realising from experience how interested the people in Meadowbank were about the various comings and goings of everyone who lived within their vicinity. Leaving the car where it was, he walked along the pavement and opened the gate of number six.

Victor didn't recognise the woman who came to the door, but that didn't mean she didn't know who he was, although he couldn't detect any sign of recognition on her face. She was in her early forties he reckoned; a short woman with blonde hair tied back in a ponytail and, judging by the flour on her apron, was in the middle of preparing the Sunday lunch.

'I apologise for disturbing you,' Victor began, 'but I've been trying to get in touch with Mr East and wondered if you had seen him lately.'

'Charlie, you mean?'

'Yes, that's right; Charlie East.'

'He's away on holiday; he left on Friday morning, in fact.'

'Oh, really, I hadn't realised.'

'He told me on Thursday afternoon and I think it was very much a spur of the moment decision,' she said, surprising him with her knowledge. It was obvious that either she was a personal friend of Charlie's or merely overly observant, 'we're actually keeping an eye on his house for him.'

'I see; did he happen to say where he was going?'

'Somewhere in France; to be honest, I can't remember the name of the place, far less pronounce it!' she laughed, 'I was never any good at French at school.'

'Well,' Victor said, 'you've been very helpful. I'll just have to wait until he gets back. Did he tell you when that was likely to be?'

'A couple of weeks, he said. Lucky man; to be able to pack up like that virtually at a moment's notice. It would be impossible for us with three young children, not forgetting our dog.'

Thanking her again and managing to get away without, he hoped, showing his disappointment, Victor returned to his car, backing out of the drive and into the road. So, he concluded, Charlie was, not to put too fine a point on it, out of contact. Something must have happened to alert him, to make him decide to make himself scarce for a while. He had told his neighbour on Thursday and that was the same day he had spoken to him, going over in his mind exactly what he had told him. About the robbery, yes, he had talked to him about that and he could remember how scathing he had been, also he'd made it abundantly clear he didn't believe one word of it. But the main part of their conversation had been Charlie's reluctance to meet him, wanting to delay the handover of those blasted packages, and the reason he gave was because of the rumours he was hearing around the town. He hadn't actually said anything specific, although he had hinted broadly enough. Perhaps he had been holding something back? Perhaps he had heard more than he'd implied? Whichever way Victor looked at it, it appeared that Charlie had started to worry about himself and decided to move out of the scene for a while. In other words, to let him, Victor York, deal with the problem on his own which Victor believed was becoming imminent and he wondered how soon it would be when he could expect another visit from Inspector Ash, or perhaps from the pair of them this time; the Inspector and Chief Inspector Brenda Masters.

*

Sunday afternoon, and Brenda and Ian were working. It was always the same in a murder enquiry; neither of them could afford to take any time off, at any moment something could come through. They couldn't wait until Monday morning and expect to pick up from where they had left off on the Saturday; it didn't work like that. The detection of a crime of this magnitude wasn't a nine-to-five job and, as much as she would have liked a free weekend, this was the way it had to be and had been practically from those early years when she had joined the force.

The call from Gerald Carpenter was put through to her at exactly three-fifteen and she braced herself for what she reckoned would be another development in this complicated case.

'Hello, Brenda,' were his first words, 'how are you?'

'I wish you wouldn't ask me that each time you call, Gerald, because the answer is always the same.'

'I know, I know; it's tough at the top.' he chuckled.

'It can be! Anyway, fire away; I'm sure you haven't just phoned to pass the time of day.'

'No, Brenda, I thought you would like to know we took Johnnie Baker into custody last night.'

'Did you now? Did you catch him in the act, then?'

'More or less,' Gerald answered, 'and only thanks to an observant resident with a social conscience and actually living next door to the pharmacy in Oliver's Battery, we were able to get there in time.'

'That's outside Winchester?'

'That's right,' he agreed, 'practically on our doorstep and that's why we could move as quickly as we did. Anyway, we caught them red-handed; there was absolutely no way they could have got themselves out of that one.'

'So, it wasn't only Johnnie Baker?'

'No, he had someone with him; meant to be acting as some sort of cover for him and did a pretty bad job of it as it turned out.'

'What happens now?'

'Well, they will both be appearing tomorrow morning at eleven and then it's up to the court to decide their fate. The ironic part of this is, Brenda,' he went on, 'we were probably just a little bit too quick off the mark, because if we'd waited until they'd emerged from the pharmacy carrying their bag of spoils, so to speak, we could have stuck something on them straight away, but it's more than likely, as neither of them have any previous convictions, they'll get away with it. Pity, but there you are.'

'There is one thing, though, isn't there,' Brenda said, 'this confirms what we already suspected; that Johnnie Baker has probably been involved in these robberies for some time. It does give us a lead; of a kind.' she added.

'Yes, that's true. I spoke to his girlfriend just before I called you, by the way. She's young, Brenda, and the news hit her hard, but whether she knew what he was up to is anyone's guess. Personally, and call me an old cynic if you like, but I find it hard to believe she could have been living with him and not know.'

'Presumably, it will all come out, Gerald.'

'I hope so.' he said, 'You've heard about Danny Howarth?'

'Yes, I have. Events are moving quickly, aren't they?'

'You could say that.'

'I don't suppose you were able to find out from either of those two who they were working for?'

'No; we asked them, naturally, but they were giving nothing away.'

'There has to be someone controlling them.'

'You're thinking about this Charlie East, aren't you, Brenda?'

'Yes.'

'I've read the profile you sent through and yes, he does sound a likely candidate, shady past and all that, but that aside, what else have we got?'

'Not a great deal,' she admitted, 'but I do feel events are beginning to move. Also, I'm fairly sure Christine Saunders' murder is somehow tied up in all of this business, but at the moment there's been no positive link. Too many loose ends, Gerald, far too many, but I'm sure we'll find a solution, given some time, plus a little bit of luck.'

'The whole case is something of a conundrum, that's for sure.' he said, 'It's not often we find ourselves working as closely as we are with so many police districts and now, with Danny Howarth's murder, it would seem Surrey is also involved.'

'Yes,' she was quick to agree, 'and ironically, each time, we come back to Meadowbank.'

'Which, unfortunately, Brenda this means more work for you and your officers.'

'I know; how right you are, but I'll ring off now, Gerald, if you don't mind. I want to have a word with Ian, but I will say this, it looks very much as if we're in a position to pull Victor York in for questioning, so I'll get back to you tomorrow.'

Brenda sat for a moment once she had replaced the receiver and before she rang Ian on the internal line. She had meant what she had said to Gerald; she did feel the case was showing some signs of moving, but she wanted to get their priorities right. The first step, was to tackle Victor York; afterwards, they could put all their energies into the main aspect of this enquiry, not that she was diminishing the importance of Christine Saunders' death, far from it, but she had a gut feeling if they could find out whoever was acting as the instigator behind all of this, they would be more than half-way there. It was all very well to suspect Charlie East, but they needed a lot more to go on than they had so far. They were up against a professional; she had no illusions about that. This whole investigation seemed to be split in two; each part, up to now, pulling away from the other; she had to, somehow or other, find a strategy, a method of how to merge them and she was positive she would be able to do this. But, how? That was the question she thought, dialling Ian's number.

'I've just received a call from Katie Brownlea, ma'am.' Ian said as soon as he came into her office and she didn't miss the expression on his face; one she recognised from a number of cases they had worked on together. He also felt they were on the verge of cracking this one; there was that familiar gleam of suppressed excitement in his eyes as he looked at her.

'Have you now?' she couldn't help smiling at him; his enthusiasm was palpable, reminding her, and not for the first time, how terribly intense she had become in hardly ever allowing herself the luxury of such a reaction. It's high time you lightened up, Brenda Masters she told herself and waited patiently for him to elaborate.

'Yes,' he smiled back at her, 'apparently, she had been worried when Danny Howarth didn't get back to her as he'd promised last Wednesday night, so she took it upon herself to drive down to London and find out what was wrong.'

'Ah.'

'Precisely; she was beginning to think something had happened to him.'

'And did she say what grounds she had for thinking like that?'

'She did give me an explanation,' Ian answered, 'but I got the impression there was something else, but what she did say was that Danny had phoned her on Wednesday morning to tell her he was planning to come to Meadowbank that day.'

'Really? And did he tell her why?'

'Yes, he did; to find Charlie East.'

'This is it, Ian! This is the break-through we've been waiting for; I'm sure of it.'

'I believe it is. However,' he continued, 'she is still in London, having, as it was to be expected, since learned that Danny Howarth's body had been identified and that we were treating his death as murder.'

'Tell me, Ian,' Brenda put in thoughtfully, putting a reign on what she was thinking and planning what they should be doing next, 'there's something puzzling me here; Katie Brownlee is married now, so why is she concerning herself so much with an old boyfriend? Also, her husband; what can he be thinking with her going off to London in the way she has.'

'She told me he was away at the moment, so I would hazard a guess he knows nothing about any of this business, but as to why she appears to be so concerned about Danny, I believe there might be a bit more to it.'

'Such as?'

'It's going back to their time with the rock group, I think. Perhaps the real truth is she is more concerned about herself.'

'You mean in case we start putting two and two together?'

'That's exactly what I was thinking, yes. Up to now, I've only spoken to her on the phone; I haven't been able to gauge what she's like; you know,' he went on, 'her facial expressions, body language, that sort of thing.'

'If you are right, and I think you may very well be, her behaviour could be construed as a guilty conscience.'

'Exactly, and that's why I believe I should go down there, to London, and talk to her face to face and perhaps speak to some of Danny Howarth's neighbours, although it might be best to clear it with Guildford first; find out who's in charge of the case. The last thing I want to do is encroach on them in any way.'

'I believe you're right, Ian. One of us will have to go there. A day should be long enough for you, wouldn't you say?'

'I would think so, ma'am, although I'm sure Guildford will already have covered virtually the same ground, except, of course, they won't know anything about Katie Brownlea, but all the same, I would prefer to have more of a hands-on approach, rather than merely reading their reports.'

'That's fine by me,' Brenda nodded, 'I'll leave that side of the enquiry to you for the present. Meanwhile, there have been a couple of developments here which you should be aware of.' and giving him the gist of her conversation with Gerald Carpenter, gratified that his reactions were the same as hers. Ian also believed the attempted robbery the previous evening could be linked to Charlie East and now, given what they had been talking about, they were coming back full circle to the extinct rock group.

'You mentioned a couple of developments, ma'am?' he prompted.

'Yes, and this may, or may not, surprise you, but I bumped into Jack Wilson last night after we'd finished here and he told me something extremely interesting. He'd been talking to the woman who owns The Bridge Cafe who just happened to mention to him that Victor York hadn't been in there for lunch on Monday, although she did see him in the car park around one o'clock.'

'But, he walked to work; there would have been no need for him to be in the car park!'

'Exactly, Ian; so, once again, I'm prepared to push my neck out and bring him in for questioning tomorrow.'

'And I won't be here.' Ian said disappointedly.

'Can't be helped,' she smiled at him, aware how much he regretted to miss out on what should prove to be an enlightening interview, 'it will be recorded in any case, Ian, and you can listen to it when you get back.'

'It will certainly be interesting to learn how he'll wriggle out of that.'

'*If* he can,' Brenda commented dryly, 'however,' she continued, 'once we have our search warrant, I'll have four of our officers over at the pharmacy; two of them to give the place a thorough search and the other two carrying out a physical stock-take.'

'We'll need a copy of the financial accounts, won't we, ma'am?'

'That's right; we will, but I can ring the accountants tomorrow and get them to fax us through a copy and as soon as we have those final stock figures it won't take long to arrive at what the true figures should be.'

'Sergeant Williams could prove useful to us in this respect;' he suggested, 'before he joined the force he took an accounts course at Winchester Technical College.'

'And then decided he'd prefer to be a police officer?' she smiled, 'Ah well; we all make choices, Ian, but, seriously, I'll take on board what you've said and make sure he's with them tomorrow.'

'That's good.'

'And, Ian,' Brenda said, 'I think it's time you and I visited Charlie East. There are a number of pertinent questions we need to ask him and, let us see how *he* squirms out of those. So,' she added, 'I suggest we do that first thing on Tuesday morning.'

Chapter Thirteen

Sergeant Alan Williams escorted Victor York across the square from the Meadowbank Pharmacy to the Police Station and straight to the interview room. Brenda took her time in collecting the various items she would need; the most important one being the tape recorder. This was no ordinary interview; what she had to ask Victor York was absolutely crucial to the case and she had to make certain it was conducted along the correct lines.

The interview room was at the rear of the building on the first floor; the only view, if one could describe it as such, being a brief and uninteresting stretch of the motorway. There was nothing comfortable about the room; not one single redeeming feature; from the off-white painted walls to the plain long wooden table in the centre, with the two chairs, one on either side. There were no pictures, not even a calendar, only a wall clock, reminiscent of one of those old railway ones, which at one time may very well have been, perhaps on some now long defunct south west railway station.

Victor York was standing with his back to the window when Brenda went in, closing the door firmly behind her and nodding to the sergeant standing nearby.

'Perhaps, Chief Inspector,' Victor York's voice, heavy with sarcasm, 'you would be so kind as to enlighten me? Firstly, the invasion by half the Meadowbank police force swarming at this precise moment over my pharmacy and then, having to suffer the indignity and, I might add, in full view of the chronically curious in this town, of being brought over here?'

'Please sit down, Mr York,' Brenda said, gesturing towards one of the chairs, 'and I'll explain.'

'I sincerely hope you can.'

'I will do my best, sir.' she replied dryly and adding under her breath, 'if you'll allow me?' Victor York positively exuded righteous indignation, not so dissimilar to what she had experienced a number of times in the past and which, all too often, could be interpreted as one of plain and unadulterated guilt. She must, she decided, try not to pre-judge him; she must, on the other hand, methodically and without bias, exactly as she had been trained to do, get on with the questions she had planned to ask him. The fact she believed he was responsible for Christine Saunders' death should not come into the equation. It was difficult, but she would manage and bracing herself for what she already realised was going to be a difficult half hour or so. Victor York would, she was certain, continue to bluff and bluster his way out of everything she put to him. She had to be prepared for that.

Brenda waited until he was seated, which he did with obvious reluctance, before saying anything further to him.

'I'm conducting a murder enquiry, Mr York,' she began slowly, selecting each word with care and watching him closely, ready for any change in his expression, no matter how subtle, 'into the death of your late assistant, Miss Christine Saunders.'

'What on earth has that to do with me, Chief Inspector? I was under the impression the reason for you wanting to talk to me this morning was concerning my business?'

'We believe there is a connection, sir, between the way the pharmacy's accounts are compiled, in particular in respect to your stock-taking of drugs and the murder of Miss Saunders.'

'What possible grounds have you for suggesting such a preposterous idea? I would really appreciate how you have arrived at such an assumption, Chief Inspector.'

'I'm not assuming anything, Mr York,' Brenda replied, her tone sharper than she had intended, but the man was so unutterably pompous; his whole manner excruciatingly over-bearing, 'but, before I proceed,' she continued, 'I think it may be in your interests to have your lawyer present this morning. I would strongly advise this.' she added quietly.

'I don't need a lawyer! Totally unnecessary!'

'The decision is yours, of course, sir, but if at any time you change your mind, please let me know and we'll curtail the questioning until he or she arrives.'

'I've just told you; I don't need a lawyer.'

'Very well, sir. This interview is a formal one and will be recorded, at the end of which I will ask you to sign your agreement to what has been discussed in this room between the times recorded. I trust I've made myself clear?'

'Perfectly clear, Chief Inspector.' the sarcasm returning, 'Now; it would seem, you suspect me of being a murderer?' he finished, leaning back in his chair and folding his arms in front of him.

'Right,' Brenda said, pointedly ignoring what he had just said, and pulling the tape recorder across the table towards her, 'we'll make a start and, remember, you may ask me to call a halt at any time.' and pressed the 'start' button: 'Ten forty-five am on Monday, the twenty-eighth May, two thousand and five,' she began, looking across at him. He hadn't changed his position, but she noticed a muscle high up on his left cheek beginning to twitch slightly. 'As I've already mentioned, Mr York,' she said evenly and not taking her eyes away from his face, 'there are two issues here I would like to address, but before I ask you any questions about what appears to be certain discrepancies in your stock figures, I am going to mention a few anomalies which could have a direct link to Miss Saunders' death. The last time we spoke was on Wednesday, when I called into the pharmacy. Do you agree?'

'If you say so.'

'I would like you to try and think back and confirm that this was the case.'

'Yes,' taking a full minute before answering, 'you came into the pharmacy last Wednesday.'

'To inform you that we were now treating Miss Saunders' death as murder?'

'Yes.'

'We discussed where Miss Saunders lunched each day and you told me she always went to The Bridge Cafe, as, indeed, you do yourself?'

'That's right.'

'We do have confirmation that she did go there last Monday, but you were not there as usual and, yet, you led me to believe differently.'

'I don't see that it matters, Chief Inspector; whether I was there or not. Everyone likes a change now and again, even I do.'

'Where did you have your lunch on Monday, sir?'

'I didn't have any; I wasn't hungry.'

'You weren't hungry?'

'That's what I said.'

'How long did you take for your break?'

'The same as always; one hour.'

'And where did you go during that time?'

'I went for a walk.'

'Exactly where, sir?'

'Oh, around the town, nowhere in particular.'

'Nowhere in particular?' she repeated.

'No, not really.'

'You were seen around one o'clock that day in the car park behind the mini-market in Bridge Street; I take it you know which one I mean?'

'Of course I do.'

'This being the same one Miss Saunders used.'

'It could be.'

'It was you, yourself, sir, who told me she parked in that car park, if you remember?'

'Did I?'

'So,' Brenda persisted, 'were you there on Monday?'

'I may have been.'

'I would appreciate if you didn't prevaricate in this way, Mr York. I'll repeat; were you in the car park at the time you were seen?'

'I don't know about the exact time, but I was there.'

'Why? Were you using it as a short-cut or, perhaps, you'd decided to take a drive somewhere during your lunch break instead of going to the cafe?' she asked him casually.

'How perceptive you are, Chief Inspector,' he said; the thin bloodless lips stretching in a poor replica of a smile, 'I did take a short drive as it happens.'

'You may have taken a drive, sir,' Brenda said quietly, 'but I don't think that could have been possible, unless, of course, you returned home first.'

'Why should I have? I don't understand.'

'To collect your car. You may have forgotten, but you did tell me on Wednesday when I spoke to you, that you didn't bring your car into town that day, preferring the exercise of walking to work.'

'You seem to know more than I do, Chief Inspector. All I can tell you is what I did during my one free hour in the day.' his voice smooth; it was going to take considerably more questions to crack this man Brenda thought, but not disheartened. She still had a long way to go before she was finished with him.

'What time did Miss Saunders leave the pharmacy?'

'At six-thirty; I believe I remember telling you this before, Chief Inspector.'

'Mr York, I meant at lunchtime; you told me you both took different times in order that the pharmacy could remain open. Presumably, she would have had her break before you?'

'Of course.'

'An hour before?'

'Yes.'

'And, presumably, she would have returned shortly before one o'clock in time for you to take your break? Is that right, sir?'

'Yes.'

'Well, if the person who saw you was correct and you were in the car park around one, I don't see how you could possibly have walked home, collected your car and been back by then.'

She had him! The muscle below the eye was moving again and she didn't think she was mistaken, but there was considerably less colour in his cheeks than there had been.

'Oh, I don't know,' he shrugged, 'I'm probably getting mixed up with the time. Whoever it was who *thought* they recognised me must have been mistaken about the actual time. It would have been nearer twenty-five minutes past or even half-past before I reached the car park.'

'And you went for your drive after that time?'

'Pardon?'

'You've mentioned you went for a drive, sir. Was this after you collected your car or before.'

'Oh, afterwards, of course.'

'Are you sure, sir?'

'Of course I'm sure; why shouldn't I be?'

'Because when you were seen, you weren't driving, Mr York; you were walking across the car park, that's why.'

'It must have been when I returned to Meadowbank in that case; your *informant*,' he emphasised, 'must be way out with her time.'

'Do you keep an address book, sir?'

'Of course; doesn't everyone?'

'And have you got it on you at the moment?'

'Ye – es;' he didn't know where she was coming from and this was exactly what she wanted, 'why do you ask?'

'May I see it for a moment?'

'Of – of course,' his voice on the edge of a stammer as he reached into an inside pocket of his jacket, 'here you are.' handing a small dark blue book to her.

'Thank you, sir.' Brenda said, taking the book from him and flicking through the pages, starting near the beginning of the alphabet until she found what she was looking for and jotting down the two telephones numbers.

'How friendly are you with Charlie East, sir?' she asked him, giving the book back to him.

'I don't know any Charlie East.'

'You have telephone numbers for a man called Charlie in your address book. Are you telling me his surname isn't East?'

'I have just this minute told you; I don't know anyone of that name.'

'Mr York,' she said, exercising all of her patience. Either he was being particularly obtuse or he considered her to be lacking in basic intelligence, 'there are two telephone numbers written against the name, Charlie; one of them obviously for a mobile and if I were to find out they did, in fact, belong to a Mr Charlie East, what would you say to that?'

'He could be called East, Chief Inspector,' he said, 'you see,' he went on, 'I never did know Charlie's surname, otherwise, don't you think I would have included it in my address book?'

'Not necessarily, sir,' she replied, 'but what I might think was you had another reason for not including the surname.'

'You've lost me, Chief Inspector. You really have.'

'I'll ask you once more, sir, and this time I'll re-phrase it in a slightly different way; how well do you know the man called Charlie?'

'Hardly at all,' he was quick, too quick, in replying; a look of smugness replacing the sarcastic expression he had been wearing since the interview began, 'he was someone I met quite some time ago. You know how it is, I'm sure, Chief Inspector, you have a chat with a complete stranger, enjoy the conversation and for some very unfathomable English reason exchange telephone numbers, probably both of you realising you will never keep in touch?'

They were interrupted at that moment by a light tapping at the door; the sergeant moving to open it. Subdued voices in the corridor reached her before the door closed again and the sergeant came over to the table.

'Sorry, Chief Inspector, but could you spare a moment, please?'

Signing off on the tape recorder, Brenda asked Victor York if he would like some tea or coffee and suggesting, when he refused, there were quite a few more questions she needed to ask him before she could officially close the interview, but he merely, without looking at her straight in the face, shook his head.

Alan Williams was waiting for her outside in the corridor and she led the way back down to her office.

'Alright, Sergeant, what have you got? By your expression it looks as though you've found something?'

'We have, Chief Inspector,' and as she suggested, sitting down at her desk, 'First of all, we've completed the stock-taking; only hand-written notes, of course, but we've highlighted the two drugs you mentioned.'

'That was quick work,' Brenda said, taking the sheet from him, 'it can by typed up later, Alan; that's no problem.'

'We made a thorough search of the pharmacy and the dispensary, ma'am, and found nothing; also on the floor above, which is used as a storeroom: old office furniture, that sort of thing and then we noticed the skylight on the landing hadn't been closed properly. There are no floor boards up there,' he went on to explain, 'only rafters and we discovered three cartons had been placed along one of them.'

'Three?'

'Yes, ma'am; we've brought them across to the Station: two containing amphetamine tablets and the other morphine phials.'

As she had said to Ian earlier, Victor York was not very clever. He really and truly believed he could get away with this she thought. Goodness knows how long it had all been going on and the fact remained he had to pass those drugs on to someone, but this last lot hadn't left the premises, either because of the recent events he hadn't had the time or opportunity or his 'receiver' hadn't been in touch with him. She would be a lot happier if she had the name of the contact. Believing he was Charlie East was not good enough; this was pure speculation and nothing else. Brenda was in a slight dilemma. She could go ahead and charge Victor

York with falsely acquiring drugs, but without hard evidence, the case wouldn't stand up in court. And, as far as Christine Saunders' murder was concerned, the evidence they had against him was insufficient and only circumstantial.

'Very well, Sergeant,' Brenda said to him, 'I'll get back to Victor York shortly, but before I do I need to make a few calculations from these figures you've given me.'

It took her less than ten minutes to do what she had to; a fairly straightforward book-keeping exercise to find out what the pharmacy's closing stock should be, using the figures Ian had already worked out, together with a copy of the financial accounts which had, earlier that morning, been faxed by Ronald Wilcox. Once she had made the calculation she was able to compare it with the closing stock figure handed to her by Alan. As she suspected, the different was substantial and far exceeding the amount of drugs found by her officers. Although she questioned the accuracy of the opening stock for the new financial year, given that the accountants hadn't carried out their own stock-taking, but had relied instead on those supplied to them by Victor York, the discrepancy was significant. There was now no doubt in Brenda's mind that only Victor York could be responsible for fraudulently altering his accounting for the stock of drugs and, collecting her notes together, took them back with her to the interview room.

Throughout the relatively short time it took Brenda to tell him what they had discovered, including how she had arrived at what his closing stock should be, compared to the check made in his dispensary that morning, not once did Victor York show any sign of surprise or even, as he done earlier, one of indignation. He remained seated exactly as he had done earlier; his arms back in their folded position. Only when she reached the end and told him she intended to charge him with fraudulently manipulating his accounts and siphoning off amounts of prescribed drugs for distribution to person or persons unknown, did she get the reaction she expected.

His chair crashed to the floor as he jumped to his feet to stand squarely in front of her. Brenda could hear the sergeant's footsteps behind her and, once he was in her line of vision, watched as he walked towards Victor York.

'Please sit down, Mr York.' she said, deliberately keeping her voice low as she looked up at him; his face now suffused with colour and the nervous tick on his cheek more prominent as he struggled to find the words to fully express his fury: 'What you're – what you are saying, is monstrous! That, I, Victor York, a highly qualified pharmacist, should be treated in this – this cavalier way – and, by a mere woman! Totally unacceptable!'

'I won't ask you again, sir,' Brenda said, 'but will you please sit down?'

Perhaps he had been able to read the determination in both her voice and expressions; she didn't know, but sullenly, he pulled the chair upright, sliding it noisily across the wood-block floor as he did so and sitting down. His reaction had told her something; Victor York had a nasty temper, but this wasn't the first time she'd had to deal with such a violent display, or to be insulted either. She was used to it and had, over the years, hardened herself to retaliating the way she may have wanted to.

'Now,' she continued, noticing that this time he was leaning forward in his chair with both hands firmly gripping the edge of the table in front of him. Everything about him told her a great deal; his surly expression, the way he pushed his head forward and the white of his knuckles as he clutched the table. Not only was he a self-opinionated and bombastic type of character, but he was also a bully she concluded and as she had learned in the past, very often a bully meant he could also be a coward. 'before we go any further, sir, I would remind you of your situation; as you are aware, this interview is an official one and every word which has been spoken in this room has been duly recorded. Also, you may now have decided you would like to contact your lawyer?'

'Later,' he muttered; barely civil, a belligerent scowl on his face and looking away from her, 'I'll phone him later; when I'm ready. I do hope you realise, Chief Inspector,' he added, turning to face her, 'you are making a very grave error.'

'Before I bring this interview to a close,' Brenda said calmly, obliquely avoiding a direct response, 'I have to tell you that the evidence we have to support the charge being made is, in my considered and professional opinion, irrefutable. It will be up to the courts to decide otherwise.'

'Hmmph. We'll see.'

Brenda stretched out a hand towards the tape recorder and with her finger on the switch brought the interview to an end: 'the interview closed at twelve hundred hours, fifteen, on Monday, twenty-eighth May, two thousand and five.'

*

Melissa, bringing Roy back from his morning walk, had seen Victor York leave the pharmacy accompanied by Alan Williams. The Market Inn wouldn't be open for another forty minutes or so and taking Roy, his coat still damp from his morning swim in the river, into the pub the back way, wondered how long it would be before this piece of news filtered through the town. Brian was in the kitchen and had made a fresh pot of coffee for them and looked up when she came in.

'Alright, love?'

'I am, yes,' she answered, 'but I'm not so sure about Victor York. I've just this minute seen him walking across to the Police Station.'

'Have you? What's up, I wonder. Perhaps he's had another robbery?'

'He could have, I suppose, but he wasn't on his own, Brian; Alan Williams was with him.'

'Well, love,' he said, passing a mug of coffee across the table towards her, 'no doubt we'll find out soon enough. I only hope,' he went on, his expression thoughtful, 'we're not in for some more unwelcome excitement in this town of ours.'

'I hope not,' she agreed, taking a sip of her coffee.

They didn't have long to wait; predictably, and immediately the front doors had been opened, the first regulars arrived; a couple of them, Brian suspected, waiting on the pavement outside until the magical hour of eleven-thirty.

'Have you heard the latest, Brian?' one of them, apparently their self-appointed spokesman, exactly as he had been a few months back when there had been all that dreadful business.

'I'm sure you're going to enlighten me, Fred.' Brian said, stifling a sigh. Here it comes, he thought; first the tittle-tattle, followed by the rumours which would have grown a hundredth fold by the time they re-opened at six-thirty. 'But, first, I take it the three of you are going to have your usual?'

'Of course,' his crony answered for him, 'we're thirsty!'

'Anyway,' Fred said, wiping the froth of beer from his lips with the back of his hand, 'as I was saying –'

'- you haven't said anything yet, Fred!'

'Give me a chance, Bert,' he spluttered, 'and I will.'

'Out with it then, Fred,' Brian prompted, 'don't keep me in suspense.'

'Well,' he paused, obviously revelling in the attention he was attracting, but also, Brian noticed, from the handful of customers who had that moment come in and were waiting to be served, 'that Victor York's been arrested!'

'Are you sure?' Brian asked him.

'Of course, I'm sure;' he replied, indignation in every nuance as he glared at Brian, 'they've found out who murdered Christine Saunders and it's him; Victor York, I'm telling you!'

'I bet that surprised you, Brian?' Fred's side-kick put in; the pale eyes bright with excitement behind the thick lenses of his National Health spectacles.

'If it's true, yes,' Brian was slow to reply; he knew what this trio was like; give them the slightest encouragement and the whole situation could rapidly escalate out of all proportion, 'but how did you find out so soon?'

'I don't know what you mean by so soon, Brian,' the intrepid Fred went on, 'but it stands to reason, doesn't it? I saw him with my own eyes being marched across to the police station earlier this morning; in handcuffs, I dare say.' he added, with a final nod of his grey head.

'Did you see any handcuffs?' Brian asked him.

'Well,' he said, 'I didn't exactly see them, but it stands to reason, doesn't it, if you think about it, Brian, as I'm sure, an intelligent man like yourself must do? We've been saying all week he's as guilty as hell and it looks as though we've been proved right.'

'It's not a good idea to jump to conclusions, you know, Fred,' Brian said cautiously, in a vain attempt to curb his enthusiasm, 'let's face it; it isn't as if we've had any official confirmation. I would suggest we wait and see.'

'Wait and see! Is that all you can say?'

'Look,' Brian said, 'you saw Victor walking across to the police station this morning -'

'- Alan Williams was with him,' Bert added, quick to support his friend, 'and that must mean something.'

'It probably does, Bert,' Brian agreed, 'but it doesn't necessarily mean he's been arrested for something as serious as murder.'

'He's been in that police station since before eleven,' Stan, their buddy spoke out for the first time, 'and I haven't seen him come out yet.'

'Stan's right,' Fred nodded again, 'he's been arrested I tell you! You won't be seeing *him* again!'

By this time, Brian had more than enough of their speculations and the fact that none of them really knew what they were talking about only added to his exasperation with them. He moved along to the end of the bar, well out of earshot; he didn't want to listen to anymore of their amateur sleuthing. He'd had enough for one morning, although, very much aware the day wasn't over yet; there would be more to come when his other regulars made their appearance later and added to their fabricated rhetoric.

'They're at it again, aren't they?' Melissa said, coming out of the kitchen, 'I could hear them from in there. They just don't let up for one minute.'

'I know,' he smiled at her, 'nothing better to talk about. They probably think life has been pretty dull around here since January and are trying to liven things up somewhat.'

'I wish they wouldn't, though.'

'They can't help it, love,' he said, putting an arm lightly around her shoulders, 'and really, no-one ever takes what they're saying all that seriously.'

'I suppose you're right,' she said, but he could tell by the doubtful expression on her face, she wasn't so sure and if he was being honest, neither did he. They may be described by the younger generation as a bunch of old codgers, but there was nothing wrong with their brains, or their memories either, he thought. They forgot nothing! Brian had been in the pub business for long enough to realise that. It wasn't as if they intended to be unkind and cause mischief; it was merely, as he'd tried to explain to Melissa, they were short of something new to talk about. Most of the time, they were wide off the mark, but just occasionally, one of them did manage to hit on the truth which made him wonder whether Fred was right and that Victor York had been charged with Christine's murder.

The pub was filling up with their lunchtime customers and Brian and Derek were kept fully occupied behind the bar and being another warm day, Melissa was doing a good trade with her cold quiches and salads. Jacqueline from Town & Country arrived with her manager, Martin Frame shortly after twelve-thirty; Jacqueline going over to Melissa to order a couple of salads, while Martin came up to the bar for their drinks.

'Something's going on across at the pharmacy,' he said to Brian, 'did you notice?'

'Can't say I did, Martin,' Brian said, wondering what was coming next. Jungle drums had nothing on Meadowbank; did everyone, he wondered, have a built-in antenna on special alert for the latest news!

'I'm surprised you didn't,' Martin went on, taking his wallet out to pay for the drinks, 'you are practically across the road from the pharmacy after all.'

'Been too busy,' Brian answered, wishing he would either come to the point or go over to join Jacqueline where she was sitting at one of the window tables. For some inexplicable reason he'd come to the conclusion Martin Frame wasn't the sort of chap he could really take to. It wasn't as though he was like his predecessor, Rodney Blake, outwardly and over-the-top campish in his mannerisms, but in many ways, Martin's manner more often than not sounded supercilious to him. 'So, what's been happening, then?'

'Mind you,' Martin began, putting the change into his pocket, 'don't get the idea I have the time to keep an eye on what's going on in the square, but it so happened I was standing at the window, having completed, I might add, a rather good sale on a property which had been on our books for rather a long time, when I saw four police officers going into the Meadowbank Pharmacy and minutes later, no more than that, one of them emerged with Victor York in tow, taking him across to the police station.'

'Another robbery?' Brian suggested, trying to keep his tone light.

'I do not think so. Not at all, Brian. This is serious, very serious indeed.'

'In what way?'

'Because, my dear fellow, they were in there for most of the morning and I caught a glimpse of the woman who's helping out at the moment -'

'- that would have been Miss York, Victor's sister.'

'Is she, oh, well, anyway, she was in a dreadful state. She was crying, Brian, most distressed she was. It's all very easy to jump to conclusions, but I would say they've arrested him.'

'We don't know that for sure, though, do we?' Brian said; honestly, he thought, Martin Frame was not so very different from Fred and his cronies. Like them, he was giving every appearance of enjoying the situation, enjoying someone else's misfortune. Not a pleasant thought and relieved when he collected the drinks and went over to their table.

'Tongues are beginning to wag, Brian.' Derek said quietly, reaching up to the shelf above their heads for some more glasses.

'Too true.' Brian said ruefully, 'And the difficult part is not to get dragged into their speculations.'

'To remain impartial you mean?'

'I couldn't have expressed it better myself, Derek.'

Chapter Fourteen

Ian Ash, having spent over an hour talking to Katie Brownlea, walked round the corner into Craven Passage at exactly the same time as Brenda, back in Meadowbank, switched off the tape recorder in the interview room.

He had met Katie in the coffee shop of the hotel where she was staying and, although she had been forthcoming about how Danny Howarth had been in touch with her to say he was on his way down to Meadowbank to try and find Charlie East and then her concern when he hadn't been in touch with her as he had promised, Ian got the impression she was holding something back and that this might very well be an important link in finding out more about how and why Danny had met his death. But, he didn't pursue it, neither did he ask her why she had felt the need to make the journey down to London as she was no longer his girlfriend; to have done so he felt may have resulted in her clamming up altogether. If anything, Ian concluded, he was no further forward than he had been from the moment he had arrived in London earlier that morning. She hadn't told him why Danny wanted to find Charlie East; in fact, she had skirted round that question quite smartly, saying he had been upset about what had happened to Mark Astley, explaining to him the unusual relationship the pair of them had had and how Danny had convinced himself that Charlie East had something to do with Mark's murder. And that was all she had said. Perhaps that was all she had known and it could, Ian thought, be the truth; she didn't know anymore. So, for the moment, he didn't have much choice, he must focus on trying to find out what happened here on Wednesday night and the only positive lead he had was what Katie had been told by one of the regulars in the Ship & Shovell.

She had given him a good description of the old boy and as soon as Ian had stepped inside the pub he spotted him; a tall, thin man, well on into his eighties, with a shock of thick white hair and, surprisingly clear blue eyes for anyone of that age and, to complete Katie's description, a glass of Guinness on the counter in front of him. But, first, Ian went up to the bar, a few feet away from the man at the far end, and ordered half a lager from the girl he guessed, by what Katie had said, would be Polly.

'Here you are, darling,' she smiled broadly at him, giving him his lager;

her wide-eyed interest in having a customer she had never seen before, immediately replaced by an exaggerated rueful expression as she had to move away and serve a couple of businessmen who had just come into the bar.

Amused, Ian looked around the room; many of the customers were dressed identically to the two Polly was now serving, both of them having collected their lunches from the food counter which looked pretty good to him, not having had much to eat since the night before. Polly switched on the CD player and the haunting voice of Annie Lennox immediately permeated throughout the room and although the volume had been turned down, there would, Ian decided, be small chance of any conversation at the bar being overheard; a good time, perhaps, to find out whether the old regular was willing to talk to him or not, although judging by the quick glances he'd been throwing at him since he came in, Ian didn't think he would be disappointed

'Are you a reporter?' were his first words before Ian had a chance to say anything; those eyes piercing through him, but he couldn't see any sign of antagonism, only a keen interest which he was making no attempt to hide. Encouraged, Ian quickly denied this and taking his identity card from his wallet, introduced himself.

'Ah!' he said, after reading what was on the card, 'Not from London though, I see?'

'No, I'm with the Meadowbank Police Force, we're in Hampshire.'

'I know where Meadowbank is, young man,' he said sharply, handing the card back to him, 'it's been in the news often enough over the last six months or so. Quite notorious it's become.'

'Some would certainly agree with you, sir.' Ian agreed, 'We are working in conjunction with the Surrey constabulary,' he began to explain, considering it would be best to be straight-on with him, feeling any prevarication would soon be spotted and then he wouldn't get the co-operation he was hoping for, 'into the investigation of the recent death of Danny Howarth.'

'I thought so.' he nodded and waited for Ian to continue.

'We understand he was a neighbour of yours?'

'Don't know how you found that out, but you're right, he was; poor fellow.'

'I wonder if you would mind answering a few questions, sir.' Ian said, 'We need all the help we can get from people who lived in the same area as Mr Howarth.'

'I don't mind; anything to help.'

'Thank you, sir. It would appear that the last time anyone saw the deceased was last Wednesday night?'

'I wouldn't know about that,' he said, 'all I do know is that was the last time I saw him.'

'What time would this have been, sir?'

'Can't say exactly, mind you, but it was probably about tennish; it was getting dark and I was on my way home from here. Danny had just pulled up outside his house which is immediately across the road from mine.' he explained.

'You say it was getting dark,' Ian said, 'can you be sure it was Danny Howarth you saw?'

'I'm sure alright; I saw him put his key into the lock of his front door, also there's a street lamp directly outside the house. It was definitely him.'

'You mentioned that you live opposite, therefore you would have been able to notice whether any lights were switched on inside his house.'

'Oh, yes,' he said, 'he didn't switch on any at first, but when someone came to the door, he switched on his hall light.'

'He had a visitor?'

'Looked like a visitor to me.'

'Can you describe what he looked like?'

'Quite ordinary really; short, stocky, light brown hair, not what you would call memorable.'

'And had you seen him around the neighbourhood previously.'

'Only earlier in the evening, not before then.'

'Perhaps he had been waiting for Mr Howarth to return home.'

'Yes, could have been; that thought had occurred to me. You see, he drew up about the same time as I left to go to the pub; around eight it would have been, but he didn't get out of his car, just sat there.'

'When you got back home; was the car still there?'

'It was, yes,' he answered, 'exactly where it had been earlier.'

'Did he go into Mr Howarth's house, then?'

'He went in alright.'

'I see, and did you, by any chance, happen to notice when he left?'

'No, I went into my kitchen after that; it's at the back of the house, and made myself a bite to eat, but later, a long time later, when I was getting ready for bed, I looked out of the front window and the car had gone.'

'The visitor's car?'

'No, no,' impatiently, 'not his, but Danny's. It wasn't there.'

'And the other car,' Ian prompted, 'did you see it again the following morning?'

'No, it had gone.'

'Have you any idea of the make, sir?'

'I have, young man,' he said stoutly, pulling himself more upright, 'I'm eighty-six, you know, and my eyesight is excellent. He was driving one of the latest Peugeots, very nice car; expensive. Also,' he added, I can give you the registration number as well.'

'You can remember it?'

'Of course I can. My memory is good as well. Always has been and God willing, will be for a long time yet!'

'You've been extremely helpful, sir, and I'm much obliged to you. Would you like another Guinness?'

'I won't say no.' he smiled his gratitude, 'I sincerely hope you get the blighter,' he went on; 'Danny Howarth was a likeable chap. He used to come in here a lot, most evenings in fact, when he'd finished working. He's going to be missed; by his girlfriend as well, poor woman. What a shock all of this must have been for her.'

'Does she live around here?' Ian asked him, for the first time experiencing a tiny glimmer of; he wouldn't go so far as to describe it as excitement, more of anticipation. Had Katie known about this woman he wondered. If she had, why hadn't she mentioned it?

'I don't think she does, but she has her business in the premises next door to where Danny lived.'

The blinds in Danny Howarth's house had been pulled down; a reminder to anyone walking along the pavement and who had known him and, no doubt, to many of the curious who had never even heard of him before the news of his murder became headline news.

A firm of lawyers occupied the premises on one side and on the other, according to the brass plaque, belonged to a Miss Myra Middleton,

Dietician, followed by a string of impressive-looking letters. The door wasn't locked and, turning the handle, Ian walked into the small reception area. The girl behind the desk looked up from buffing her already perfectly manicured fingernails to ask how she could help him. Not the brightest of receptionists he thought, and couldn't help comparing her with young women around her age who worked in the various offices in Meadowbank. They may lack the polished sleekness of their city counterparts, but at least they did give the appearance of enjoying their work. He told her his name and asked if it was possible to speak to Miss Middleton and, reluctantly putting down her nail file, picked up the receiver and after pressing a couple of buttons languidly spoke into the mouthpiece: 'There's an Inspector Ash in reception, Miss Middleton; he would like to see you.' waiting, her heavily made-up eyes staring past him, before replacing the receiver and picking up the nail file once again.

'You can go through.' she said to Ian in her Sloane-like drawl which he found utterly grating, immediately wishing he was anywhere else, but in the centre of London where he felt, not only out of place, but totally alien. Perhaps I've been living in the suburbs too long he decided, stifling a sigh.

'Would you mind telling me where Miss Middleton's office is?' he asked her, doing his best to keep the exasperation from his voice.

'Sorry; I didn't realise you hadn't been here before. It's through there, the first door on the left.'

Don't bother to get up off your neat little bum Ian thought, following her instructions; that would be too much to expect!

Ian had no pre-conceived impression what the girlfriend of Danny Howarth would look like, but having met Katie Brownlea, he had assumed Myra Middleton may be a similar type. He couldn't have been more wrong. Not only was the woman who stood up as soon as he came into the room and now walking towards him, a number of years older than Katie she didn't resemble her in the least. Where Katie was small, no more than five-foot two, with a mass of straight raven-black hair and elfin features, Myra Middleton must be at least a foot taller, slim, short ash-blonde hair and her eyes, not blue like Katie's, but emerald green. She was an attractive woman; not pretty in a conventional way, but quite striking with a peaches and cream complexion, but more than anything what really struck him as they shook hands, was the expression in her eyes. Here was a woman he decided who was deeply unhappy. He also sensed she was proud and it would take a lot to penetrate that shell of aloofness. Whether this was the result of losing Danny Howarth or this was the way she normally appeared, he had no idea.

'It's good of you to agree to see me, Miss Middleton.'

'That's alright, Inspector,' she answered, 'I'm actually between consultations at the moment. So,' she went on, gesturing for him to take a seat; not at her desk, but to one of the softly upholstered chairs in the centre of the room, 'how do you think I can help you in your enquiries into Danny's death?'

'I suppose it is rather obvious why I'm here.' Ian said, taken aback by her forthrightness; he hadn't expected that.

'Well, it is,' she smiled and although it didn't quite reach her eyes, it did improve her features; he caught a quick glimpse of what she would look like in happier circumstances, 'I can think of no other reason why you should be here; you want to know more about Danny, who he was friendly with, that sort of thing.'

'How long had you known him?' Ian asked her, deciding to come straight to the point. He had to start somewhere and he felt he was very much groping in the dark, trying to find something, no matter how insignificant it may seem, which would give him some much-needed background.

'Not so long ago; it was about this time last year. I had finished work for the day and was just leaving when he moved into the house next door.'

'Did he tell you much about what he did before? We know he was in a rock group about four years ago; at least that was when they broke up, but not much else.'

'He did mention the group, but I don't think they were together for all that long and then shortly afterwards he set up on his own organising concerts; first in the north of England and then latterly in London.'

'Did he tell you any of their names, Miss Middleton?'

'A couple of them, yes; there were four of them altogether, but he told me about Mark Astley and the girlfriend he had at that time, Katie Brownlea.'

'But nothing about Johnnie Baker?'

'That was the name of the other one? No, I don't think he did.'

'Does the name Charlie East mean anything to you, Miss Middleton?'

'No, should it?' and as soon as she spoke, he knew she was lying. It wasn't only the speed in which she answered, but it was the way she lowered her eyes. This lady, Ian thought, looking at her more closely now, was not accustomed to telling lies, but she had. She had heard of Charlie East, but for some reason which he intended to find out, she wasn't admitting it.

'There's no reason why you should have, but we have reason to believe he could have been behind the rock group, possibly acting as their manager, although,' he added, hoping she wouldn't be smart enough to see through the fabricated half-truth, 'we are still looking for evidence to substantiate this.'

'Danny never mentioned him.'

'I see,' he said; this time she hadn't lied, but she did know Charlie East; that was for sure.

'How long have you lived in London, Miss Middleton?'

'Not all that long,' she answered, 'since two thousand and one. Before then, I was living in the South of France. In Nice.' she added.

'You were working there?'

'I was studying actually and I was fortunate to have a husband who was able to make that possible.'

'But, you're not married now?'

'No, Inspector,' she said quietly, 'I was widowed; my husband committed suicide.'

'I'm sorry.'

'Please don't be; it took me a long time to recover, first the shock and then the stigma I felt I was carrying. You have to understand, Inspector, having a husband who has taken the ultimate decision to end his life, doesn't exactly make one a comfortable dinner guest.'

'It must have been a difficult time for you.'

'It was an extremely difficult time,' she agreed, 'but I got over it, just as all my well-meaning friends told me I would. *Cela Vie*, Inspector.' she shrugged her elegant shoulders.

'You are aware, I presume, of the recent death of Mark Astley?'

'Yes,' she was being cautious now; he would have to tread more circumspectly.

'Did Mr Howarth discuss this with you?'

'I wouldn't say he discussed it with me,' she answered, 'only to say how upset he was about Mark's death.'

'Nothing else?'

'No – should he have said anything else?'

'I was wondering if he had any ideas of who may have been responsible.'

'If he had, he didn't confide in me, Inspector. All he did tell me was how they had grown up together and how distressed he'd been when he heard the news, he didn't say anything else.'

'And, Katie Brownlea?'

'Yes?'

'You mentioned that he'd told you she had been his girlfriend in the days when they were in the group; was he still in touch with her?'

'Oh, I don't think so.'

'You're sure?'

'How can anyone be sure about something like that, Inspector? All I can tell you is what I believed.'

'Have you met Katie Brownlea?'

'I think you know perfectly well I have.' she smiled at him.

'I have no grounds for surmising this, you know,' he said, 'and although I met her earlier today, she didn't mention your name.'

'So,' she asked, frowning, 'why are you here? How did you know about me?'

'It wasn't all that difficult,' it was his turn to smile now, 'I was in the Ship & Shovell earlier and a gentleman, a staunch regular there I would imagine, told me about you; he didn't mention your name, but said you were a friend of Mr Howarth's and how upset you must be at hearing about his death.'

'Oh, I see. I was jumping to conclusions; one shouldn't do that, should one?'

'Most of us are guilty of that.'

'I suppose we are.'

'Going back to the man, Charlie East, Miss Middleton.'

'Yes?' the wariness returning to her eyes.

'You've said that Danny never mentioned his name to you, but did Katie Brownlea?'

'Yes, she did.'

'I thought she may have done,' Ian said and thinking it really was like extracting blood from a stone. There was something deeply imbedded here, but to try and literally delve right down to the bottom was proving practically impossible, 'because,' he went on, 'apparently Danny had conveyed to her that he was sure that Charlie East was involved, not going so far as to say that he actually carried out the murder, but he felt he was, in some way, guilty; that was only his opinion.'

'Katie said the same to me, Inspector.'

'And, Miss Middleton,' Ian continued, 'this is why we need to find out more about Charlie East; it's police routine, and unless we do and are able to talk to him, we will not be able to eliminate him from our enquiries if it should turn out he is entirely innocent. You do understand, don't you?'

'Of course I do. But, I don't believe I can help you, Inspector.'

He was about to leave her office, his hand already on the door handle, when he turned round to face her: 'Your name, Miss Middleton?' he asked, 'After your husband died did you revert back to using your maiden name or was Middleton your husband's?'

'No, it was Prescott. He was called Walter Prescott and I thought it best with all the furore which followed his suicide, especially as I had decided to stay on in France for a while, to go back to my maiden name.'

'Not an easy decision to make.'

'Under the circumstances, Inspector, not all that difficult and I've had time to convince myself that Walter wouldn't have minded.'

*

Ian arrived back in Meadowbank shortly before seven. Brenda was in the process of packing up for the day, saying she had a dinner appointment, but taking the time to tell him that Victor York had been charged, not with the murder of Christine Saunders as they'd discussed, but with falsifying his stock figures and siphoning off drugs from his pharmacy.

'We didn't have enough evidence against him, Ian,' she explained, 'as much as I wanted to pull him in on the murder charge. I know you agree with me he's guilty, but we need much more. Meanwhile,' she added, a small smile hovering on her lips, 'he's out of action.'

'I can well imagine how he must have reacted to that.'

'In one word, Ian;' she said, 'badly, but then I didn't really expect anything else from him. He was contradicting himself with practically everything he said. For the time being I thought it wiser to leave it; eventually, we'll have what we want. Anyway, Ian, you look tired, which is hardly surprising; why don't we meet up tomorrow; perhaps after we've paid that visit to Charlie East and you can tell me what you were able to glean today.'

'That's alright by me, ma'am,' he said, 'and you're right; it's been a long day, but not entirely unproductive.'

'Good, but it can wait, can't it, Ian.'

'Of course it can,' he agreed quickly, sensing she wanted to get away; at the same time wondering, although it was none of his business, who was taking her out for dinner. There was an air of suppressed excitement about her this evening which he had never seen before and he didn't think it would be one of her female friends she would be meeting either.

'Incidentally,' she said, 'Gerald Carpenter phoned this afternoon; Johnnie Baker has been given three months.'

'We didn't expect that, did we?'

'Not really, but from what Gerald was saying it would seem they wanted to set a precedent; no doubt because of all these pharmacy robberies.'

'A word of warning, you think?'

'Could be, Ian,' Brenda said, 'but as to that, well,' she added, switching off her computer and picking up her bag from the desk, 'we are police officers and our brief is to find the culprits, apprehend them and hand over what evidence we have and the rest is up to the courts. And, as I'm sure you've thought many times, if we're not happy with the final outcome, there's nothing we can do about it; the law will have spoken!'

How right she was Ian thought, following her out of the building. All the same, given that Johnnie Baker had no previous convictions, the verdict was surprising. Also, with him in prison it was going to make it more difficult to question him about those other robberies, in particular with the one on the Tilsly estate, and the courts could very well consider he had served sufficient time with these three months.

It was too early to go home and, feeling in the need of some convivial company, Ian decided to have a drink and for a change, instead of The Market Inn, driving along to Bridge Street. The Bridge, as usual, was busy, with customers spilling out on to the narrow pavement with their drinks and, making his way over to the bar, he recognised a few familiar faces, one of them Terry Simpson. Ian had had a drink with him a number of times over the last few months and had a growing respect for him. Terry had been through a lot; that old scandal with Brian Morrison's first wife, followed immediately by the break-up of his own marriage and then coming back to Meadowbank and picking up the threads of his life again. It can't have been easy for him.

'Good evening, Ian,' Terry greeted him, 'can I get you a drink?'

'I'd like a lager please,' Ian smiled, 'I'm extremely thirsty.'

'Had a hard day?'

'Not particularly, but I've been up in London for most of it and that in itself was pretty exhausting. I don't know how you cope, Terry; driving up there every day.'

'Oh, you get used to it,' he grinned, 'besides, it's always a good feeling to get back here.'

'I know what you mean,' Ian agreed 'that's exactly how I felt as soon as I drove into the square earlier.'

'Mind you, Ian,' Terry went on, passing his beer to him, 'although I'm not saying my job can't be stressful at times, I don't think it can possibly compare with yours.'

'Oh, I don't know,' raising his glass, 'most of it's routine.'

'And long hours.'

'And long hours.' Ian grimaced, then noticing with pleasure that Jennifer Stevens from the local Planning Office had just come in. She was with her friend, Jacqueline, and both of them spotted him at the same time, Jennifer giving him a quick wave of recognition. It had been some weeks since he'd seen her and each time he had been reminded of how he longed to know her better. The attraction, even from when he'd first met her, had always been there and often he would catch her looking at him in a speculative sort of way and he had hoped she may feel the same way, so why, he wondered, looking at her now as he made to go over to them, was he prevaricating in this ridiculous fashion? Why didn't he ask her out for a meal? Nothing difficult in that. It wasn't only the fear of rejection which held him back; more that if he were to try and further their friendship, she would all too quickly, once she had experienced how unsociable his working life really was, grow weary of never knowing where he would be at any given moment. Goodness knows, Ian had seen enough marriages fail among his colleagues and invariably this had been the main reason: being constantly on call if they were working on a case; not being able to plan far ahead; having to cancel dinner arrangements at the last moment, all of which eventually led to disillusionment and spiralling down to the final irretrievable break-down of their lives together.

'He who hesitates is lost, you know, Ian.' Terry said at his side; a lop-sided smile on his face.

'You don't miss much, do you?' Ian muttered, not realising he was being so obvious and to hide his embarrassment, once he'd said hello to the two women, went back to the bar and ordered some more drinks.

'It's not such a common name, is it?' Jacqueline was saying when he re-joined them, 'but I can't help wondering if Danny Howarth was related to the couple who're buying Rodney's house.'

'He could have been, I suppose; what do you think, Ian?' Jennifer asked him.

'He was as it happens;' he said, feeling slightly uncomfortable. It was always like this when knowledge he'd acquired at work encroached into his private life, all of which meant he was unable to act naturally and had to decide how much he could or should say, 'he was Cyril Howarth's son; from a previous marriage.' he added.

'Sorry, Ian,' she smiled at him sympathetically, 'I think we'll understand if you'd rather not say anymore.'

'No, it's alright,' he said, 'I'm not giving anything away which isn't already fairly common knowledge.'

'He was in here last week.' Terry said.

'Who;' Jacqueline asked him, 'Mr Howarth?'

'No, Danny. It was Isobel who recognised him actually, from when he was in Meadowbank some years back; this was while I was still in the middle-east.'

'Of course, there was a photograph of him in one of the Sunday papers; he was a good-looking guy I thought and reminded me of Gilbert O'Sullivan.'

'That's exactly what Isobel said,' Terry commented, 'strangely enough, he was in a rock group then.'

'Apparently, he was still in the music business;' Ian supplied; another piece of non-sensitive information he could mention, remembering they'd said that in the newspaper report, 'organising concerts; that sort of thing.'

'I wonder if Charlie East is in the same line of business.' Terry said thoughtfully.

'Why should you think that?' Ian asked him, his interest quickening and unable to believe his luck in hearing Charlie East's name mentioned.

'Because they came in here together last Wednesday, that's why. I thought then they were an oddly matched pair, to be friends, I mean, so perhaps it was through their work they knew each other.'

'Possibly.' and that was all Ian would permit himself to say. This was a further step forward; confirmation that Danny did meet up with Charlie East. What did the pair really talk about he wondered, certainly nothing to do with a joint interest in the music industry, that was for sure, if he was to believe what Katie Brownlea had told him and then there was Danny's girlfriend, Myra Middleton. She was definitely hiding something about Charlie and the more Ian thought about the conversation he had with her, the more he was coming to think whatever it was didn't concern Danny Howarth. It was quite telling the way Charlie East's name kept occurring; all it needed now was to hear that he knew Victor York. That would give Brenda what she was looking for to proceed further into Christine Saunders' murder. Hoping now they would change the subject and, Jennifer, who had been watching him closely for the last couple of minutes, intuitively came to the rescue.

'I see they're getting on with the riverside development across the road; I guess at the rate they're going, they should have completed everything before the end of the year.'

'I hope you're right, Jennifer,' Jacqueline said, 'we already have two or three clients seriously interested in some of the houses.'

'Good business, eh?' Terry smiled at her.

'Well,' she returned his smile, 'put it this way, Terry; the buyers will get the house of their dreams and everyone else involved will receive a slice of the cake.'

'Neat!' Jennifer laughed.

*

The restaurant in The Royal Oak was busier than usual for a Monday evening, with many of the tables being taken up by a seminar being held in the hotel over the following few days, but Mike Harper, having booked into The Royal Oak earlier that afternoon had already anticipated this and had taken the precaution of reserving a table for Brenda and himself. She was only ten minutes late arriving, but he didn't mind. He, of all people, should understand the difficulties of trying to leave work without being held up at the last moment. Mike had lost count of the times this had happened to him, even more so when he had been transferred to New Scotland Yard, but having, over the years, built up a veneer of tolerance. In many respects he could appreciate Brenda's position as Chief Inspector in Meadowbank could mean she was in even more demand than she would be in London, where there was always a significant back-up among fellow officers.

'I'm so sorry, Mike,' she said, kissing him on the cheek, 'but I got side-tracked.'

'Don't apologise, Brenda. There's no need; honestly.'

'Phew! Life at times does seem to be one long unrelenting rush; not that I need to tell you that.'

'Relax,' he smiled, pulling out the chair opposite, 'I've ordered champagne. I trust that meets with your approval?'

'Champagne; how marvellous! Sounds like a celebration.'

'The lady's worth it,' he said, 'so, let us enjoy it, but first of all, I haven't asked how you are. It seems an age since I saw you last; phone calls are not quite the same, are they?'

'I know they're not, but –'

'– don't say another word; I understand.'

The champagne arrived and poured expertly by David Johnson, the head waiter, followed by the menus. Mike made the suggestion they have the rack of lamb with Jersey potatoes and fresh garden peas; all of which she was eager to go along with. He wanted this dinner to be a special one, not only for her, but for them both. There were a number of things he wanted to say, but the atmosphere and the timing had to be right. He had known Brenda since they'd been at cadet college; they had still been in their teens, far too young and immature to think seriously about any future together and then, as was inevitable, their careers gradually took over. Both of them had been ambitious, although Brenda had made the decision to stay in her home town, while he had chosen instead to be in London. They had tried to stay in touch but it had proved impossible and eventually and sadly, they had drifted apart: he to marry which ended disastrously and Brenda somehow, although he didn't know how, a pretty woman like her, had so far avoided marriage and had, instead, reached the rank of chief inspector at such a young age.

'You're looking exceedingly thoughtful, Mike.'

'Sorry, I don't mean to be. I'm reflecting, that's all.'

'On what was or, on what might have been?' she smiled gently at him; she always did have an uncanny knack of knowing what he was thinking.

'Clever, perceptive woman.'

'It doesn't do to dwell too much on the past, Mike.'

'You're right, of course.' he said, raising his glass to her, 'Here's to us, Brenda; the future.'

'To us and,' she added, still smiling, 'the future.'

'You haven't asked why I'm here, in Meadowbank.'

'No, I haven't, have I? So, Mike Harper, why are you here?'

'Brenda, the last think I want to be this evening is to come over heavy. I've done a fair amount of thinking over these last few months and, at the risk of scaring you off, I would like us to try and get to know each other again.'

'We're a lot older now.' was the only comment she made.

'Twenty years; is that so long?'

'Not really.' she answered, taking a sip of her champagne.

'So, what do you think?'

'There's nothing I would like better, Mike; you probably realise that, but –' she hesitated for a second, '- I suppose it's this distance thing. You're in London and I'm here. How can we possibly see more of each other?'

'Have you thought anymore about asking for a transfer?' he asked her tentatively, not wanting to put any pressure on her, 'We did talk about it back in January, but I haven't liked to mention it to you again. I do realise it would be a big decision to make.'

'I have thought about it, Mike, quite a bit as a matter of fact and I do think it's time I moved away from here. Apart from my job, there is nothing to keep me in Meadowbank. Also, I believe I would enjoy the challenge; I've often felt stymied in this town as I've already mentioned to you.'

'Perhaps I'm being selfish,' he said quietly, 'hoping you would make such an important change, even going so far as to consider applying for a transfer down here myself; to Winchester or Southampton.'

'No, Mike, please. That wouldn't be right; I'm sure of it. Think about this seriously; would you really be happy living and working away from London?'

'I'd be with you though.'

'That's no answer Mike Harper,' she said softly, 'and you know it.'

'Okay, I'll hold my hand up. I was prevaricating; I apologise and you're right, Brenda, I wouldn't be entirely happy and I would be even more unhappy if that discontentment would affect our relationship.'

'There you are then. You've answered your own question. If, in your honest opinion, consider I would fit into the city life, and provided I was fortunate enough to be working right in the hub of things, I'm prepared to take the chance.'

'You would?'

'I've just said so, haven't I?' but she was smiling at him.

'Wow!'

'Is that all you can say?'

'I'm not going to let you go this time, Brenda and that is a promise.' his expression instantly becoming serious.

'Shall we have another glass of this delicious champagne on the strength of that?'

Chapter Fifteen

Ian pulled up outside Charlie East's house in Stockbridge Road; Brenda, from where she was sitting in the passenger seat, had a clear view of the property, her first impression being that it had a deserted look about it. The Venetian blinds at all the windows on the ground and first floors had been dawn and the doors to the double garage closed, all made it fairly obvious to her that Charlie East wasn't at home. One look at Ian's doleful expression told her he was thinking the same. Nevertheless and realising, without having to say anything to each other, they would have to go through the motions of ringing the bell, no matter how fruitless, they stepped out of the car and on to the pavement, only to find when they reached the gate that it was securely locked.

Momentarily stymied, accepting they had no option but to return to the Station, a woman, pushing a buggy and with another young child at her side, emerged from the house next door and, closing her gate behind her, came hurrying towards them. Brenda instantly recognised her; she was David Johnson's daughter: Sue she was called, although Brenda didn't know her married name.

'Chief Inspector Masters.' she called out, slightly out of breath.

'Hello, Sue,' Brenda said, 'I knew you had married, but I'm sorry, I don't know your husband's name.'

'It's Jones,' she explained, 'I married the oldest son; Barry.'

Brenda went on to introduce Ian to her and asking if she had met her new neighbour, although aware that Charlie East had only been in Meadowbank for a short time.

'We have, yes,' she said, 'we're keeping an eye on his house for him, actually. He left the keys with Barry and we thought it best to lock his gate. There's nothing wrong, is there?'

'We were hoping to have a word with him; it's in connection with a case we're working on.' Brenda answered obliquely.

'Charlie's on holiday, Chief Inspector,' she answered, 'he left here on Friday morning and I don't think he'll be back for at least another couple of weeks.'

'We hadn't realised,' Brenda said, 'I don't suppose you know where he's gone?'

'Well,' Sue gave a rueful smile, 'he did tell me the name of the place; it's in France, you see, and never having heard of the town before, I'm afraid I can't remember the name. I have been racking my brains since Sunday, actually,' she went on, 'because a friend of his who had also been hoping to see him, came to our house, but again I wasn't much help.'

'A friend,' keeping her voice casual, which wasn't easy when every nerve was telling her that this could be of importance to them, 'did she give you her name, Sue?'

'It wasn't a woman, Chief Inspector,' she answered, 'it was Mr York from the pharmacy. Mind you, it wasn't until after he'd gone I remembered who he was. I don't really know him; we always use White's.' she added.

Back in the car again, Ian at the wheel, they drove the short distance back to the square. He took his eyes briefly from the road to look at Brenda: 'Did you expect the caller to be a woman, ma'am?'

'As it happens,' she smiled at him, 'I thought it may have been Felicity Carter.'

'We have rather neglected her, haven't we?'

'You could be right,' she agreed, 'but as we know she was told on Sunday that her boyfriend had been arrested and I thought, wrongly as it turns out, that she may have been trying to get in touch with Charlie. After all, he appears to know Johnnie Baker; well enough to have a drink with him, that is, and she could have thought he may be able to do something to help.'

'And before then he had already left Meadowbank.'

'Exactly.'

'He does seem to have the ability of making himself scarce, doesn't he, but do you think he'll come back, ma'am?'

'I would say so. He's no fool, Ian. He knows we have nothing on him and if he did decide to stay away, well, it would immediately alert us that he had something to hide. No, I think he'll be back and somehow I rather doubt he's gone to France as he told his neighbour.'

'Why do you say that?'

'Because,' Brenda said, 'the man is a controller; there's no doubt he's up to something. I would suggest primarily it's drugs; that would be the most lucrative after all. Also, if you remember that profile on him, not only has he been able to avoid the law on more than one occasion and that's only as far as we're aware, it would seem he always gets someone else to do his dirty work. Perhaps that's the secret of his so-called success, Ian, although it does depend on the way you view it, so I think he's probably in England; London most likely, where he can keep an eye on what's happening.'

'We have the link we've been waiting for with this latest development; Victor York knew him.'

'That's right,' she nodded, 'it sounded to me as though Victor York was getting more than a little anxious. Charlie East has been in Meadowbank for a month and from what we've managed to pick up; those two haven't been seen in public together. This town is very much a village, but I don't need to tell you that, Ian.'

'And, ma'am, those drugs we found on his premises; compared to the amount siphoned off this year, it was a relatively small cache. He had to have had someone he could off-load them to each time and Charlie East seems a likely candidate.'

'That's the way I'm thinking, Ian.' Brenda said quietly.

By now, they were outside the Station; being fortunate enough to find a parking space not too far from the main door: 'I'll write up my report from yesterday, ma'am, but there is one piece of news which you should find interesting.'

'Yes?'

'Danny Howarth did meet up with Charlie East early on Wednesday evening; they were in The Bridge.'

'Well, well,' unable to keep the smile from her voice, 'that circle of ours is every nearly complete.'

*

It was after nine that night when Brenda called Ian. This, in itself, was unusual; she had always tried to avoid phoning him after they'd finished for the day, but what she had to say was, she considered, worth it, knowing in advance Ian wouldn't object.

'First of all, Ian,' she said immediately he'd answered, 'I apologise for phoning you so late -'

'- that's perfectly alright, ma'am,' he was quick to reassure her, 'I've just finished watching the news, and as usual nothing but doom and gloom; I was about to make myself a bit of supper and then, perhaps, have an early night.'

'You'll get your early night, Ian; I can promise you that,' she said, 'although we'll need to have an early start tomorrow.'

'Yes?'

'I've read your report,' she went on, 'makes interesting reading, especially Danny Howarth's girlfriend; her background, I mean.'

'She knows Charlie East,' Ian said, 'I'm sure about that.'

'Quite well, I would say, Ian, could even go as far back as their student days and might very well prove relevant to this case, especially if as you suggested she showed a reluctance to be more forthcoming.'

'You have some ideas, ma'am?'

'I didn't, Ian, until I got a call from New Scotland Yard a few minutes ago. I'd contacted them earlier,' she explained, 'and I was right,' she continued, 'Charlie East is in London.'

'Really?'

'Yes,' she said, 'apparently, when he bought the house in Meadowbank he still held on to his property in Chelsea and, without making it obvious the Yard confirmed he's been staying there since the end of last week. They're keeping a watch on him and if he should leave, they'll be back in touch with us.'

'So, where do we go from here?'

'Well,' she paused to take a deep breath, 'I had to get in touch with Surrey constabulary; after all the murder of Danny Howarth is their case.'

'I know.'

'They're being very co-operative, but let's face it,' she said, 'this is what it's all about in a crime of this nature: we've got three murders to solve and each of them occurring in different parts of the country.'

'You're including the death of Christine Saunders?'

'I am, yes. You agree?'

'Of course.'

'Alright then; as I was saying, we all have to work together on this and as I've thought, right from the start of our enquiries, our man, namely Charlie East, is the main instigator. Need I say anymore?'

'Not really.'

'Good,' Brenda said, 'so, once again, we are in agreement. We drive up to London first thing in the morning; I don't think for the time being we can do very much more from here.'

'You want to meet Myra Middleton?'

'You're right; I do. I sincerely hope I'm wrong, but I believe that lady could be putting herself in an extremely vulnerable position.'

'You mean,' he asked, 'she could be blaming Charlie East for her husband committing suicide and now for Danny Howarth's murder?'

'You'd come to that conclusion as well, then?'

'I began to think that as soon as she mentioned her husband. She is distraught; there's no doubt about that and as you've said she could be in danger; not only to herself, but to Charlie East.'

'Alright, Ian, I'm taking on board what you're saying and you could very well be right and this is why we need to move quickly. This whole case is about to break and I feel when it does it won't, for a change, be here, in Meadowbank, but very likely in London. We do have three key people there already, Ian.'

'Three, ma'am?'

'Yes, Charlie East, Myra Middleton and –'

'– Katie Brownlea.' he put in quickly.

'Spot on, Ian. That is, if she's still in London and hasn't gone back up north, but somehow I rather think she will be.'

*

It was now Wednesday, and Katie had thought by this time she would have been back home, acting the dutiful wife and waiting for Ben to return from Singapore, but it didn't turn out like that. It wasn't only talking to Inspector Ash on Monday, although she had found that unnerving enough, waiting for him to refer to her time with the rock group and even when he didn't, continuing to worry, but it was more than that. She hadn't disliked him; he had been easy to talk to and not many more years older than herself either. He had listened while she had done her best to explain why she had decided to drive down to London to try and find out why Danny hadn't been in touch with her as he had promised, and he hadn't once prompted her or, after she had finished, asked her many questions. He had, it's true, shown an added spark of interest when she mentioned Charlie East's name, but again, hadn't pressed her; hadn't asked how well she knew him and seemed satisfied when she told him she hadn't even met Charlie. Katie had intentionally not mentioned Myra's name, deciding there was no point. But, yesterday afternoon and again in the evening, when she had tried to phone her on the mobile number Myra had given her, there'd been no answer, she began to question the wisdom of this. And, again this morning, still not getting any response and unable to stand the suspense any longer, she took a bus to Trafalgar Square and walked along what was becoming a familiar route to Myra's office.

The girl she had seen on Saturday was in reception and looked up from behind her desk with a vague expression of half-recognition. No doubt wondering where she had seen her before Katie thought and she asked if it was possible to see Miss Middleton.

'She won't be back until Friday.' Brief and to the point; obviously not given to any form of niceties, Katie concluded, and zilch training in social graces either. 'I can make an appointment for you for next week, if you want,' she continued, 'but not until Friday at the earliest. I've had to rearrange all of Miss Middleton's appointments for this week.'

'She's not ill, is she?' Katie asked, but not expecting to extract anything further from her.

'Not as far as I know.' came the predictable response.

'I've been trying to call her on her mobile,' Katie said, although realising she was probably wasting her breath; there was very little else she was going to get from this apology for a receptionist. 'but without any luck. Do you happen to have her home telephone number?' she asked her, 'It is rather important I speak to her.'

'Sorry,' she said; her whole expression devoid of any interest, 'I only have her mobile number, so I can't help you, can I?'

'When did you last see her?' Katie asked, somewhat gratified to find the direct question had by some miracle penetrated.

'Oh, Monday afternoon, actually,' she drawled, her heavily outlined eyes focused at last on Katie, 'it was after she had the visit from the police.'

'The police?' knowing that she was very likely playing into this silly girl's hands, but she couldn't help it. The very word 'police' had acted as a catalyst, with a number of connotations instantly occurring to her and each one more outrageous than the other.

'Yes; a really good-looking guy; an *Inspector* of Police,' she emphasised and,' obviously making the most of what she had to say, 'he was with Miss Middleton for a very long time; in her office, naturally.' she added, obviously miffed not to have been able to hear what they had been talking about.

This had to be Inspector Ash; in fact, who else, Katie thought, but how on earth had he found out about Myra?

'Look,' Katie said, moving closer to the desk, 'I know this is probably none of my business, but I am worried about Miss Middleton.'

'Are you?' the bland expression, this time unexpected and lacking even a token of friendliness.

'I am, yes,' Katie replied, this time choosing her words carefully. Perhaps she had been wrong and the girl's reaction was the way she behaved with everyone who came into the office, but even so, she should perhaps be more circumspect in the way she phrased her questions. That dark shadow of Charlie East was never very far away these days; she was probably over-reacting, but better to watch what she said all the same. Charlie's tentacles stretched far; Danny had told her that also, and as far-fetched as it might seem, how did she know that Charlie East wasn't aware of Myra's existence? This is crazy thinking, Katie concluded; really crazy, she had absolutely no grounds for surmising anything of the sort. Okay; Myra had received a visit from, presumably Inspector Ash, and the talk with him had further distressed her and she'd quite simply decided to take a few days off work.

'I've been wondering when I saw you before,' the girl said, 'I spoke to you on Saturday, didn't I?'

'That's right,' Katie said, 'I was looking for a friend of mine -'

'- Danny Howarth,' she interrupted, animation in her expression for the first time, 'you were looking for him, weren't you?'

'I was.'

'He was murdered, you know.'

'I do know that.' Katie said quietly and with a supreme effort trying not to lose her temper. She had to be one of the most crass and insensitive people she had ever had the misfortune to meet. Poor Myra, having someone like this working for her.

'Well,' she shrugged, 'as I've already told you, I can't help you. You'll just have to wait until Friday to see Miss Middleton.'

'Do you have her home address?'

'I might.' the return of the drawl; honestly, this girl was behaving unbelievably, far over-stepping the role of receptionist; her manner having changed in a matter of seconds to one of insolence.

'If you have,' Katie said, continuing to keep her voice level, 'I would be grateful if you could give it to me.'

'I'm afraid that's against company policy,' she glibly replied, 'it isn't allowed to divulge the addresses of colleagues and certainly not the address of an *employer*.' Why, Katie wondered, totally puzzled by this time, was she being so damned rude? And, she thought, as for this company policy stuff, that really is a load of rubbish! Was the girl merely being obstructive or didn't she want Katie to know where Myra lived.

'I understand,' Katie said, tired now of playing games and moving towards the door, 'but I'm sure I'll find where Miss Middleton lives from someone more obliging.' And, before the girl had a chance to make any kind of response, Katie had opened the door and was back outside on the pavement and walking rapidly away from the building. What an out and out cow! And then she remembered the girl telling her on Saturday that she had only recently started working for Myra; last week she had said, wondering how she'd managed to get the job as receptionist, especially as it was plainly obvious she lacked the necessary qualities. Katie knew from experience, when she had been to any employment agency to look for work, how detailed their application forms had been and how long it used to take to complete. Perhaps it's different in London she thought, trying to put the last ten minutes out of her mind, as she got closer to the Ship & Shovell and to what she hoped was normality.

'Hello, darling,' Polly greeted her as soon as she was inside; she had no problem with her memory, Katie was relieved to find, 'you look a bit hot and bothered.'

'Oh,' she tried to smile, 'I've just had a rather unpleasant encounter, but I'll be alright.'

'That's terrible,' she sympathised, 'I'm really sorry to hear that, darling. Anyway, what would you like; something to buck you up?'

'A white wine, please; that should do the trick.'

'When you were in here on Saturday,' Polly said, reaching up for a glass, 'you were asking about poor Danny, weren't you?'

'That's right; I was.'

'I can't tell you how terribly upset we all were when we heard about what happened to him. You must have been as well?'

'I was, yes. It was tragic.'

'Quite tragic, darling,' she said, filling the glass and handing it to her, 'he was such a terrific guy. Really talented too, and no side to him either.' she added.

'I've been trying to get in touch with Danny's girlfriend,' Katie explained, taking a grateful sip of her drink, 'but I've heard she's taken a few days off.'

'I'm not surprised; she must be utterly devastated. They were such a lovely couple. Came in here quite often they did.'

'I don't suppose you have any idea where Myra lives, do you?' Katie asked her.

'I don't know exactly,' Polly said, 'all I do know is that she recently bought one of those apartments in a converted old mansion in Holborn. I think the apartment block is called the Lincoln Apartments, probably because it's not far from Lincoln's Inn Fields.'

'I should be able to find it alright.'

'You won't have any problems,' she assured her, 'and it's best if Myra has someone with her at a terrible time like this. When you see her, darling, tell her how sorry we all were to hear about Danny and that she's very welcome to call in whenever she feels like a chat.'

As Polly had said, Katie soon found the Lincoln Apartments, only a relatively short walk from the bus stop at Holborn Circus. A woman, outside the main door, polishing the plaque, looked up when she saw her.

'Can I help you, dear?' she asked.

'Well, I hope so,' she answered, surprised how helpful most people were in London; not in the least standoffish as they had often been described from where she lived up north, 'I'm looking for a friend of mine, Myra Middleton; I've been told she lives here.'

'That's right, dear, she does; the third floor, in fact. I should know,' she smiled broadly, 'I keep her apartment spick and span for her. But,' she went on, 'you've just missed her.'

'Oh, that's a pity.'

'Why not phone her, dear? I'm sure you'll have a mobile; everyone seems to have one these days. Even I have one, but only because my son bought it for me.' she added.

'I've been trying, but I can't get any answer. All I can do is call round later.'

'You do that, dear. I've no idea where she went, of course, because she didn't tell me. Mind you, don't get the idea I'm the nosey type, because I'm not,' she explained, 'but I was out here, doing my bit of polishing, when she got in a taxi and it so happened I heard where she wanted to go.'

'Not to the airport I hope,' Kate said, although not really believing Myra would have been, but more to avoid asking the woman directly.

'Not unless they've moved it,' laughing at her own joke, 'no, dear, she asked the driver to take her to Cheltenham Terrace and I know that Cheltenham Terrace happens to be in Chelsea. Probably visiting someone.' she suggested, returning to the plaque and giving it a final polish, 'Must get on, dear; I can't stand here chatting all day. Anyway, I hope you're able to see your friend later.'

Katie watched the woman walk up the short flight of steps and on into the building; the glass swing doors closing behind her. For several seconds Katie remained where she was, standing quite still, staring at, without actually registering, the steady stream of pedestrians hurrying past her, while her mind did somersaults. Charlie East once owned a property in Cheltenham Terrace. This could not be a coincidence; it couldn't be. Myra must be on her way to see him. Katie tried to make some sense of the way her thoughts were going; when she had given her Charlie's name on Sunday, Myra had not said she knew him, but she must have, otherwise how could she have discovered where she might find him. Danny wouldn't have told her; he had found out that Charlie was now living in Meadowbank, so why would he have mentioned the house in Chelsea? It didn't make sense. And then, another memory from Sunday surfaced. It had been when Myra was about to leave the coffee shop; she had already risen to her feet, picked up her handbag and said something, the possible importance of it not registering at the time, but now, Katie was able to read into what those few words could have meant: "I was serious when I told you to be careful, Katie," she had said, "Charlie is a dangerous man." She had said this so emphatically, as though she knew it to be true; not only because she thought he may have had something to do with Danny's death, or Mark's either, if it came to that. Also, it had been the personal way she had spoken his name. If she had never heard of him before, surely she would have said that Charlie East is a dangerous man; not Charlie is a dangerous man?

She couldn't spend the remainder of the morning like this. She had to do something, but what could she possibly do? Apart from Myra, she had only confided in one other person so far, by now totally discounting what she had said to Johnnie last week, and that was Inspector Ash, but he would be back in Meadowbank and she was here, in the centre of London, facing a problem she had no idea of how she was going to tackle. She could always behave like an ostrich; go and have lunch and come back later in the hope that Myra would have returned or, the simple solution and the easiest; to drive back up to Manchester and forget about everything. Put it all out of her mind and get her own life sorted out. But, she knew she could never do that; she had liked Myra and the fact that she may have, while not lying, withheld the truth from her, must have meant she had a very good reason. Also, when she had last seen her on Sunday, although she had calmed down a little, she wanted to make sure she was alright, more especially now, as according to the receptionist it looked as though Inspector Ash had been to see her and this visit may have intensified the trauma she was suffering over losing Danny. She couldn't desert her, therefore she must think of something.

*

Myra paid off the taxi outside number twelve Cheltenham Terrace and walked up to the front door and rang the bell. She didn't have long to wait before the door swung open and the man she hadn't seen for almost fourteen years was standing in front of her with the remembered sardonic expression on his still-handsome face, which, characteristically, was giving nothing away.

'Myra Prescott!'

'I'm Myra Middleton now, Charlie,' she said, 'after Walter died I went back to using my maiden name.

'And, why,' he asked, 'has it taken you so long to visit an old friend?'

'Unless you wish me to conduct this conversation, which, incidentally, could take some time, standing like this on your doorstep, I really think it would be much better if you were to invite me in.'

'Of course, Myra,' he said, stepping to one side and gesturing for her to go in, 'that is, if you're not afraid to enter the lion's den?' his laugh, hollow and forced, and which in the early days when she had been young and naive enough to have been in awe of him, would have instantly punctured her built-up confidence, reducing her no doubt to a nervous wreck, but not anymore. Charlie East had lost his power as far as she was concerned. For the very first time in her life, Myra felt she was in control of the situation and one, not contrived by anyone else, but by her and this was exactly how she wanted it to be.

'You said it, Charlie,' creating a smile which she was sure would appear equally as false as his laugh, 'I didn't. Quite frankly, I never did see you as a king; of a jungle or otherwise.'

He made no comment and led her into a room leading directly off from the hall: a large, well-proportioned room; highly polished wood-block flooring; pale walls with few paintings, all of them water colours and two high casement windows facing the street which was quiet, with very little traffic and looking across towards a private garden where she could see behind the dark-green painted railings a clump of apple trees, their branches thick with blossom. A peaceful scene, far removed from her inner turmoil. In spite of her earlier bravado, she had neglected to make allowances for how she would react to seeing Charlie again after all these years and for several seconds her mind travelled back along that painful road: from the day after the trial when he had made a speedy and predictable exit, leaving, or so he had thought, no clues as to where he was heading, right up to when she had found Walter; only a matter of days from when he had been released from prison, slumped across his desk in their study in Nice. A self-inflicted drug overdose, they had told her; taken while he was mentally disorientated and suffering from a deep and chronic depression for which he'd refused to seek medical help.

'Would you like a drink, Myra?' he asked her, moving over to a cabinet in the corner of the room and taking down a bottle of whisky from one of the glass shelves.

'No thanks, Charlie,' she said, 'this isn't a social call.'

'I didn't believe for one moment it was,' he said mildly, his hand hovering above the bottle, 'but I would have thought a drink for old times' sake wouldn't have gone amiss. You used to enjoy a scotch, Myra, if my memory is correct.'

'Normally,' she answered and not sitting down as he'd suggested; not from anything he'd said to her, but in the way he'd waved, obviously wearing his hospitality hat, to one of the four olive green armchairs placed in an obvious designer-like way along the edges of a fringed Chinese rug, 'I would have liked nothing better, but now, is not the right time.'

'Very well, but I take it you won't mind if I have one?'

'I don't mind at all, Charlie.'

Myra watched him as he poured a generous measure into a crystal glass and with the same unfathomable expression on his face, took a deep sip of the amber liquid. Although she had no idea what he was thinking or what he was going to say next, there was something she could interpret quite clearly: Charlie East was nervous. Incredible although this might be, she could tell by his body language she had unnerved him and from past experiences when she had been in his company, that in itself, was no mean feat. He really had no idea why she was there; why she had arrived, unannounced, after all this time. There was a tautness along his jaw line which there was no way he could disguise, neither did she miss the way now and again he would look away from her, as though reluctant to have any eye contact. So far, she had an advantage over the man she had loathed for so long and she intended to make the most of it.

'I presume,' he said at last, lifting the glass once more to his lips, 'you're going to get round to explaining why you're here?'

'Charlie,' she said, giving him no indication she had heard him, or even that she had any interest in what he had just said. If he was as nervous as she thought, that was his problem, not hers. She had recovered from those first moments of unease of having come face to face with him again and allowing herself to be dragged back, in memory only it was true, but she had been on the verge of wavering, of changing her mind, but she'd had a new burst of strength. She would see this through; she had to.

215

'when Walter committed suicide,' she went on, 'for a very long time I held you responsible.'

'Why? You were in the court that day; you heard all the evidence. Walter was guilty; there was never any doubt about that. Therefore,' he shrugged, in exactly the way she knew he would, 'Walter had to pay the price for being found out. Five years of imprisonment, Myra; not so long in the full scale of things.'

'To some people, you could be right, Charlie,' she said quietly, 'but you, like a modern-day Houdini managed to extricate yourself. You were just as guilty as Walter and you know it.'

'Of course I was; that should go without saying, but they didn't have sufficient evidence to support their original charges against me and -'

'- and you got off scot-free.'

'Succinctly put, Myra. I got off scot-free.'

'Exactly as you had before that time; in Hong Kong.'

'My word, you have been doing your homework.'

'Over the years, Charlie, I have made it my business to find out all I could about you and your dubious and crooked past.'

'Strong words.'

'They may be strong words, but they happen to be the truth.'

'So what; they're history now.' another shrug, 'Why, may I ask, are you getting so excited about all of this retrograde stuff? Pointless, if you ask me?'

'I'm not asking you, Charlie. Not only have I looked into your background, even since those first days when you and Walter were in college, I have known exactly where you've been, although I must admit this latest move of yours to a town in the middle of Hampshire did manage to escape me, but somehow I didn't really believe you would have permanently left London. You're a city man, Charlie. You need to be in the centre of what is going on. You would never bury yourself in the country; just not your scene at all.'

'You haven't answered my question, Myra?'

'Which was?'

'Why all this sudden interest in my existence; why not let sleeping dogs lie. Walter's been dead for thirteen years now; you've made a new life for youself. What does any of this old shit matter?'

'Alright, Charlie, I'll answer your question. Up to a few days ago, this 'old shit' as you so eloquently described it, was no longer important to me and had, in fact, reduced itself to something which once happened in my life, but then I lost Danny; a man I loved dearly and I believe you are responsible; whether directly or not makes no difference to me.'

'Ah.'

'Yes, as you say, ah!'

'Now, we are getting to the crux of your dilemma, Myra.'

'This is not *my* dilemma, Charlie; I would prefer to describe it as *your* dilemma!'

'You don't say?' sarcasm now coming to the fore.

'I do say, Charlie. What I would like to know is why you decided in your infinite wisdom,' she, too, could exercise a certain degree of sarcasm which, even to her ears, sounded unpleasant, 'to arrange Danny's tragic death -'

'- just a minute, Myra -'

'- No,' she interrupted, 'I will not wait a minute. You wanted Danny dead; he was a threat to you; to your miserable low-life and, like anyone else who posed a threat to you and your self-elevated and false position in society, had to be destroyed. Danny went to Meadowbank to find you last Wednesday and I believe he did and the last time he was seen alive was late that night outside his house in London.'

'You are talking nonsense, Myra; absolute nonsense.'

'Am I?'

'Of course you are. What you've been saying is pure fabrication and entirely without any foundation whatsoever. It's obvious to me that the death of this man has affected your reasoning, Myra. Surely, you must realise you're not behaving rationally and to think I had anything to do with his death is, quite frankly, ludicrous.'

'I have never been more rational in my life, Charlie. I came here to extract something from you and I'm not leaving until I achieve that!'

'What are you talking about, woman? Extract what?'

'Extract an admission that you were involved in what happened to Danny.'

'I think, Myra, before you say anything further, it would be best that you leave. This whole conversation is absolutely pointless.'

'Perhaps then,' she said, unzipping her bag and taking out Walter's Berretta; the gun she had found among his personal possessions shortly after he had died, never believing she would ever actually be doing what she was at this moment; pointing it directly at Charlie East. 'this will further our pointless conversation, Charlie.'

'Are you mad?'

'No, quite sane, in fact.'

'Give me that gun, Myra; you don't know what you're doing.'

'Don't tell me what to do, Charlie. Now, it's my turn; either you give me the information I've asked for, or I will kill you.' she said, at the same time releasing the safety catch. It took her several moments to realise what had happened, but within seconds she felt herself slipping and then falling down, hitting her back against one of the chairs. Charlie was standing over her with Walter's gun in his hand and this time it was being pointed at her.

'Right,' he snarled, his whole face distorted with hatred, 'Get up! Slowly and believe me, I won't hesitate; I will most definitely fire this gun and I won't miss either. It will be self-defence, Myra. Remember, you threatened me and no-one, I repeat; no-one threatens me and lives! Now, get to your feet!'

As she pulled herself upright, the front door bell rang.

He didn't move, neither did he take his eyes away from her: 'Now,' he hissed, 'walk over there, away from the window and stand next to the wall.'

She did as he said, noticing that the rug had shifted and realising that was what he'd done; he'd caught her unawares when she had been fumbling with the safety catch and nudged the rug with his foot, causing her to lose her balance.

'Aren't you going to answer whoever is at your door, Charlie?'

'Shut up!' as the bell rang for a second time.

Chapter Sixteen

Ian was on the approach road to Chelsea Bridge, having, since leaving the motorway, been trying, and failing to overtake a souped-up and aging Vauxhall Cavalier, when his mobile rang.

'Damn!' he muttered under his breath, at last being able to pull out and overtake the Vauxhall.

'It's alright, Ian,' Brenda said, 'I'll take the call for you.'

'Thank you, ma'am,' he answered, passing the mobile to her, 'I don't know where all this traffic comes from!'

'Neither do I.' she smiled sympathetically, grateful he'd suggested before they left Meadowbank earlier that morning that he did the driving, and pressing the on-switch of his mobile.

'Hello,' the voice; young and barely audible above the continuous roar of vehicles on either side of them, 'it's Katie Brownlea, here.'

'Hello, Katie,' Brenda said, 'Inspector Ash is driving at the moment, but go ahead; that is, if you can; the reception isn't good.'

'Oh,' a crackling pause and Brenda began to wonder if they'd been cut off and then Katie was back, accompanied by so much static it was almost impossible to hear her: 'I'm really worried about Myra Middleton,' she said, 'Danny's girlfriend. I believe Inspector Ash spoke to her on Monday when he was here –' more crackling; louder this time, then just as suddenly, it went and the line cleared, '- were you able to hear me?'

'Just about,' Brenda answered, 'you're concerned about Miss Middleton, but first of all, Katie where exactly are you?'

'I'm still in London; not far from Holborn tube station. I've been trying to get in touch with her, but she hasn't been answering her phone and then, a few moments ago, I was told she'd taken a taxi to Cheltenham Terrace –' another pause and this had nothing to do with the bad line.

'Yes, Katie?' Brenda prompted her.

'Well,' Katie went on and Brenda could hear the long intake of breath as she spoke, 'Charlie East used to live there. That's when I started to get really worried. I'm sorry, -' running out of breath and giving Brenda the impression she was anxious to say what she wanted to before the connection went altogether.

'It's alright, Katie,' Brenda said, 'I managed to hear all of that. We're not far from Cheltenham Terrace; it shouldn't take us more than five or six minutes to get there.'

'What should I do?' Katie's voice now fast disappearing, 'I can't stay around here not knowing whether Myra is alright or not.'

'Holborn is some distance from here,' Brenda said, at the same time trying to decide what would be best. They needed to talk to her, but their main priority was to reach Charlie East's house, remembering what Ian had said the other day; that not only could Myra Middleton be in danger, but equally, Charlie East. She had yet to meet the woman; therefore it was impossible to gauge the extent of her grief over the death of her boyfriend. How much was this tied up, she wondered, with the friendship she and her late husband would have had with Charlie and which had ended so disastrously. 'I think it best you make your way over here, Katie,' she said, 'and I would suggest you take the tube; it will be more direct. We have your mobile number, remember, and if we need to, we can always get in touch with you.'

'I hope nothing has happened to her,' Katie said, 'Myra never told me she knew Charlie.'

'We're doing the best we can,' Brenda said, trying to reassure her, but how could she when they had no idea what was going on. By now, having crossed the bridge and turned left into Royal Hospital Road, the traffic, she was glad to see, had thinned out considerably, and by the time she had switched off Ian's mobile, they were in Cheltenham Terrace.

'You got the gist of that, Ian?'

'I think so,' he said, pulling up a few hundred yards before the house.

'Before we go along there,' she said, taking out her own mobile from her shoulder bag, 'I'll give Chief Inspector Harper a ring; if Charlie East has had any visitors, he should have already have been told,' and dialling Mike's number before she had stopped talking.

'Mike? It's Brenda; Ian Ash and I are in Cheltenham Terrace.'

'Good; I was on the point of calling you, Brenda,' he said, 'our man is in there and ten or fifteen minutes ago he received a visitor.'

'That would have been Myra Middleton.'

'Danny Howarth's girlfriend?'

'That's right. Katie Brownlea phoned us; she'd heard that Miss Middleton was on her way here. That's how we know.'

'Alright, Brenda,' he said, 'I hear what you say. We've had a couple of officers posted outside East's property since early this morning, but apart from this one call we've had from them, Myra Middleton has been his only visitor so far this morning.'

'We don't want to tread on your pitch, Mike,' Brenda said, 'but I think we should proceed. Quite frankly, I don't like the way this is developing. Myra Middleton has known him for a number of years. Could be, she is an extremely bitter woman, harbouring some kind of grudge for all we know and that could mean trouble.'

'First losing her husband and presumably blaming East and now the murder of Danny Howarth?'

'Something like that, yes.'

'You could be right,' he said, 'but be careful. Sorry, Brenda, I shouldn't have to tell you that, but given the man's track record, he remains an unknown quantity and we don't know just how dangerous he is.'

'Perhaps we are about to find out.' she said, bringing the call to a close and putting the mobile back in her bag, 'Alright, Ian, we won't waste anymore time; we'll get this over with. It could be,' she added, as they walked along the pavement towards the house, 'that Katie is concerning herself unnecessarily. How do we know Myra Middleton hasn't kept in touch with Charlie East?'

'We don't know.' Ian replied; his lips set firmly in a straight line which told her he was as keen as she was to bring this case to a head.

'All the more reason,' she said, 'to try and keep an open mind. We know something of his background, but precious little about Myra Middleton's, only what she has chosen to tell you. This visit, Ian,' she went on, 'will have to be played very much off the cuff, so we'll just have to wait and see how he reacts and take it from there. I must admit I don't like this way of working.'

'It's a bit like going in blind-fold.' he commented dryly, coming to a standstill outside the door of number twelve.

He rang the bell and they waited for three or four minutes, but there was no response. Brenda, who was standing slightly behind him, stepped to one side to get a better look through the window to the right of the door. Venetian blinds, although in mid-position obscured a good part of her vision and only being able to make out it must be the lounge going right to the back of the property to French windows overlooking a walled garden.

'Try again, Ian,' she suggested, 'I'm going to take a walk round to the back and see if there is any sign of life. He's in there and eventually he'll have to come to the door.'

There was a narrow paved path running in front of the property and curving round the side to end up at a high, wooden gate. Lifting the latch, Brenda stepped into the garden she'd seen from the window. An extremely quiet neighbourhood she thought, considering they were virtually in the centre of London. She was now at the back door; frosted glass, making it impossible to see properly inside. Once again, this time from a different perspective, she was looking into the lounge. There was no sign of life. There was nobody sitting on one of the chairs in the centre of the room and waiting for the uninvited caller to leave. Charlie East had to be to be in there somewhere! Also, Myra Middleton; the woman she had yet to meet, where was she? Ian would have rung the bell again, but in spite of the warm day, there wasn't a single window open on the ground floor, making it impossible for her to hear; not only the bell, but any movement or voices from inside. She tapped on the glass. Nothing; complete and continuing silence. She tapped again, this time louder, but still no response and then her mobile rang: 'Hello, Brenda; it's Gerald here.'

'Hello, Gerald.'

'Not called at an awkward moment, I hope? I phoned Meadowbank and they told me you would be in London today.'

'I don't know whether you would exactly describe it as an awkward moment or not, Gerald, but Ian and I are outside Charlie East's house and, although we've been told he's inside, so far he hasn't come to the door.'

'I'll keep it brief then,' Gerald said, 'but I thought you would be interested to hear that Victor York made a full confession this morning; not only to Christine Saunders' murder, but he's blown the whistle on Charlie East. Apparently, he'd been supplying Charlie with drugs for a number of years. Quite a detailed, and, especially for Charlie, a very damning statement. Not that it's likely to reduce Victor York's sentence, of course, but I believe the bottom line is he made it out of pure vindictiveness. He knew he was going to go down and saw no reason why Charlie shouldn't join him.'

'You couldn't have given me better news, Gerald,' she said, 'and you know what this means, don't you? We now have something positive to pull him in for questioning and I wouldn't be surprised if there wasn't a great deal more to come. Charlie's been in the game for a long time and it might be possible that Victor York could act as a catalyst. What we need now is for Johnnie Baker to come forward and tell us more than he has done so far.'

Re-joining Ian, she told him the latest development watching for and not being disappointed to see his expression of suppressed excitement, realising he was as frustrated as she was by the slowness in the way events had been moving for more than a week.

'We'll try for the last time,' Brenda said, 'and if he still refuses to come to the door, I'll give the Chief Inspector another call. The very nature of this enquiry isn't primarily for us, in Meadowbank, to handle.'

'There is considerable over-lapping, though.'

'True.' she agreed, watching him reach up to press the door bell, this time keeping his finger on it for several seconds and this time it worked. The door was opened, but only halfway and not by Charlie East, but by a tall, slender, blonde-haired woman. It was the haunted expression in her eyes, which alerted Brenda that there was something very wrong, but before she could say anything, the woman spoke to Ian: 'Inspector Ash?' the two words sounding too high-pitched to Brenda's ears.

'Yes, Miss Middleton,' Ian said, pitching his voice higher than usual and Brenda realised he was thinking along exactly the same lines as she was: someone had scared Myra Middleton practically to the edge of hysteria. The build-up of tension surrounding the three of them was almost tangible and she knew from experience one wrong move could prove disastrous.

'I'm Chief Inspector Masters,' Brenda said to her, 'we were hoping to speak to Mr East.'

'I'm sorry –' Myra began, her attention now fully focused on Brenda.

' – Chief Inspector,' a voice, further back in the hall, interrupted her, 'this visit of yours is indeed a timely one!' and Brenda, recalling the description Ian had given her of him, knew the man now walking up the hall towards them, was Charlie East.

'Mr East?'

'Indeed, who else, Chief Inspector,' he smiled; a benign smile which she didn't like, and watched as he moved further forward until he was standing squarely in front of them both, 'and I think it would be best if you have this.' he finished, handing her a Berretta pistol.

'Your property, Mr East?' she asked him, taking the gun from him and giving it to Ian.

'Certainly not,' the smile remaining, 'it belongs to Miss Middleton who came here this morning for the sole purpose of using it to threaten me, but fortunately, I was able without a great deal of difficulty to overpower her. She may be a novice when it comes to any expertise in handling firearms, but her intentions were plain enough to me.'

'Do you wish to bring charges against Miss Middleton, sir?'

'I don't see the point,' he shrugged, 'Miss Middleton is, in my estimation, a hysterical female and possibly in need of some medical help, but then who am I to judge? I'm no psychiatrist.'

'Mr East,' Brenda went on, using the same low level in her voice as she had done from the beginning, 'there are a number of questions we would like to ask you in connection with the recent arrest of Mr Victor York.'

'Victor York? Who's he?'

'Sir,' Brenda said, her voice becoming sharp and wondering whether he had noticed or sensed her instant dislike for him. So much for her advice in telling Ian they should keep an open mind, but she was finding it extremely difficult as she looked at him, 'we haven't come to London this morning to play games. Now,' she continued, interested to note that her tone was affecting him, if the way in which his eyes narrowed was anything to go by; presumably trying to size her up, 'we'll go inside, shall we; unless you would prefer to accompany us to New Scotland Yard?'

During this one-sided exchange, Myra had remained silent, as had Ian, but Brenda hadn't expected him to say anything, not yet. It had become an unwritten agreement between them from when they had started working together that he would leave the initial questioning to her and this method had worked well. Ian had seemed to know instinctively the right moment when he should intervene and, on watching people's reactions, especially when they had something crucial to hide, she had learned how it, invariably, threw them off-guard and she didn't think it was going to be any different this time.

'Victor York,' Brenda said, when the three of them were in the lounge and sitting at the long glass-topped table at the far end of the room in front of the French windows she had seen earlier, 'was arrested on Monday and is being held in Winchester awaiting trial. The charge being the manipulation of the stock figures of his pharmacy accounts and systematically siphoning off large quantities of drugs.'

'Interesting, Chief Inspector,' he said, leaning back in his chair and adopting what appeared to her as a much-practiced position of appearing relaxed and totally in control of the situation, 'but what has all this got to do with me?'

'We believe, sir,' Brenda said, selecting her words carefully and not wanting to bring the questioning to a head prematurely, it has a great deal to do with you.'

'This is pure fabrication. You've charged this man; Victor York, you say he's called and you're scrabbling around for some evidence to support the charge. You can't fool me, Chief Inspector.'

'It is not our intention to fool anyone, sir. Are you still saying you don't know Mr York?'

'Do I have to repeat myself?' a glimmer of anger flickering across his features, but she knew it would take more than what she'd said so far to make him lose his temper.

'If you would, sir, but before you do, you may wish to call your lawyer. It is your prerogative.' she added.

'I know perfectly well it is my prerogative. But, there's no need and when I do, I'll make that decision.'

'Do you know, sir; those were almost the exact words used by Victor York when we made the same suggestion to him. However,' she continued slowly, 'do you insist in saying you've never heard of him?'

'That is what I said and that is what I meant.' Charlie East said, pronouncing each word separately; the eyes now no more than slits as he stared across the table at her.

'Sir,' Ian put in, 'how well do you know Johnnie Baker?'

'What! What sort of question is that?'

'Quite a simple one, I would have thought;' Ian said, 'how well do you

225

know him?'

'I don't know anyone called Johnnie Baker; at least not that I can recall.'

'Perhaps we'll be able to jog your memory, then. You own two properties in Meadowbank?'

'Wrong.' a puzzled frown appearing; the quick change in tack had disturbed him. 'For your information, I recently bought one of the town houses in Stockbridge Road.'

'You are a director of Aztec Financial Services, aren't you, sir?'

'*Managing* Director,' he corrected.

'You didn't retire from the board when you moved to Meadowbank?'

'No, I didn't. I intend to continue taking an active part in the full running of the business; that's the reason I kept on this property as I have to be in London at least twice a week.'

'We'll go back to Johnnie Baker for a moment.' Ian said.

'How many times have I to tell you I don't know the man?'

'I would suggest you hear me out, sir,' Ian warned him, 'before you say anything further because we know differently.'

'I'm sure you're going to enlighten me, Inspector Ash.' his expression changing once again, this time with an ingratiating and fixed smile.

'I intend to;' Ian said quietly, 'a week last Saturday I was in The Market Inn and you were there, talking to Johnnie Baker.'

'It's possible, I suppose. I talk to a number of people when I call in to any pub for a drink, but as I've said, the name means nothing to me.'

'Although you were on your own with him, sitting at one of the tables?'

'Naturally, I do remember talking to a young man and, if as you say, it was that evening, it still doesn't mean I knew his name.'

'In case your memory has failed you, sir,' Ian pressed on and Brenda watched Charlie East even more closely. She had worked out where Ian was coming from, what he was going to say next, and hopefully, they would get the right sort of reaction they were looking for, 'your company, Aztec Financial Services, purchased a property in Meadowbank six months ago, namely twenty-eight Market Square, which is currently being rented out to a man you say you've never heard of. I'm talking about Johnnie Baker, Mr East.'

'Oh!' the second shrug making its languid appearance, '*that* Johnnie

Baker.'

'Sir,' Brenda broke in, 'I will repeat; we are not here to play games. Also, I would put it to you that you have known all along we've been talking about the same person. There are not two Johnnie Bakers in Meadowbank. You have already confirmed you don't know Victor York, but we believe this is not true. You *do* know him and have done for many years. Earlier this morning, Victor York made a formal confession to the murder of his assistant, Miss Christine Saunders and in his revised statement he has told the authorities that each cache of drugs from his pharmacy were handed over to you for distribution; all except the last ones and those were found on his premises. It is our strong belief, Mr East, that the misappropriation of these drugs and the murder of Christine Saunders are connected. Now, do you want to make a call to your lawyer?'

'I will later.' he said, tight-lipped and at last beginning to show signs that his former confidence was waning. He was going to sit this out, Brenda thought, right to the end. They were a long way off cracking his resolve, but they would, she was certain of that.

'It is our opinion, sir; you would be well advised to do so.'

'Is it now?'

'Yes, it is. This morning,' Brenda went on, 'we have mentioned to you the names of two men, both of whom you have denied knowing, even after we pointed out to you we have obtained proof to the contrary. I am now going to mention a third one and before, as with the others, you say the same, I would suggest you think carefully before doing so.'

'Go on, Chief Inspector; I'm intrigued.'

This time,' she said, 'I will re-phrase my question differently; when did you last see Daniel Howarth?'

'I – er –', stumbling now; she could almost read his mind, but she didn't say anything, only waited for his next fabrication, 'I can't remember.' he answered at last and the only other sound in the room was that of Myra Middleton's sharp intake of breath.

'Oh, so you did know him, then?'

'Vaguely,' he waved an arm dismissively, 'but it was some time ago. I never knew him all that well.'

'You knew he was dead?'

'Yes, I read about it.'

'No natural death, but that of murder.'

'Only what they said in the newspaper.'

'Which wasn't a great deal, was it, Mr East? But, someone obviously knows considerably more of how it happened; how his body had fallen from the burnt out wreckage of his car at the Devil's Punchbowl in Surrey.'

'Presumably.'

'This happened late last Wednesday night; you would have read that also in the newspaper?'

'Of course.'

'Where were you on Wednesday night, sir? In London or at your other property, in Meadowbank?'

'I was in Meadowbank.'

'And in the evening; did you go out?'

'Yes, I went for a drink.'

'Where?'

'Pardon?'

'Where did you go for your drink, Mr East?'

'Oh, I see. The Bridge Inn.'

'Are you able to remember what time this would have been?'

'Not precisely; around seven I think.'

'It was before seven, sir, six-thirty in fact; they had just opened and you were seen coming into the pub with Danny Howarth.'

He was momentarily spared making any response by the sharp ringing of the front door bell.

'I'll go, Chief Inspector.' Ian said, standing up and walking down the length of the lounge towards the hall. Brenda heard the front door opening, followed by Mike's voice and then Ian's. Minutes later, Mike, followed by Ian, came into the room and silently beckoning over to her. Keeping his voice lowered he said: 'Ian Ash has given me a brief resume of your questioning, Brenda and with what I've been told less than an hour ago, I think we'll have sufficient on him now to make an arrest. Alright if I take over from where you've both left off?'

'Be our guest.' Brenda said quietly, but she wasn't smiling. It was always like this towards the end of a case, no-one taking for granted that a satisfactory outcome was going to be guaranteed. Within seconds, minutes, well constructed evidence could shift, putting a totally different emphasis on everything. This last thirty minutes or so had not been easy. Brenda, not only from reading the profile on Charlie East, but from the first moment she had seen him earlier, had reached the realisation that here was a man well used to confrontation, to professionally squirming out of situations where a person with considerably less expertise would have tripped himself up verbally right at the start of the questioning, but Charlie East was more than clever; he was like a master chess player; he had the ability to see, think and plan ahead, knowing in advance where the next move was coming from, but she concluded, walking over to the table with Mike and Ian, perhaps the man had reached the end of his particular crooked road. She sincerely hoped so. A cat only had so many lives, so how many did Charlie East have? Sitting down and listening as Mike introduced himself.

'This is ridiculous!' Charlie said, his voice raised for the first time, 'What is all this charade?'

'You would be wise, Mr East,' Mike warned, ignoring the outburst, 'to take care of what you say. Inspector Ash has informed me you have no wish at the moment to call your lawyer.'

'And I still don't! Whatever you're trying to pin on me won't work!'

'I would like to remind you, sir, you are in an extremely serious position. However, it's your decision whether you want your lawyer here with you or not. Also, I will be taping the remainder of this interview.'

'Tape as much as you like.'

'We will be doing that, I can assure you. Now,' Mike went on calmly, 'I want you to tell me where you were on Thursday night, the 17th May.'

'I'd have to look in my diary to be certain,' grudgingly given, 'but I think I was here, in London.'

'Very well and did you spend the night here or did you return to Meadowbank?'

'I would have spent the night here and then driven down to Meadowbank the following morning.'

'You didn't go to Manchester that night?'

'Certainly not; why should I have gone there?'

'I'm hoping you would be able to tell us that, sir.'

'Well, I didn't.'

'On that Thursday night, Mr East, you were seen leaving the flat in London Road, in Manchester at approximately eleven-thirty, the one tenanted by Mark Astley. The following morning Mark Astley's body was found inside the flat. It was believed at first he had died from a drug overdose, but it was later proved that the drug had been administered to him. Mark Astley was murdered. His next door neighbour had heard what sounded to him like a scuffle, but he had been too nervous to investigate and it wasn't until a member of the cleaning staff found the body the following morning that the incident was reported.'

'And you think I'm responsible?'

'Are you, sir?'

'I damn well am not!'

'Had you perhaps been visiting Mark Astley, had a whisky with him; there was an empty bottle found beside the body, and after a few drinks became involved in an argument which had gone out of control. Was that what happened, Mr East; the stronger man won?'

'Whoever says he saw me there that night is either lying or else he has an over-developed imagination.'

'Your name, Mr East, has been cropping up far too often recently. I'll recap for you, shall I?' and going on before Charlie East had time to protest, 'There have been three murders within days of each other: first, Mark Astley, followed by Christine Saunders and thirdly, Daniel Howarth. We've received confirmation from Winchester that Victor York has confessed to the murder of his assistant, Christine Saunders, so that leaves the other two unaccounted for – for the present. We'll go a little further back, four years to be exact, when a number of robberies in the south of England were taking place; the culprits were never apprehended, although the police did have their suspicions, which weren't enough. It was believed they were carried out by a group of people; three men and one woman, Mark Astley, Johnnie Baker, Danny Howarth and Katie Brownlea. Now four years later, a further spate of robberies has been taking placing: drugs being stolen from pharmacies through the south of England. Johnnie Baker was arrested a few days ago, actually caught red-handed. Another name kept cropping up: Christine Saunders' boss, Victor York –'

'- excuse me, but the door was open.' Katie Brownlea said, taking a tentative step into the room, followed immediately by a police officer: 'Sorry, sir,' he said to Mike, trying to catch his breath, 'I was across the road and I'd only just noticed her.'

'It's alright, Sergeant. If you could wait outside, please.'

'This is Katie Brownlea, sir.' Ian told him, keeping his voice down.

'Right,' Mike nodded, 'you'd better sit down, Miss Brownlea now that you're here.'

'I didn't mean to intrude, but I was worried about Myra. You're alright, aren't you?' she asked her.

'I'm fine.' managing the smallest of smiles, but whether Katie was reassured or not Brenda couldn't tell.

'Miss Brownlea,' Mike said, obviously trying to pull the meeting back into more orthodox and manageable lines, 'you are the young woman who was with the rock group; the one who spent the summer of two thousand and one touring the south?'

'Yes, that's right,' she said, giving a deep sigh, 'you know all about it then?'

'Never sufficient, Miss Brownlea. However, I'm going to ask you one question.'

'Yes.'

'You knew the man the members of the group reported to, didn't you; the same person who they handed over the goods they had stolen to after each robbery.'

'I only knew his name; I never met him. Mark was always the one who did that.' so quietly, Brenda had difficulty in hearing her.

'And what was his name?'

'Mr East; Charlie East.'

'Thank you, Miss Brownlea.'

'What the hell is this?' Charlie yelled, pushing back his chair and jumping to his feet, his face red with fury. A put up job! That's what it is! A put up job!'

'Mr East,' Mike, his voice as calm as it had been since the moment he'd come into the room, 'please.' waiting until Charlie, straightening his chair, sat down again. 'Thank you, and remember this meeting is still being taped. Before we were interrupted, you understood everything I said?'

231

'Quite clearly.'

'Very well. I now charge you, Mr Charles East, with suspicion of murder on two counts; Mark Astley's on Thursday, the 17th May and Danny Howarth's on Wednesday, the 23rd May.' and continuing to include the further charges of instigating and arranging the breaking and entering of various commercial and private properties in the south of England between two thousand and one up to the present day and to the receiving and distribution of drugs.

He finally came to the end, switched off the tape and they all watched in silence as Charlie East was escorted off the premises by two officers and into the waiting police car. He had made no further comment and although white-faced and keeping his eyes straight ahead he still managed a slight swagger as he left the room. The Charlie Easts of this world, Brenda thought, looking across at Mike, didn't go down without a fight, knowing in advance the fighting would be carried out in the court room between the defence and prosecutor lawyers. There was nothing more any of them could do to ensure the final outcome would be as they hoped. With his money, Charlie East would employ the best defence lawyer. He'd obviously done it before and in spite of the volume of evidence against him, they knew in advance what could happen in the final reckoning.

'Do you think he'll get off with it all, ma'am?' Ian asked her once they were in the car and on their way back to Meadowbank.

'That's anyone's guess, Ian; he might,' she added, 'but as far as we're concerned our investigation has reached its conclusion; there's nothing further we can do to ensure whether he does go down or not. Of course he's guilty, but from now on the whole business is in the hands of the law. In other words, we've done our part. For the moment he's well and truly cornered and it could be he'll be able, with the assistance of a clever lawyer, to extricate himself.'

'Although we have a witness to say they had seen his car parked outside Danny Howarth's house last Wednesday night.'

'Oh,' Brenda sighed, 'I hear what you're saying, Ian, but no doubt Charlie East would be able to come up with a plausible explanation for that; anything in fact to exonerate himself.'

'You mean that someone may have stolen it, gone for a joy ride?'

'It does sound ridiculous, Ian, put like that, but we know full well that his lawyer would produce something which would be impossible to disprove.'

'Frustrating.' he commented, making to join the slip road on to the motorway.

'For us, yes, but to Charlie East no doubt one more challenge in an eventful life. Who knows, Ian, this time he just might be the loser.'

Other titles by Margaret Alty:

Tangled Web – ISBN: 978 1 84549 422 3

Jenny – ISBN: 978 1 84549 442 1

Camouflage – ISBN: 978 1 84549 478 0

The Last Orange – ISBN: 978 1 84549 560 2

A Meadowbank Mystery

Murder in Meadowbank – ISBN: 978 1 84549 494 7

Double Act – ISBN: 978 1 84549 537 4 560 2

All published by arima Publishing.

www.ingramcontent.com/pod-product-compliance
Lightning Source LLC
Chambersburg PA
CBHW051643260626
47170CB00004B/1314